PAINT,
GOLD AND BLOOD

By the same author

PAINT,
GOLD AND BLOOD

MICHAEL GILBERT

1817

Harper & Row, Publishers, New York
Grand Rapids, Philadelphia, St. Louis, San Francisco
London, Singapore, Sydney, Tokyo, Toronto

This book is published in Great Britain by Hodder and Stoughton, a division of Hodder and Stoughton Ltd.

FIRST U.S. EDITION

LIBRARY OF CONGRESS CATALOG CARD NUMBER 89-45078
ISBN 0-06-016206-6

89 90 91 92 93 RRD 10 9 8 7 6 5 4 3 2 1

PAINT,
GOLD AND BLOOD

PART ONE

PRELIMINARY SKIRMISHING

There is always, in every school, something nasty going on somewhere, even in places where hanky-panky is not tolerated. Growing up is, for some, a messy business. There are new experiences to be sampled, exciting sins to be dreamed of, prizes to be fought for. There is cheating, lying, greed, envy, sloth, wrath in as much abundance as in the House of Commons or a Cathedral Close. There is also idealism, romance, joy.

John Thorn, Headmaster of Repton 1961–8;
of Winchester 1968–85.

1

It must be unusual for a boy who is three months short of his seventeenth birthday to be nearly seduced and nearly murdered within the same twelve hours, yet this is what happened to Peter Dolamore one April day on the north coast of France.

He had spent the first fortnight of his Easter holidays in a visit to the Château de Lambrécie, east of Valeyrac, in the northern tip of the Médoc peninsula.

The claret which this château produces is not one of *crus classés* (though it commands a ready sale in the markets of Bordeaux) but the château is noted for other things than its wines. Its owner, Joseph Wellborn, a francophile Englishman, was a millionaire, a fact which did not make him outstanding in an area full of the wealthy owners of world-famous vineyards; but he was also the possessor, by inheritance, of a famous collection of pictures. "Much more valuable," he would say deprecatingly when showing them to his visitors, "than the château which houses them or the vineyards which surround the château."

Peter could estimate their value from the precautions which Mr. Wellborn took to guard them. He had never been in a house which was bolted and barred so thoroughly at night; and looking from the window of his turret bedroom he had seen either Hervé or Michel-Ange, who took it in turn to act as night watchman, patrolling the grounds followed by the big Alsatian shepherd dog, Bruno.

All in all it had not been a happy visit and he had been glad to be able to confine it to four days, on the grounds that it had taken him five days by bicycle to reach the château from Dieppe and would take him as long to return. His host had been formidably polite about this, as about everything. He had known Peter's mother, a de Clissac, and he appreciated the fact that Peter spoke impeccable French; which was not surprising, since he had lived the first eleven years of his life with his mother in the St. Germain-en-Laye suburb of Paris.

The chance which had produced the invitation to the château was the fact that Peter was a school friend of Lisa Shilling, Joseph's niece, although this did not much improve the *entente*, since there were many matters on which Joseph did not see eye to eye with his elder sister.

"The B and S is scrumptious," Peter wrote to his friend Stewart Ives. "But I spend most of my time hoping I'm not going to drop some fearful brick. I get out as much as I can. The country round here is fairly uninspiring, though it's fun watching the boats battling their way up the Gironde and there's miles and miles of forest behind the château; that part's pretty gloomy, actually. The second day I was here I went for a walk in it and got lost and was late for dinner. Didn't make me popular. All in all I'm glad I'm leaving on Monday. I told them it would take me five days to the Channel, but I think I can do it in four, which will give me a free day for ancestor hunting."

There was no need to explain any of this. He and Stewart had known each other long enough to correspond in a sort of shorthand. He would understand that B and S stood for 'browsing and sluicing' and he knew about the de Clissac family.

In accordance with this ambitious programme, on the Thursday evening Peter had pedalled into Sassencourt-le-Mauconduit, between Etretat and Dieppe, leg-weary and saddle-sore, but content. Two of the intervening nights had been spent in friendly farms and one in a dry ditch, at no cost to his pocket, and he reckoned he could afford to pass the last two nights of his trip comfortably if not luxuriously. The Hôtel Commerce, a medium-sized establishment behind the market square, had seemed to be just the ticket. He had nearly fallen asleep over the dinner table, had creaked upstairs to the tiny room in the attic which had been the only accommodation available and had tumbled into bed and into the depths of untroubled sleep.

On opening his eyes his first idea was that he was in hospital. When he had last been there, following the removal of his appendix, he remembered being tidied up for the consultant's morning rounds. Two strong nurses had seized the bedclothes and tucked him in so tightly that he had hardly been able to breathe, let alone move. On this occasion the only difference was that there was one girl doing the tucking. Owing to the narrowness of the room, the other side of his bed was jammed against the wall.

He tried to sit up, said, "Hey!" and then, in his best French, "Am I a sardine to be enclosed in a tin?" He had noticed the girl on the previous night serving in the dining-room and had heard her addressed as Claudette. She had a lively street-urchin face; but this, as he was able to observe as she bent over him, was the only boyish thing about her. He thought she was not much older than he was.

She said, "Little idler, do you realise that it is now ten o'clock and that I have been ordered to make your bed?"

He said, "Surely you would be able to do it more effectively if I was not in it?"

He had managed to wriggle his shoulders clear of the bed clothes. This was unwise. He had forgotten that he was sleeping, as he normally did, naked. Claudette inspected what she could now see with approval.

Although no girl had ever made such a direct approach to him before, he was not unaware of the impression he made. His widowed mother, being a Frenchwoman, had discussed the matter with her son. She had said, "Some English girls fall for the typical French male, with his black hair, his virile face and his air of maturity and attack. French girls, on the contrary, are often *accablées* by the young Anglo-Saxon who has, as you well have, *mon petit*, blond hair, a *nez camus* and a general look as though he had just been hatched from the egg. You will have to guard your virginity carefully."

Peter had been ten at the time of this pronouncement and had not taken it too seriously. Afterwards it had acquired a certain solemnity as being one of the last occasions on which his mother had spoken to him. She had been in bed at the

5

time, with the onset of the leukaemia that had killed her. She had died a month later.

On his recent journey through France, at the farms where he had lodged, he had had an opportunity to confirm what his mother had said. When entering a strange household he usually concealed his knowledge of French and he had been able to understand the unguarded comments which the female members of the family had made.

"If I let you out of your nest," said Claudette, "you must naturally pay a forfeit. It will not be too disagreeable, I hope. One kiss. Are you willing to pay such a price?"

"If I must," said Peter hoarsely.

She slipped one arm under his bare shoulders and brought her face down towards his. She said, "Has no one taught you how to kiss? Open your mouth, baby." Her tongue had come out and was probing for his.

'This is all very well,' said his inner monitor, 'but if I do get out of bed, she'll be able to see only too plainly what my feelings about her are.' And then again, 'What does it matter? Why not give her what she wants?'

Someone was shouting from outside. It sounded like the manageress, a dragon of a woman. "Haven't you finished up there?"

"Nearly," said the girl, disengaging herself and hurrying across the room.

"Have I to come up and give you the back of my hand? There are a thousand things to do."

Peter was, by this time, propped up on his elbows. This offered a clear view of him down to his navel. Claudette examined it with increased pleasure. she said, "Tonight? Yes? I sleep alone. My room is at the end of the passage."

"Yes," said Peter breathlessly.

"What are you doing up there?"

"Nothing, nothing. I am coming. Old cow."

Peter extracted himself from the bed and dressed thoughtfully. By the time he got down the dining-room was shut. He breakfasted at a café in the Square and turned his attention to the Michelin Guide.

The fourteenth century church of St. Brieuc des Caves which stands in

6

*a somewhat isolated position on the eastern side of Sassencourt possesses
a number of interesting features. Originally it served as a chapel to the
de Clissaque family and stood within the boundaries of their domain. It
contains many of their tombs, armorial tablets and funerary inscriptions.
At the beginning of this century it was adopted as the parish church of
Sassencourt and Pont d'Ancrette. There are larger and more imposing
churches in the district, but this one continues to attract not only its
own congregation, but numerous visitors, on account of its possession of
a triptych, gift of an early de Clissaque, attributed to Niccolò Frumenti
and known as the Triptyque Scholastique, on account of the fact that
the centre panel only is the work of Frumenti, the side panels having
been executed by two pupils, one of whom, Paulo Agostino, attained to
an even greater repute than his master.*

He had had enough of bicycling in the last four days and
decided to walk to the church, which he found nearly a mile
out, on the side road to Gerville. A flagged path led from
the road to the west door, which was locked. He was not
discouraged. He knew that a side-door would usually be left
open on week days, the main door being reserved for use on
Sundays. The southern side of the church was blocked by the
presbytère, a much later building, almost as large as the church
itself. He therefore tried the path which ran clockwise round
the building and found an unlocked door at the end of the
north transept.

The interior was dim and silent. The walls were thick and
the windows were small and heavily crusted with old stained
glass. There was no sign of the 'numerous visitors' mentioned
in the guide book. Peter, who had had some experience of
French churches, had armed himself with a torch.

He spent ten minutes admiring the Frumenti triptych.
The centre piece was the Virgin and the Holy Child. On
the left were three, rather stylised, Magi. On the right a
group of very human shepherds gaping up into the sky,
with wide-open mouths. He tore himself away from this
to examine the de Clissaque inscriptions and memorials.
He started on the left of the transept and worked his way
towards the eastern bay behind the high altar. Most of the
plaques commemorated male members of the de Clissaque
family who had predeceased their wives. In one case he

noted that the widow, *femme obéissante et soumise*, had evidently thought it wrong to survive her Lord and had followed him *respectueusement* within three months. Other ladies had taken a more robust view and he noted Catherine de Clissaque who had survived her husband by forty years, outliving eight children and thirteen grandchildren who were all entombed in the same vault. 'Quite a girl,' he thought, writing down the names of the children in a note book he had brought with him.

What he was looking for in particular was information about the later members of the family, whom he could link up with his known maternal grandfather and great-grandfather. Unfortunately there seemed to be a complete gap after the third quarter of the eighteenth century. This, he realised, was due to the fact that many members of the family would have perished in the Terror; others would have been driven abroad, to live for twenty-five years in penury, their estates confiscated and divided in such a way that it had been impossible to ask for restitution when the Bourbons had returned.

These transcriptions had taken time. It was after four o'clock and his torch was showing signs of weakening before he reached the corner of the south transept. What he saw there looked promising. To start with, it was comparatively modern, a *cercueil* mounted on a low pediment; and the first name he saw on it had the modern spelling, 'de Clissac' and the date of death he deciphered as MDCCCXXXIII.

"Eighteen thirty-three," said Peter. "That's more like it. If I could read the rest of it I'd be getting somewhere."

The inscription ran right round the lid of the coffin. Unfortunately the box-like structure of a confessional had been erected close to its far side, but there was just room to squeeze between the back of the monument and the wall. To get in he had to shift a brass vase. He pulled it out and inserted his slim person behind the pediment. He hoped that his torch was not going on the blink altogether. He had squatted down to bring his eyes level with the lettering, when he heard two people coming.

At first he thought it was one man, whose shoes clattered on the floor of the south transept. Since the only entrance to this transept was a door at the end which led out to the *presbytère*, he assumed that it was the *curé*. This was confirmed by a glimpse of the black *soutane* as the man swept past. Then he heard the second footsteps, much quieter. Someone wearing rubbers on his shoes had come through the side-door and was approaching. There was a murmur of greeting and then, to Peter's dismay, both men made for the confessional.

This was divided into three narrow compartments, the centre one for the priest, the outer ones for the penitents. He realised that, squatting where he was, he was going to be able to hear every word of the newcomer's confession. This was intolerably embarrassing. He decided to extract himself and slip out of the church. Then he changed his mind.

He knew the set words the penitent would be expected to use at the start: *'Mon Dieu, tu es bon. Je t'ai offensé. Pardonne-moi mes péchés'* and the soothing reply: *'Que Dieu notre père vous montre sa miséricorde.'*

But here came a very different opening. Before the man could speak the priest said in the sharp voice of one who seeks to be authoritative, but is secretly afraid, "Is everything arranged?"

"Down to the last detail," said the newcomer. The French was fluent, but Peter knew, from accent and intonation, that he was a foreigner.

"I will unlock the door in the north transept after midnight, but when you leave you are to give it the appearance of having been forced."

"Of course."

The dialogue then moved on to money. It seemed that half of an agreed sum had already been handed to the priest. A dispute developed over when, and how, the second half was to be paid. Peter decided that he would wait no longer. He could guess that the object of the thief was the Frumenti triptych, which was the only thing of value in the church. The prospect of its theft did not trouble him. It would no doubt end up in a museum and be seen by even more people. What was upsetting him was the voice of the newcomer. It had a hard, callous undertone which chilled him. He had no desire to be caught eavesdropping by the owner of such a voice.

He unfolded himself, slipped his torch into his pocket and started to edge out. He had forgotten the brass vase.

His foot hit it and sent it, ringing and clattering, into the aisle.

Abandoning any attempt at secrecy, he took to his heels.

He skirted the high altar and the pulpit beyond it and fled for the door in the north transept which both he and the newcomer had used. If he could get through it safely he was sure that his speed across country would see him safe. His prayer was answered. Not only was the door unfastened, it was standing ajar. He kicked it open and crashed through, almost into the arms of the man who was standing outside.

It was still quite light. For a long second they stared at each other, then Peter turned and dodged back into the church. It was an instinct of self-preservation, but it was a mistake. He should have trusted to agility and stayed outside. As he ran back, down the north aisle and into one of the pews, he heard the voice of the first man. He had not troubled to pursue him. He had taken up his position at the west end of the church and now said, in the voice of one accustomed to obedience, "Lock the door, Mahmoud and come here."

Peter realised exactly what they were going to do.

Both men had torches. They were going to move down the side aisles, examining the pews in turn.

He tried to think.

Unless the priest helped them, they could only take one of the aisles each. This left him a limited field of manoeuvre. As they advanced down the side aisles he could, by using the centre aisle, move ahead of them. What was going to happen when he reached the end was something he tried not to think about.

At that moment the priest reappeared. He came out of the confessional, turned to the right and moved, with evident caution, into the south transept. It was clear that he had no desire to play any part in the unpleasant finale. He was making for home.

By now Peter, moving on hands and knees down the centre aisle, had reached the altar rail. He thought, for a moment, of hiding in the pulpit, but his wits, which worked well in an emergency, told him that to cower in the pulpit would be stupid. They also showed him a possible chance of escape.

He could hear the priest, who was the only one of them wearing hard-soled shoes, creaking his way along the south transept. He had guessed, from his voice, that he was elderly and timid. By the time he reached the presbytery exit Peter was a few yards behind him and coming up fast. Fear lent force to his attack. He launched himself at the priest's back, bringing him to his knees, hurdled his body, slipped through the half-open door and slammed it behind him.

The passage ahead of him made a turn to the right and then the back door of the presbytery was ahead of him. It had been left ajar. As Peter went through it into the hall he could hear the pounding of his pursuers on the flagstones of the passage. He slammed this door, too, and heard it shut behind him with a satisfactory click. He reckoned it would take the men a few seconds to get the key from the priest and open it. This was fortunate, because the front door was both locked and bolted. By the time he got it open the pursuit was surging into the hall.

A short path led to the road. Beyond the road was a hedge, which he burst through. Beyond the hedge an open field. Dusk was already deepening into night and he reckoned he was safe, but he crossed three fields diagonally before he stopped.

A beautiful silence.

He crouched in the ditch he had landed in, getting his breath back and allowing his heart to stop bumping. When he stood up and started to walk his legs felt oddly weak. The road which he had crossed led to Gerville. He would stick to the fields until he got there. Then he could work out a round about way back to Sassencourt. Better to arrive there after dark since one of the men could recognise him.

It was eight o'clock by the time he reached the hotel and he could hear the clatter of knives and forks and the sound of cheerful voices from the dining-room. Claudette, who must have been watching for his return, came out with a pile of plates. As soon as she saw him she dumped them, seized his arm and dragged him into a small room which was used for coats and hats. Her intentions were not amorous. She was a badly frightened girl.

She said, "You must go."

11

"Why?"

"Quickly, quickly. I have packed up your things."

She showed him his knapsack, which she had hung behind the door.

Peter, who was beginning to be infected by the girl's terror, said, "Please explain. What have I done?"

"You have done nothing. It was the two men."

Peter knew now what was coming and his heart began to bump.

"They came here, enquiring. They have been to the other two hotels as well. All the other people here are regular visitors, so they were interested in you. They will be back again, soon."

"Who are these men? What are they doing here?"

"They are Iranians, it is thought. They have been around for a week or more. It is clear that they have some project in mind. Probably criminal."

"But," said Peter, conscious that his throat was dry and that he was beginning to squeak, "This is absurd. You mean that they are known criminals, murderers perhaps. Why are they not taken into custody?"

"It was my brother who told me about them. He is in the *Police Judiciaire* at Fécamp. He said that when he reported their presence to his own chief he was told to take no further action. It seems that the order came from the headquarters in Paris."

"You mean that they are free to do what they like? That they could attack me – kill me perhaps – and no one would do anything about it?"

"If they killed you," said the girl unhappily, "then I am sure that notice would be taken of it."

"Which would be a lot of use to me."

"It is because of his feelings in the matter – he does not like the interference of the politicians in police matters, you understand – that my brother is willing to help. He has a car in the courtyard. We have put your bicycle in the back. If you give me one hundred francs that should be sufficient for a room for two nights and one dinner. I will tell madame some story – "

"I shall have to think of somewhere to stay for the night."

"No need. The night boat from Dieppe, my brother says,

12

goes at ten o'clock. You will be in plenty of time if you leave now."

"That seems the best plan, then," said Peter. He was extremely relieved at the idea of getting away. He gave Claudette his last hundred franc note and the kiss that she seemed to expect. Then she hurried him by a back passage to the yard in which a Citroën tourer was parked.

The brother was a saturnine young-old man in the dark grey suit which seemed to be the uniform of the French detective branch. He gestured to Peter to sit beside him and they drove away. As they were passing through St. Valéry he said, "I should advise you not to pay too much attention to what my sister says. She gets odd ideas into her head sometimes."

"Yes, indeed," said Peter. Silence fell again until they reached St. Veulette. Then the young policeman said, "You were wise to leave. They are not agreeable characters, those two. They are not Frenchmen, you understand. They are foreigners. From Iran."

Peter hesitated before asking the next question, but curiosity was stronger than discretion. He said, "Is it true that they enjoy some sort of protection?"

This produced a very long silence. Then the young man said, "If I were the *Commissaire*, in charge of the *Brigade Criminelle*, maybe I could answer your question." A pause, whilst they negotiated the narrow main street of St. Aubin. Then, "As it is, I can only offer a surmise. As you know, the Ayatollah Khomeni lived for a number of years in France. He had many friends. When he left France to eject the Shah, some of them went back with him. But others did not. They remained here."

Nothing further was said until they were approaching Dieppe. Then Peter took his courage into both hands once more. He said, "As long as these two men do nothing criminal, you leave them alone. But if you *knew* about a crime they were planning, you'd stop them?"

"What sort of crime had you in mind?" There was no trace of friendship in the voice. It was French officialdom speaking.

"Well, burglary. Or theft." He added a brief account of his adventure.

"So you *know* that they plan to steal something? And you *know* what that thing is?"

"Well," said Peter, "I don't exactly know. But I've every reason to think – "

"What you think does not interest me. Only what you know."

"In that case," said Peter, "I suppose – "

"Unless you have definite information, it is better to keep quiet."

"If that's the way you want it."

"I am saying it in your own interest, you understand. I see that your boat is already in. It is never crowded at this time of night."

While Peter was wheeling his bicycle up the gangplank it was not the question of accommodation that was worrying him. It was the question of food. He had suddenly realised that he was furiously hungry. Only a breakfast of coffee and croissants stood between him and the dinner he had snoozed over more than twenty-four hours before. There was a cafeteria on board, but it was shut and deserted. He returned to the quay and found a bar open. The only available food was ham sandwiches. He bought three of them, returned on board and settled down at the back of the saloon, which filled up gradually as the hour of departure approached.

He was wondering what he was going to do when the boat reached Newhaven, which it was scheduled to do at one o'clock in the morning. His uncle's rectory was at Dollingford Parva, five miles outside Chichester. Normally it was approached by train from London and onwards by bus. Neither form of transport would be available at one o'clock in the morning. And even if he did succeed in persuading someone to give him a lift he would hardly be welcome at the Rectory at such an hour.

He had finished his sandwiches and the boat was moving, before the solution occurred to him. There must be a boat train to take passengers up to London. Once he was there he could kill time by finding an all-night restaurant which would fill the gap left by the sandwiches and then he could take an early train to Checkington, where Stewart Ives lived with his

14

aunt. There was no difficulty about arriving at that house at any hour of the day or night. Mrs. Pye was so engaged in local affairs and charitable works that she hardly noticed what went on inside her own home.

This seemed to Peter such an admirable solution that he fell asleep, waking when the boat reached Newhaven.

2

"I observe," said Stewart Ives, "that Sassencourt is described on the map as 'Le Mauconduit'. If that means what it sounds like it's pretty nearly what you went in for, wasn't it?"

"Nearly," said Peter sadly.

"Just as well you didn't. She'd probably have given you V.D."

"Oh, I don't think so. She wasn't a prostitute."

"Or maybe presented you with a little bouncing bastard. I can't see your uncle paying a paternity allowance, can you?"

"The truth is, you're green with jealousy."

"Not jealous. Disappointed in you. After all the thought I've devoted to your upbringing – "

"Well, what would *you* have done?"

"Taken what was offered. On the spot."

"With that hag bellowing upstairs at her?"

"Distracting, I admit."

Breakfast was over in the dining-room of Mrs. Pye's house. Though he and Stewart were both orphans and were both looked after by a guardian, this household was as complete a contrast as could be imagined to the formality and economy of the Dollingford Parva Rectory. Not his uncle's fault, Peter was fair enough to admit. If you had practically no money, that was the sort of life you had to live. It had been an act of Christian charity to house him after his mother's death. And his uncle had done more than house him. In the holidays from school he had coached him skilfully enough to secure him a Foundation Scholarship at Chelborough. There were only three such scholarships, all handsomely endowed and producing enough money to pay the entire fees, so that his schooling was, practically, free.

"Where is your aunt?" said Peter.

"She's gone down to prepare the Vicarage hall for a Youth Club meeting. At least, I think it's the Youth Club. It might be the Mothers' Union."

"She keeps at it, doesn't she?"

"Like her nephew," said Stewart complacently.

"Oh. What are you doing today?"

"Going up to London. To Southwark to be precise. Would you like to come, or are you too tired after your exhausting experiences on the other side of the Channel?"

"It depends what you're going to do."

"Well, I'm not going to visit the Bishop. Though I might do, sometime. He's a distant relative on my mother's side. In fact, I plan to call on a Mr. Leonard Terry."

"I might as well come along."

Peter knew that when Stewart was determined to be mysterious it was a waste of time asking him questions. His technique, on such occasions, was to wait until Stewart condescended to explain what he was up to, as he invariably did in the end.

His French trip had left him practically penniless, but it was an understood thing that when they went out together Stewart paid for everything. He had a generous allowance from his aunt. They went by train to Victoria and by underground to Shadwell station on the East London Line. On the first branch of their journey Stewart talked about computers and on the second about birds. Peter deduced from this that the project in hand was secret and probably disreputable. From Shadwell station they walked eastward along Cable Street, following the river. London was recovering from an unpleasant winter, and the sun was shining convincingly for the first time that year.

They stopped at the corner of Juniper Street opposite a gaunt building of yellow brick and blackened tiles. A large notice said 'South London Mission'. A smaller one said 'Please use the side entrance. Wipe your feet'.

"Good Lord," said Peter, "so that's *our* mission. I often wondered what it looked like."

As in many public schools, the boys of Chelborough supported a mission. Their interest in it was peripheral. Members of the staff visited it from time to time; boys hardly ever. For the most part their support was limited to the subscriptions which

17

they, or their parents, handed in at the start of each term. With this money the missioner, Father Elphinstone, kept the Mission Hall heated and lighted and supplied such of the local talent as cared to attend with cocoa, darts and table-tennis. Earlier in his career he had been more enterprising. He still shuddered at the memory of a continental visit, some years before, with twenty of his charges. Half of them had left the party as soon as they landed at Calais and had set out to explore France in their own way. Five of them had ended up in the hands of the police and two in hospital. One was still missing.

The missioner welcomed Stewart, whom he evidently knew, and was introduced to Peter.

Stewart said, "I'm afraid this is only a flying visit, Father. I really came to get the current address of one of your lads – Leonard Terry."

"Len Terry. Yes. He used to be one of our regulars. Now that he's left school we don't see so much of him. When I last heard of him, he was living with his brother Ronald at – let me see, yes – the address I have for them is fourteen Barnabas Street. That's a turning off the Causeway."

When they were going, he said, "I wish you could persuade more of the boys to visit us. Then they might get a better idea of what we're trying to do."

"I'm afraid it's just the term's subscription to most of them."

"Even that's falling off," said the missioner sadly.

Stewart, who had got up, sat down again. He said, "Tell me about that, padre."

"What is it you wanted to know?"

"About the financial position."

"We publish our accounts each year," said Father Elphinstone doubtfully. "I send the school six copies. The details are all there."

"I expect so. But they go to the headmaster and the bursar and people like that, don't they? We boys never see them."

"Actually I send them to your chaplain, Alvin Brind. Doesn't he distribute them?"

Stewart looked at Peter who said, "I've never seen a copy.

Mr. Brind is our housemaster – we're both in School House – so if anyone had seen them it should have been us."

"Well, if you're really interested, I've got a copy here."

"Please," said Stewart. "And earlier years, too, if you've got them."

"Yes, I could manage that. This is a copy of the accounts for last year. I could look out earlier ones and send them to you if you'd tell me what you have in mind."

Stewart was studying the simple roneoed document which Father Elphinstone had produced. He said, "You have four sources of income, is that right? Local collections – that would be bazaars and raffles and things you get up locally I imagine?"

The missioner nodded. He did not seem to notice that Stewart had not answered his question, or if he noticed, made no comment.

He said, "We had a Christmas party last year, which was very successful. And one or two raffles. And a local fund-raising drive. We collected just over £2,000 altogether."

"Then I see there's a grant – that's from our general school funds – two thousand pounds. And a grant from your own diocese of one thousand, eight hundred. And last, and a good deal least, boys' subscriptions – one thousand and seventy-five."

"That's the one I'm anxious about. When you look at the earlier accounts you'll see that it used to be much higher. For many years it was around one thousand, eight hundred pounds. Actually that was what fixed the diocesan contribution. I'm afraid that if they see the boys are falling off, they may take the view that if the school is losing interest in the mission it's not their function to support it. I had a hint to that effect when the Archdeacon visited us last autumn."

Stewart seemed to have been doing some sums. He said, "I don't know exactly what our numbers are, but they're near enough six hundred. If each boy gave a pound a term – which used to be the understood thing – that would bring you back to one thousand eight hundred a year."

"That would be excellent. But I don't see how you'd set about it."

"The spirit of competition," said Stewart. From the way in which he said it Peter knew that some devious ploy was in the offing. "When our Chaplain sends you the term's contribution, which he collects, does he give you the house totals, or does he send it as a lump sum?"

"As a lump sum."

"What I had in mind was that we ought to publish the figures for each house separately."

"I've no doubt he'd let you have the breakdown if he knew what you were planning to do. An excellent idea, if I may say so – "

"Why on earth," said Peter as they were walking away, "did you rouse the old boy's hopes? You know perfectly well that Brindy won't tell us anything. Or let us help. He loathes us both. He'd be very happy to get rid of me."

"Of both of us," said Stewart. "I've long been a thorn in his flesh. Or if I haven't been, it's not for want of trying."

"He can't get rid of you, unless you do something pretty stupid."

"It isn't easy to get expelled these days," agreed Stewart. "Too much ghastly tolerance. Not like the good old days when you could get hoofed out for almost anything."

"Whereas he can get me out by giving me bad reports. If they're bad enough, my scholarship gets taken away and my uncle would have to remove me. He wouldn't have a hope of finding the fees."

"Yes. You told me about that. And didn't I advise you not to worry? To have a bit of confidence in the Stewart Ives Service."

"I don't see what you can do."

"You and Father Elphinstone! Doubting Thomases the pair of you."

"You can't make Brindy give me good reports if he doesn't want to."

"We shall see," said Stewart. "There are more ways of killing a cat than drowning it in cream. I have begun by making a few enquiries. To start with, I have discovered *why* Alvin is so anxious to displace you."

"I thought it was just because he didn't like me."

"Not so. There are wheels within wheels. Do you know a spotty drip called Dakin?"

"I think I've seen him slouching round the corridors. What about him?"

"Didn't you realise that his mother is sister to our Bishop?"

"No, I didn't."

"That special scholarship you've got. It lasts for four years and only three boys can hold them at a time. Right?"

"Yes."

"But if one of the holders happened to leave before the four years was up, his place is taken by the next boy on the waiting list."

"And that's Dakin?"

"Correct. And if he gets his scholarship a year early and if the Bishop finds out, as no doubt he will, that it's all due to Alvin's disinterested efforts, that puts him in good with his ecclesiastical boss."

"I suppose all clergymen suck up to the Bishop."

"It's more than sucking up. Alvin has got aspirations. He's looking for promotion."

"How on earth do you know that?"

"One of my many accomplishments," said Stewart modestly, "is the ability to read writing upside down. It needs a bit of practice, that's all. The last time I was hauled up and given a dressing down I was able to absorb some of the carbon copy of a letter to the Bishop's Chaplain which Alvin had carelessly left lying on his desk. It wasn't conclusive evidence, because I could only see the address and the opening paragraph. But it pointed in that direction."

"I must admit that if I am going to be sacrificed I'd rather it wasn't for the advancement of our housemaster."

"My best efforts," said Stewart, "shall be devoted to saving you from immolation."

Number fourteen Barnabas Street looked no different from number twelve and number sixteen. A stamped earth forecourt, a flight of holy-stoned doorsteps and a brass knocker, in the form of a mermaid, on which Stewart beat a hearty tattoo. This produced no response until a first-floor window in number twelve opened and a lady with her hair in curlers poked her head out and said, "Lay off, carncher. I'm tryin' to watch the telly."

"Sorry, madam," said Stewart. "I was looking for Len Terry."

"If 'e's attome, which I'm not sure 'e is, you'll find him rahnd the back."

Stewart said, "I'm much obliged to you, madam." The old lady slammed down the window and returned to her television set. The boys penetrated a passage which held a motor scooter, a dismembered bicycle, a rabbit hutch and a birdcage. Emerging into the back yard they heard the sound of an electric drill from a lean-to shed at the end.

Here they found Len Terry. He stopped work when they came in. The missioner had said that he had recently left school, but with his white face and deepset eyes he might have been any age, thought Peter, from fifteen to thirty. He greeted Stewart by punching him on the chest and said, "Oo's the mucker?"

"This is Peter."

"Pleesetermeetyer," said Len. Peter grinned, which seemed to be the only possible answer.

"Come along to join the class 'ave we?"

"A watching brief only," said Stewart.

He had been carrying an army knapsack. From it he took two cartons of cigarettes and laid them on the work bench.

"Thass right," said Len. "Good boy. Pays his school fees in advance. What's on the menu for today?"

"I'd like to go on with the motor car. Last time we'd got to starting it without the key."

"Right. Lessee if you remember what I told you, or we shall 'ave to go through it again."

Stewart screwed up his eyes as though he was trying to remember a piece of repetition and said, "Join the live terminal of the battery to the coil and put a spanner or a screwdriver across the solenoid."

"*Not* a spanner," said Len reproachfully. "Want to electrocute yourself? A screwdriver, with a wooden handle."

"Sorry. Of course. A screwdriver."

"But before you start any larks like that, you've gotter get the bonnet open."

"That was where we left off last time."

"Right. And to get the bonnet open you've gotter get the car open, in most models, that is. In the good old days, it was apple pie. Why? Because cars had door handles that stuck out. Slip a piece of pipe over the handle and exert pressure. Not so now. Nowadays you've gotter use your intelligence. Think it out. First thing is, try the boot. You'd be surprised how many people lock all four doors and leave the boot undone. Well, let's suppose it is locked. Whatyer do next?"

Stewart turned the matter over in his mind. Exactly, thought Peter, as though he had been faced by a problem in geometry to which he was certain he knew the answer, but couldn't quite put his finger on it.

Finally, he said, "From what you've taught me, Len, I'm certain I couldn't deal with the lock of a modern car. So the answer must be to get, say, a loop of wire through one of the windows and jerk up the retaining catch."

Len shook his head reproachfully. "You've got brains," he said, "try usin' 'em. Wass the first question you've gotter ask yourself? *'Ow much noise can I make?*"

"Of course. If noise doesn't matter, no need to fiddle. Smash the window and put your hand through."

"Right. But suppose you can't take a chance on making a lot of noise?"

During the next ten minutes Len, by explanation and demonstration showed how many ways there were into a car which was apparently securely locked. He was a born teacher. Better, Peter considered, than most of the masters at Chelborough.

At the end of this time he said, "Thass all for today. Gotter get on with some real stuff."

The real stuff was on the bench at the end of the shed. It was a model of a 1905 De Dion Bouton car. The undercarriage had been completed and Len was now putting in some delicate work on the chassis.

"Is that your hobby?" said Peter, opening his mouth for the first time. It was clear that he had said the wrong thing.

23

"'Obbies," said Len scornfully, "are for characters like you 'oo can, no doubt, afford them. I'll get two 'undred smackers for this baby."

"And the man you sell it to will sell it on for four hundred," said Stewart.

"Thass the way it goes," said Len. "See you soon."

"Not very soon, I'm afraid. We go back to school next week."

"Keep you boys at it, don't they?"

Peter managed to bottle up his curiosity until they were in the train on the way home. Then, as they had the carriage to themselves, he uncorked it.

"What on earth," he said, "are you up to? Are you practising to be an amateur cracksman? An up-to-date Raffles, something like that?"

"Nothing like that at all. What I'm doing is, I'm broadening my mind."

"You mean you're going to write crime books?"

"I might. The field's a bit overcrowded at the moment. A lot of women have taken it up. Elbowed the men out."

"If you're not going to commit crimes or write about them, then what's the point of it?"

"Let me ask you a question. What do *you* propose to do when you leave school?"

"My uncle wants me to go into the Church."

"Do you want to?"

"No."

"Then don't. Many a young man has had his life ruined by being shanghaied into a job he doesn't really like. What's your own choice?"

"That's the trouble," said Peter. "There aren't all that many jobs I could do."

"In fact, you haven't made your mind up."

"Not really. Have you?"

"Certainly not. It would be premature." Stewart leaned back in the corner, extracted and lit a cigarette, ignoring the no smoking notices and offered one to Peter who shook his head. He had tried smoking before, but had never seemed to get the knack of it.

24

"I am," said Stewart, "a flower, with my petals wide open awaiting the arrival of a butterfly or a bee to pollinate me and make me productive."

"You talk a lot of balls."

"Not so. I am quite serious. Ask yourself this question. Is anything that you are being taught at school going to fit you in any way to survive in the battle of life? A battle in which, let me tell you, there are an increasing number of losers nowadays."

"Well – I suppose – if I was going to be an accountant it might be a good thing to learn some simple arithmetic."

"Adding and subtracting?"

"That sort of thing."

"All done by machines now. Think again. What about all that Latin they're stuffing into you?"

"I did wonder about that," said Peter. "Learning Latin is supposed to make you write better English."

"A bit second-hand, isn't it? Now consider the things that I am learning from Len. For instance, he taught me how to use a public telephone without putting any money in. Useful, you must admit. You might have an urgent telephone call to make, matter of life and death, and no money with you. Then we had a session on locks. He didn't try to teach me to pick them. That takes time and is a lot more difficult than books make out. What you have to do is collect keys of different sorts and file off most of the wards, or bevel the edges down. I've already got more than fifty and I'm adding to them every day."

"I suppose that could be useful," Peter admitted.

"And I'll tell you one of the first things he taught me. If you've worked out in advance what you're going to do in any circumstance, you do it automatically, without having to stop and think. Now suppose some evening you're up to something and a man looms up in the dusk and challenges you. What do you do?"

"I run away."

"Absolutely wrong. You do that, he'll run after you and as like as not he'll catch you. No. You run straight at him, with your head down, aiming for his stomach. Three advantages. Your head's the hardest part of your body and his stomach's the softest part of his. It'll hurt him much more than it hurts you. Then, if you do the job properly, he'll be in no state to chase you. Last but not least, if you've kept your head down he won't be able to recognise you."

Peter thought about this. He said, "I must admit there was one moment outside that French church when that idea would have been very useful."

"Exactly. Then you agree that the course I'm adopting is sound and sensible."

"No, I don't. I think you're a nut case. And you'll probably end in jail. That looks like our station coming up."

"I trust," said the Reverend Dolamore, at breakfast, two mornings later, "that you enjoyed your trip to France."

"It was very interesting," said Peter truthfully.

"You left before your school report arrived. I have it here, with a covering letter from your housemaster."

"If Brindy's sent a letter as well, I imagine it's because he couldn't get enough nasty comments into the report."

"It's not an encouraging document," agreed his uncle. "And, as he points out, it may have serious repercussions on your future."

"You realise he's doing it on purpose."

"I don't follow you."

"I mean that he wants me to do badly so that he can get the scholarship switched to a protégé of his own."

"I'm sure you must be wrong. No schoolmaster wants a boy to do badly."

"If he didn't want it, why didn't he let me take the 'A' Level subjects I asked for? French and Maths – and you can take the History of Art as an extra. I could do all right in all three of those."

"He explained when he made the choice. It would do no good for you to take French. You could get a high mark, but no effort would be called for. What you needed, he felt, was the toughest subjects possible. As the hymn says, 'Not for ever by green pastures must you idly rest and stay. But must smite the living waters from the rocks about your way'."

"No shortage of rocks," said Peter. "If I do have to leave

at the end of the summer term, aged just seventeen, with no 'A' Levels, or very poor grades, how do you think I'm going to earn my living?"

"You're quite sure you don't wish to take orders? I could arrange with my own Theological College to take you on very easy terms – "

"It's a kind thought, but absolutely not. I should make a hopeless parson."

"It's not financially rewarding," agreed his uncle, looking sadly round his shabby living-room. He was a kindly man of limited intelligence and was fond of his nephew. "Had you any ideas of your own?"

"If I could manage to stay on for another year and leave at the end with a respectable lot of 'A' Levels in sensible subjects like French and Maths, I expect I could get a teaching job whilst I was looking round for something better."

"If you did lose your scholarship grant I might manage, perhaps, to find the fees – "

"You might," said Peter, with unexpected firmness. "But I shouldn't let you do it. I'd run away if you tried. No, we shall just have to hope for the best."

His uncle sighed and said, "By the way, didn't you tell me you finished your French trip at a place called Sassencourt? There's something in the *Telegraph* might interest you."

The Paris correspondent of the *Daily Telegraph* had passed on a report in *France Nord-Ouest*. It was headed; 'A Heartless Crime'.

It recorded the theft from the parish church of Sassencourt-with-Pont d'Ancrette of its chief treasure, a Niccolò Frumenti triptych. The *curé* had discovered the loss when he came into the church for mass. It appeared that the thieves had forced the church door on the previous evening and had taken down and broken up the triptych, feeding the beautiful woodwork into the stove. They had then left with the three canvasses. Unhappily for him one of the local farmers, André Renouf, had been returning home. He had evidently seen the men emerging and had challenged them. They had struck him repeatedly with some heavy weapon, forcing him to his knees and had finished by kicking him on the head and leaving him in the ditch beside the road. Fortunately his family, alarmed at his non-return, had come to look for him. If he had spent the night in the ditch he would almost certainly have died. As it was, he was too shocked to give any detailed description of his assailants. He said that there were two of them and he had the impression that they were foreigners. The Commissaire of Police from Etretat had announced that every effort would be made to apprehend the men concerned. He suspected that they were members of a gang who had committed more than one theft of pictures and other artistic objects in different parts of France. He had invited the assistance of the Département des Trésors Nationaux in Paris. The details of the paintings had been circulated to every museum and gallery in France and to a number of foreign institutions. Any attempt by the thieves to profit by the fruits of their sacrilege and violence would almost certainly lead to their apprehension.

"Brutes," said his uncle. "I'm glad you didn't run into them."

"So am I," said Peter.

3

"The man who set this puzzle," said Peter, "must have been brought up on a diet of Thackeray and Trollope. 'Pointed heroine'. That must be 'Sharp'."

"Of course," said Stewart, who was not really listening to him.

It was early evening in the first week of the summer term. Stewart was reading an Army & Navy Stores catalogue and Peter was struggling with the crossword in the *Guardian*, which he used to purloin from the reading-room. He could normally finish *The Times* crossword in thirty minutes, the *Guardian* in twenty. This one seemed to be causing him some trouble.

"'Downhill cleric', looks like 'Slope'. Was there a clergyman called Slope?"

"Search me," said Stewart.

"It might be 'Slips'."

"Toss for it. Do you think Alvin would object if I bought a drill and plugged it into the electric light?"

"He'd blow a fuse at the very idea."

"I'm afraid you're right. All the same, I think I'll take a chance on it."

"What do you want it for?"

"It's got a metal-filing attachment. Just the thing for my key collection. Come in. Don't trouble to knock. Ives and Dolamore keep open-house."

This was to a cheerful bulldog called Henry Bear. He was head of the house. He looked worried.

He said to Peter, "Brindy wants a word with you, Dolamore. Better hurry along. He's not in a very good mood."

"So what?" said Peter. "I'm not in a very good mood myself. Do you think Brindy reads Trollope?"

"The only novels I've ever seen in his study are Agatha Christie and Edgar Wallace."

"I feared as much. With a housemaster like that, are you surprised that the intellectual standard of the house is so abysmal?"

He departed. Bear sat down, looked at the nearly completed crossword and said, "Peter's a bit of a brainbox, isn't he?"

"He's adequately furnished in the top storey, yes."

"I wish you and he would take life more seriously."

"My dear Henry, I was telling Peter only the other day that I devote many of my waking thoughts to the question of what we are going to do when we leave school."

"I'm not talking about leaving school. It's now I'm worried about. Do you know what Brindy wanted to discuss with me? House prefects; there are two vacancies. I suggested you for one of them."

"I don't imagine our Alvin fell over backwards with pleasure."

"He said you were a disruptive influence."

"Did he though?" said Stewart. He sounded delighted. "What was discussed next in your *tête à tête*?"

"He said that *his* choices were Measures and Whitlock."

"Measures and Whitlock. It sounds like the name of a shop doesn't it? A rather superior chemist's. I'm sorry. I diverted you. What did *you* say?"

"I said that Measures was all right. But that Whitlock was a wimp."

"I would guess that he's got about as much backbone as a stick of spaghetti. Boiled spaghetti. I hope you told Brindy that."

"Of course I didn't. I just said I'd rather have you. Then he stumped me by asking if I'd discussed the idea with you and I had to say that I had and you'd turned it down. 'Just as I thought,' said Brindy. 'He takes nothing seriously. He could be a good athlete if he took the trouble. But I never see his name in any house team.' I had to remind him that you represented the school at racquets. 'Exactly,' said Brindy. 'A selfish game which gives him the maximum opportunity for showing off.'"

"O wad some power the giftie gie us, to see ourselves as others see us," said Stewart who may not have known much about the Victorian novelists, but was able to find a quotation from Burns for most occasions.

"He's right, you know. You could be a useful cricketer if you gave your mind to it. You've got a good eye, a strong wrist and sound nerves. Must have, to play racquets the way you do."

"But why should I devote these talents to futile games like cricket and football? Flannelled fools and muddied oafs."

"You're mad," said Bear. The way he said it, it sounded like a compliment. He knew that Ives was not someone to provoke. As one of the editors of the Chelburian, the school magazine, he exercised considerable power in the school. This publication appeared half-way through each term and, under its current directors, had been so outspoken that the headmaster had been forced to censor one of the items in the last issue. This had not prevented the unauthorised version from obtaining a large and much treasured circulation.

Peter came back as Bear departed. He said, "Well that's that. It looks as though this is my last term."

"An ultimatum, was it?"

"Pretty well. A slight improvement in Latin. Nothing to write home about. History, results appalling."

"And all the History reports written by the Reverend Alvin Brind himself."

"That's right. Even if I did succeed in producing some decent work, it'd be easy enough for him to pick holes in it."

"Which particular period of history is he expounding to your form at the moment?"

"Charles the second and James the second."

"Rather an interesting period to have lived in, I always thought. If you could avoid being killed by the Great Plague or burnt to death by the Great Fire. Look at Pepys. Having it off at the back of the church during the sermon."

"We don't get that sort of thing from Brindy. Just politics and treaties and dates."

"Cheer up," said Stewart. "I had a letter from Father Elphinstone this morning. Copies of the earlier mission

31

accounts and other material of interest. The wheels are beginning to turn. Listen hard and you will hear them grinding."

Mention has been made, in describing Peter's visit to the Château de Lambrécie, of the fact that its proprietor, Joseph Wellborn, did not entirely approve of his elder sister, Mrs. Shilling. This disapproval stemmed from her marriage.

In Joseph's opinion there had been one point only in favour of Frederick Shilling as a husband. The fact that he was a very wealthy man. The debit side massively outweighed the credit. Frederick was German, was Jewish and had notoriously made his money from trade.

His grandfather, Hermann Schilling (the 'c' was dropped later) had come to England in the golden nineties of the last century. The principal product of his firm was buttons. ('Buttons! I ask you!' said Joseph). However, this was a period in which ladies wore a great number of buttons on their dresses and Hermann flourished. Later he turned to more general drapery products. But the buttons were neither forgotten nor forgiven. They cost him the chance of membership of more than one London club.

Hermann's son, Walter, had restored the family reputation by performing creditably on the western front as an infantry soldier and by confining his connection with the family business to pocketing its profits. He had married a very minor member of the aristocracy. His son, Frederick, had lived entirely on inherited wealth. Lisa was the only offspring of his union with Constantia Wellborn.

When Frederick had died of a cardiac aneurism, whilst attempting a difficult putt on the thirteenth green at Sunningdale, Joseph had proposed that his sister and her nine-year-old daughter, Lisa, should come to live with him at Lambrécie. He pointed out the advantages of a girl being brought up in France and dilated on the superiority of the French educational system and his own capacity for acting as a substitute father. He did not mention the additional consideration, that it would have suited him very well to have had a finger on the Shilling fortune. He was a rich man himself, but the expenses of keeping up the château were considerable and were getting no less.

His sister would have none of this. She had no opinion of French education and valued her independence. For the next seven years Lisa had lived at home and attended a desultory succession of small private schools. Mrs. Shilling was in some ways a stupid woman, but she had enough sense to realise that her daughter had inherited a lot of her father's shrewdness and, as she would add when discussing her with her friends, his obstinacy.

When Lisa was sixteen and some more formal education had to be considered, a number of reasons had led Mrs. Shilling to consider Chelborough. It had been one of the first boys' public schools to admit girls to its sixth form and had by now attracted a sufficient number ('of the right sort,' said Mrs. Shilling) to form a separate house for them. Moreover, she had approved of the woman in charge of the girls' establishment, a Mrs. Marble ('not quite a lady, but very nearly, and motherly, but firm'). Since she only met Mrs. Marble on the single occasion that she visited the school she cannot be blamed for misreading her character. Lisa, from daily contact, was able to form a more accurate opinion.

"She's a bitch," she said when discussing her with Stewart. "Only she manages to hide her bitchiness under layers of oily charm."

Stewart said, "A *fausse bonne femme* in fact."

Mrs. Marble controlled the eighty pubescent females who formed her unruly household with the help of an assistant, a Miss Troop, known to all as Troop the Snoop. This lady instructed in swimming and eurhythmics, kept her eyes open and acted as Mrs. Marble's spy.

She had already reported that she found the conduct of Lisa questionable. She had not been able to put a finger on any particular act of insubordination. It was her general attitude to authority.

"She's a proper little bolshie," said Miss Troop.

"I don't think," said Mrs. Marble, with one of her professional smiles, "that we can found a complaint on such general grounds. What does she do? Does she talk a lot with the boys, or with any particular boy?"

"They all talk to each other before class and after class.

And in some cases, no doubt, during class. I have suggested that the girls should sit apart from the boys in the form rooms, but my suggestion has not been listened to – as usual."

"Well," Mrs. Marble had said, "if any particular instance should come to your notice – "

She would have been interested if she could have been in Stewart's study at the conclusion of morning school that day. Enter, left, Bartlett, a precocious boy of fourteen carrying an envelope. Judging it by its deckle edges and light pink colour it could, without exaggeration, have been described as a dainty missive. He announced, with a leer, "I was slipped this by one of the girls to give to you."

Stewart examined first the envelope, dispassionately, then Bartlett, with distaste.

"You're a proper little procuress, aren't you?"

"If you say so," said Bartlett. He sidled out and made for the school library where he took out the POY – RY volume of the *Greater Oxford English Dictionary* and looked up 'procuress'

(1) A female advocate or defender
    (Not very promising, but wait.)
(2) A woman who makes it her trade to procure women
    for the gratification of lust.

Bartlett said, 'Coo' and smacked his lips. Like most of the boys he greatly admired Stewart. He confided this titbit of information to his best friend who said, "Did you see what was in the note?"

"Of course I didn't, you fool, it was stuck up."

"Fool yourself, you ought to have steamed it open." After which invigorating exchange they repaired to the school dining-hall to stoke up. For the last three years feeding by houses had been abandoned and a buffet system for the whole school had been introduced in its place, much to the general satisfaction.

When he had read Lisa's note Stewart, who was careful about such matters, burnt it and deposited the ashes in the wastepaper-basket. There was no need for a written answer. If he agreed with her proposal he would nod his head when they met in class that afternoon. If he disagreed he would shake it.

He considered the matter carefully. Getting out of the house after lock-up presented no difficulty. One of the sets of bars on the ground-floor windows had been carefully attended to and opened as smoothly as an unlocked door. More to the point was the fact that Brind would be out for the evening. He had been invited to dinner by the Archdeacon, a social occasion from which he was unlikely to hurry away. This piece of news came from Brind's maid, Annie, a well-tried and reliable source of information.

Next he considered the suggested meeting place. The shed behind the pavilion was normally locked. Probably one of his keys would open it easily enough, but here, again, fate was on his side. Brind had recently procured the sacking of the young man who acted as assistant to the cricket professional, Tom Jennings. He was called Barker and was currently working out his month's notice. The dismissal was not entirely unjustified. Barker was the possessor of a vocabulary which fascinated the boys and either amused or offended the staff according to their feelings about such matters. Brind, overhearing him in full spate, had been outraged. Also he suspected, although he had no actual proof, that it was Barker who had forced one of the boxes in the chapel and removed part of the Easter offering.

Barker was, naturally, one of Stewart's allies. If asked to oblige he would certainly leave the shed unlocked. So far, so good. Yes, a nod was called for.

Lisa's problem was not so easily solved. She knew that Mrs. Marble, after a good dinner and at least half a bottle of wine, would retire to her sitting-room with the port decanter. The view of the house was that she was usually more than three parts cut before she went to bed each night. This may have been an exaggeration, but she would certainly be far too sleepy to be making any rounds inside or outside the house. Miss Troop was another matter.

She had her own sitting-room and bedroom in the wing of the house, but these were rarely occupied until a later hour. The earlier part of the evening she would spend attending the meetings of one or other of the school societies – she was a member of all the reputable ones – or, if there was no meeting, in a general prowl around the premises.

A nuisance to one and all.

Since the discipline of the boys was not her concern she took no action with regard to the occasional all-male smoking or drinking parties which she encountered, but her sentry-going had made her acquainted with lying-up spots. On this particular evening she had visited the gym changing-rooms, the shed behind the armoury and the attics above Big School, which were full of the scenery and props of past theatrical performances. In none of these had she found anything except silence and solitude; though had she probed a bit further into the attics she might have discovered the captain of cricket under a backdrop of Elsinore Castle instructing one of the small boys in the facts of life.

Coming out of the hall she stood, for a moment, looking out over Big Field. It was a misty night of early May. Rugger posts had disappeared and the ground was getting ready for the sports. In one corner she could see a row of practice hurdles had been set up. She saw something else. At the far end of the field, where the heavy roller was parked beside the pavilion, a shadow had moved. Or was it her imagination? She paused to think about it.

To go straight across to the pavilion would involve traversing the whole length of the field, in which, as she knew, there were a number of traps, dangerous on a night of such poor visibility. She had no desire to break an ankle falling into the long-jump pit. But there was an alternative. If she retraced her steps and made her way to the front gate she could reach the rear of the pavilion via the main road. She had seen no further movement. If it had been someone there, they had either gone home or they had disappeared into the pavilion. Either way, no hurry.

In fact Lisa and Stewart were not in the pavilion, but in the shed at the back. They were lying side by side on an unrolled pitch cover and both of them were smoking. Whilst he enjoyed a cigarette, for once in his life Stewart regretted this. If Lisa had not been smoking it would have been much easier for him to roll over and start some serious petting. At the moment they were restricted to conversation.

"Of course Marble is butch," said Lisa. "Look at the way she dresses."

36

"If she's butch," said Stewart, "what's her line in meat?"

"Usually some soppy junior girl. Certainly not the Snoop."

They both had a giggle at the idea of Miss Troop being anybody's *petite amie*.

"Snoop's a sadist. Do you remember Peggy Ashford, two terms ago? She positively *hounded* her out. She'd like to get her teeth into me, too."

"We're both afflicted," said Stewart. He described the manoeuvres by which the unspeakable Brind was trying to oust Peter and promote his own career at the same time.

Lisa listened with interest. Her feelings about Stewart were ambivalent. He was exciting to be with and fun to talk to. Streets ahead of other boys in that respect. (Her best friend, Virginia, had said about a boy they both knew 'Driving me home in his car after the dance, Tom did nothing but talk. And you'll never guess. He talked about *cricket*.') Stewart would certainly not have talked about cricket and had a smooth approach to the opposite sex. He was a grown-up boy in some ways, surprisingly juvenile in others; but did she want him to demonstrate his technique on her? The cigarette was a useful prop. It was giving her time to make up her mind.

She said, "It makes it difficult to believe in religion, doesn't it? I mean, when you meet clergymen like Brindy. Poor little Peterkin. Such a nice boy. He looks as though butter wouldn't melt in his mouth."

She seemed, thought Stewart, with a touch of resentment, to be more interested in Peter than in him. He said, "Don't be fooled by his innocent appearance. Look what he got up to in France."

It was a story worth telling and Stewart told it well. By the time he had finished Lisa was propped up on one elbow staring at him. She said, "He told you all that?"

"Yes."

"In strictest confidence, I should imagine."

"Well – yes."

"Then *why* have you told me? How do you know I'm not going to repeat it to all the other girls in the house?"

"I don't think you will."

"But you don't *know*."

Until then they had been speaking in whispers. But Lisa was so indignant that she had forgotten caution. Miss Troop, who had reached the back of the pavilion, heard the voices. They were coming from the shed where nets and other accessories were stored. And one of the voices was a girl's.

She did not hesitate. She was a muscular product of Bedford Physical Training College and unafraid of any likely opposition. As she strode forward the toe of her sensible shoe hit a stone and sent it spinning against the door a second or two before she got there.

The warning, though short, proved fatal to her plan. It gave Stewart time to get onto his feet. He saw the figure framed in the doorway and without a moment's hesitation ran forward and butted with his head.

Miss Troop gave out a sound which was half-way between a gasp and a scream and fell over backwards onto the gravel path. She was winded, shaken and wildly indignant. It was several minutes before she could scramble to her feet.

Then she started to think furiously.

'If the girl had been one of the members of the house, she had got such a start by now that she would have climbed back by whatever route she had got out. But she might not have had time to clear up all evidence of the escapade. Her clothes might be torn. She might be bruised or cut. She hoped she was.'

She had dropped her torch when she fell and it was no longer working. This meant that she had to go carefully until she reached the road. Then she broke into a vigorous canter. Speed was vital. Every second was important. When she burst into her sitting-room she found Mrs. Marble asleep in front of the fire with a half-empty decanter on the table beside her; and not only asleep, but snoring gently.

Miss Troop was in no mood for formality. She grabbed Mrs. Marble's arm and shook it. Mrs. Marble opened her eyes, took one look at her assistant and said, "My goodness. What *have* you been up to?"

"Never mind about me. It's the girls. Or one of them. We must go round all the dormitories and cubicles now."

"Whatever for?"

Miss Troop was conscious that time was being wasted. This upset her and made her less coherent than usual. However, in the end Mrs. Marble seemed to have grasped the essentials of her story. She said, "What makes you think that one of our girls was involved?"

"I heard her speak."

"Could it not easily have been a boy. Until their voices break they sound quite girl-like."

Miss Troop had not thought of this and it made her angrier than ever. She said, through clenched teeth, "I *know* it was one of our girls. When they – when I was knocked over – I heard her giggle as she ran past. It was definitely an upper-class giggle."

Mrs. Marble considered this. She said, still showing no signs of stirring from her chair, "I would hardly regard that as conclusive. But even if it was, have you considered the effect you will produce if you go round the house looking like that?"

"Like what?"

"Have a look in the glass."

This was the first time Miss Troop had thought about herself. She took a quick look and could not help agreeing. Her fall had not only torn the sleeve of her anorak, it had left a deposit of mud on her chin and a long scrape down one side of her face.

"You must clean yourself up first," said Mrs. Marble. "And I should advise an application of disinfectant to that scrape. There may be bits of gravel in it."

"And by the time I've done that," said Miss Troop bitterly, "the girl will have tidied herself up, too, and will be pretending to be fast asleep."

Mrs. Marble was a tactician. She said, "You're right about that. I'll tell you what I'll do. I'll have a word with the headmaster first thing tomorrow morning and he'll speak to the housemasters. They may have some idea who the boy was and that could lead, in turn, to the girl."

With this Miss Troop had to be content.

"I agree with you," said the headmaster. "If Miss Troop's suspicions are well-founded, it was a disgraceful episode. Involving a physical attack on a member of the staff."

"Deplorable," agreed Mrs. Marble. But she thought that the headmaster did not sound desperately upset.

"I will certainly ask the housemasters for the names of likely candidates. There are only a limited number of boys who are sufficiently mature to – er – date girls. Or," he added, being a realist, "for the girls to wish to date them."

"When Miss Troop spoke to me last night, headmaster, it did occur to me to wonder whether she had acted wisely in rushing straight in. If she had returned to the school for help it should have been possible to apprehend the culprits without difficulty. I didn't say so at the time, because she was clearly upset. But it does seem to me that she behaved imprudently."

"Indeed," said the headmaster. "And if she raises the matter with you again, I think you should tell her so."

That night he repeated the whole episode, in detail, to his wife. When she heard about the upper-class giggle she laughed so much that she almost rolled out of bed.

On the following morning the headmaster found an opportunity to speak separately to all of his housemasters. Apart from the Day Boys' House and the Girls' House there were seven boarding-houses at Chelborough. The heads of four of them thought about the matter and reluctantly scribbled down the names of half a dozen boys each who might be sufficiently attracted by the selection of females on offer to take the trouble to break out at night for an assignation. The head of the fifth, who was young and idealistic, denied that any of his boys would behave in such an unseemly way. The head of the sixth, who was elderly and disillusioned, said that the senior boys in his house were so busy chasing the smaller boys that they had no time to think about girls.

It was only the Reverend Alvin Brind who unhesitatingly nominated a single candidate. He said, "I have no evidence that anyone was out of the house that evening. Indeed, I make it my personal responsibility to see that all doors are locked at seven o'clock. Anyone who has a legitimate reason to be out has to come through the private part of the house and explain himself to me."

"Quite so," said the headmaster patiently.

"However, if it were shown that, despite my precautions,

a boy had succeeded in breaking out I should not be at all surprised to find that it was Ives."

"Stewart Ives," said the headmaster. "You really think so?"

"I do."

"A remarkable boy in many ways. One of the finest racquet players we have had in the school for years."

"I would have more confidence in him if he devoted his talents to team games."

"It's a curious thing," said the headmaster ignoring this, "that in every generation there seems to be one boy whose name is familiar to everyone from the youngest to the oldest. He may not be outstanding at work, or a cricket or football colour or one of the nominal 'bloods' in the school hierarchy, but he is what television would no doubt class as a 'personality'. In Ives' case it might be something to do with his editorship of the school magazine, although we've had enterprising editors before who have left no particular mark on the school. No. It must simply be a question of character. It did occur to me to wonder – although, as you know, I never interfere in these matters – why you had not made him a house prefect."

Brind, who had listened with ill-concealed impatience to these remarks said, "You talk about character, headmaster. Surely the real point is whether it is a good character or a bad one. I find him a disruptive influence. And, for all his talk, one who accomplishes very little."

41

4

"Action!" said Stewart. "The hour has struck."

Peter looked up suspiciously. He had found a puzzle in one of the intellectual monthlies which involved the solution of interlocked anagrams in English and Latin. It was the sort of challenge which he enjoyed.

It was some days after the Miss Troop episode, of which Stewart had given him an abbreviated account. He was now busy filing and shaping the wards of the growing selection of keys which lived under a loose plank in the study. He said, "We are going to commit a burglary."

"*We* are?"

"It's a two-handed job."

"Couldn't you get Barker to help you? He can't be sacked twice."

"No. The job must be done by us."

"You're mad," said Peter. "And I don't see why I should get involved in some lunatic scheme which will probably end in you getting not only sacked, but jailed as well."

"There's gratitude for you," said Stewart.

"What do you mean?"

"Here am I working my fingers to the bone, metaphorically speaking, to save you from having to leave Chelborough in disgrace at the end of term and you are not prepared to lend a hand to help. Really, words fail me."

Peter stared at him. "What are you talking about?"

"I have concluded that the only way of proving certain suspicions which I have about our housemaster, is to examine his papers."

"Oh, if it's *Brindy* you're going after – "

"Did you think I was going to rob a bank? No, no, just a

simple domestic crime. All the same, it will need thought and care. Most crimes do. Let me show you."

He extracted from the table drawer a sheet of paper on which he had started to draw a plan of the private side of the house.

"Few boys have been subjected to more heart-to-heart talks and improving homilies from Alvin than myself. Standing demurely in front of his desk, listening to his remarks on purity and the team spirit, I allowed my eyes to wander, from time to time, over his study-cum-sitting-room and its fixtures and fittings."

As he said this Stewart was filling details into his plan.

"I also, as you may remember, joined the Geographical Society and the Computer Club last term. Both bodies hold evening meetings and I was thus able to go out and return through the private part of the house. On one occasion when Alvin was absent I penetrated to the kitchen quarters and had a most interesting talk with Annie. I was then able to complete my ground-floor plan particularly the kitchen and scullery. However, let us concentrate, for the moment, on the study which forms, as you will see, a sort of no-man's-land between the school side of the house and the private side. It has French windows leading out to the garden and two doors. One on the school side, the other on the private side. This is our battleground. Now let me test your tactical sense by asking you a question. When we are engaged in the study, which of those doors would you lock?"

"Easy," said Peter. "Lock the private side-door and leave the school side one open."

"Easy, but wrong. We lock them both. We also leave the French windows open. Should Alvin come down from his bedroom it will take him some time to deal with the private side-door, even if he has a spare key, since we shall have left the key in that lock, on the inside. In the end I think he will give up and decide to come in through the boys' part of the house and enter the study that way, perhaps hoping to use his spare key. Whichever course he adopts we shall have plenty of time to replace any papers we have disturbed and to depart through the French windows, leaving the swag behind us."

"The swag?"

"Certainly. In case we are interrupted, we are staging the episode as an outside job. There are a number of silver objects in the room. Photograph frames, candlesticks, athletic cups and so on. All these we shall have placed in a sack, which we lay ready in the flowerbed outside the window. That is the picture we are painting. The burglar, alarmed by the arrival of the householder, has dropped the sack there and fled. You will now see, incidentally, why it is necessary to lock both doors. The burglar would certainly have done that as a safety precaution before commencing operations."

"You talk about locking doors. Where's the burglar supposed to have got the key? Or did he bring duplicates with him?"

"Unnecessary. Annie tells me that when Brindy goes to bed he locks the school side-door and leaves the key in the lock. Our burglar finds to his delight – as I have ascertained to be a fact – that this key also fits the private side-door. Excellent. He locks it as well and leaves the key in *that* lock. Now he cannot be disturbed from either direction."

"I suppose that means that we shall have to break in through the French windows."

"Indeed no. They are very securely fastened. We could only open them from the outside by breaking the glass and since Brindy sleeps in the room above, that would be unwise. At one time," added Stewart dreamily, "I did think of introducing a powerful sleeping-draught into his bedtime cup of cocoa – "

"For God's sake!" said Peter.

"But I decided, in the end, that the practical difficulties ruled it out."

"So I should bloody well hope. You might have poisoned him."

"I should not have regarded that as a disaster. But don't worry. A far simpler solution presented itself when I inspected the kitchen. The window of the scullery has a primitive catch which will be easy to force. We enter through it, pussy-foot along to the study and lock *both* doors, leaving the key in the private side-door. We then open the French windows, place

44

the various silver articles outside in a sack and are comfortably placed to proceed with our work."

"Which is?"

"We concentrate on the desk. If what I'm looking for is anywhere, that's where we shall find it. Both the upper drawers are likely to be locked. There's no question of forcing them. The noise involved rules that out. We must hope that one of my special keys will do the trick."

"When do we start?"

"Shortly after midnight tonight."

Peter gulped. His mouth was suddenly dry.

"Annie tells me that Alvin is an early bedder. I did wonder whether perhaps she went to bed with him, but I don't think his tastes lie in that direction."

Peter, feeling a worm as he did so, said, "Am I really going to be much help?"

"Certainly. I shall need you to give me a leg up through the scullery window. And anyway, as it's all for your benefit, you should be glad to help."

"I don't quite know what you're hoping to find. But if I'm going to be useful, of course I'll come."

"I felt you would want to. We will, of course, wear gloves. Rubber gloves will be best. I have two pairs. Even more important is the question of footwear. I gave a lot of thought to this. In the end I found, put away in a cupboard at home, what seemed just the job." From his box he produced two pairs of felt overshoes. "I think Mr. Pye must have acquired them on one of his trips to Canada. They're made to wear over your shoes. Try them on. They are quite silent and leave no identifiable print. You find them comfortable? Good, then I think that's all. Unless you have any suggestions."

"No," said Peter. "You seem to have thought of everything."

He wished he could have sounded more enthusiastic.

He and Stewart shared a small, three-bed room with a West Indian boy known to his friends as Snowball. He was snoring as they crept out of the room. Once they had started, it wasn't too bad. They left the house by the unbarred window, circled the school building and opened the scullery window without

45

difficulty. Peter hoisted Stewart up and was pulled up by him. Stewart had a torch. Peter had a sack which they had scrounged from the mower-shed behind the pavilion. They reached the study safely, took the key out of the school side-door and locked the private side. Then they drew back the curtains and opened the French windows.

The moonlight, flooding through, enabled them to work with only occasional use of the torch. Peter felt the tension of the moment like a movement in his body. It was different from that time in the church in France. Then he had been frightened. Now he was excited. He was conscious all the time of their housemaster, asleep in bed, in the room directly above them. He almost hoped that he *would* wake up and come down. Would he be wearing pyjamas? It might be a nightshirt. His legs would stick out like matchsticks. Peter was so engrossed with this idea that he allowed two of the candlesticks he was packing into the sack to clink together. This drew a venomous hiss from Stewart, who had been trying key after key in the lock of the right-hand drawer.

After that he was more careful, but he realised that he was happier than he had ever been in his life before. For the first time he had slipped outside himself and could see himself, not as a tiresome bundle of sensations, but as an interesting person, doing an important job, redolent with prospects of triumph and disaster. It was to happen again, more than once, but he never forgot this first entrancing revelation. It reminded him of the first time he had been allowed to taste a top-class claret, but it was more potent than any wine.

He realised that he had been neglecting his part in the affair. All the silver he could lay hands on was now safely stowed in the sack. He carried it to the window and stepped outside. As he lowered it into the flowerbed he fancied he saw someone moving in the hedge at the bottom of the garden. The movement was not repeated. Probably it was the clouds playing tricks with the moon.

When he got back into the room, Stewart was using his torch to examine the contents of the drawer he had succeeded in opening.

46

He said, putting his mouth close to Peter's ear, "See what I've found here."

It was three small packets of papers, each with an elastic band round it. Peter thought they were sets of accounts. They went into Stewart's pocket. The only other papers seemed to be form lists and reports. He turned his attention to the second drawer. No trouble this time. The same key opened it. He took out five notebooks bound in green cloth and two larger books with red covers. Stewart handed Peter the torch and started to flip through them. Peter could tell by the expression on his face that he was pleased.

Scarcely moving his lips he said, "Treasure trove." He handed Peter the green books, took the red ones himself and jerked his head towards the open window. They crept out into the moonlight, crossed the lawn and went out through the gate in the hedge. It was close to the point where Peter thought he had seen someone moving. When they were clear of the garden he mentioned this. Stewart said, "Easy to imagine things at night."

A few minutes later they were back in their study. Before leaving it, they had fastened a doubled blanket across the narrow lancet window, taping the edges carefully to the woodwork. Stewart switched on the lamp and they dumped the books and papers onto the table.

The green notebooks were five diaries, each one covering one calendar year. Not all the days were filled up. In some there was very little. In some one word. In some nothing at all. The last one had been written up to the beginning of the previous week. All of them were in some form of shorthand.

The two red ones were cash books. They went back for several years before the diaries started. The entries in sums of money were straightforward. The explanatory items appeared to be in the same shorthand as the diaries.

"Now," said Stewart, "we have a lot of work to do." The clock in the tower added a full stop to this sentence by sounding the hour of one. "And we've got less than five hours to do it in."

"You mean – ?"

"It is on occasions like this I am sorry that I'm not a spy. If I was, I should be armed with one of those dinky little cameras. Hold it over each page, click the shutter and Bob's your uncle. Being ill-equipped we shall have to use a more primitive method."

"Copy it all out?"

"I'm afraid so."

He took some unused notebooks out of the cupboard and said, "We'll tackle the diaries whilst we're fresh. Remember, it's got to be an exact copy. With shorthand the least little squiggle can make a difference."

"All right," said Peter. "Let's get going." He knew that this was a job he could do better than Stewart. His mind was more precise and his hand was neater.

After a bit he said, "'Tisn't all in shorthand, have you noticed? Some of the proper names are written out in full. Redcliffe. Isn't that the dewy-eyed young cleric who preached a sermon last term? Got some sort of job at the Cathedral."

"He's the Bishop's chaplain. And here's Compton-Smith. He's the precentor. We're moving into deep ecclesiastical waters. Push on."

Peter became so absorbed in the work that the slow passage of the hours between night and morning swung past unnoticed. He had finished two of the books and was half-way through the third when a sound made him look up.

Stewart was asleep, his head on the table. He was snoring gently. Peter was delighted.

'I might not,' he said to himself, 'have Stewart's dash and flair, but I have more stamina.' He had always suspected that this was so. Now he could prove it. Without disturbing Stewart he slid the book he had been working on from under his hand, drew it across the table and added it to his own pile.

Stewart grunted, sat up blinking and focused his eyes on Peter. He said, "Sorry, I must have dropped off for a minute."

"For two hours actually," said Peter.

"What!"

"It's a quarter to five and I've finished. Hadn't we better be getting the stuff back?"

He indicated the five green and the two red books neatly stacked on the table. Stewart gaped at them. It was the

48

first time Peter had seen him at such a disadvantage and it increased his affection for him.

"You're dead right," said Stewart. "No time to lose." They went back by the same route. The only thing that had moved in the study was the moonlight, which now shone coldly on the open drawers of the desk and the mantelpiece despoiled of its silver ornaments.

Stewart said, "They have served their purpose and must go back exactly where they came from. I hope you can remember."

"I think so," said Peter. When he said this he was standing by the window. "There's just one snag. Someone seems to have moved the sack."

Stewart was so shocked that he almost forgot to whisper. He said, "Are you sure?"

"I know exactly where I put it." He was speaking slowly in an effort to control his own panic. "I can see the dent in the earth where I dumped it. Come and look if you don't believe me."

"Clear up in here first." Stewart was putting back the three small paper packets in the right-hand drawer, arranging them exactly as he had found them. Next he locked the right-hand drawer, put back the green and red books in the left-hand drawer and locked that. Then he sat, for a whole minute, quite still.

"For God's sake," hissed Peter, "let's get out of here."

"Pause for thought," said Stewart.

After a further agonising minute during which Peter saw policemen racing across the lawn, headed by an infuriated Brind, Stewart seemed to make his mind up. He gestured to Peter to stand still, unlocked the private side-door and went out. He was away for two minutes, which added two years to Peter's life. Peter guessed that he was relocking the scullery window. When he came back and had relocked the door he gestured to the French windows and they went out.

"We'll leave them open," he said.

When they were back in the study and had removed the blanket from the window, Stewart stood looking out. Dawn was coming up and the buildings on the other side of the

49

quadrangle were starting to show, black against the grey sky.

"What happened?" said Peter. "Who moved the sack?"

Stewart said, without turning round, "It's obvious, isn't it? Just think for a moment. Barker goes away today. It was Alvin who got him kicked out. His obvious riposte would be to pinch anything of Alvin's he could lay hands on and take it with him."

"Of course," said Peter. The relief was overwhelming. "You must be right. So he was the person I noticed in the hedge. He probably pushed off when he saw the light of your torch inside the room and came back later to try his luck again. And when he saw the sack put out ready for him," Peter could hardly finish for the hysterical laughter bubbling up inside him, "he must have thought it was Father Christmas."

"It's no joke," said Stewart, swinging round. Like all tacticians he disliked having his careful plans upset by the brutal intervention of chance. "I've got to think this out. On the whole, it may be to our advantage. I don't suppose Barker was half as careful as we were, so any signs that were left will be his signs, not ours. And he'll clearly be the number one suspect. But if he's been sensible enough to bury the silver somewhere and leaves it alone for six months, they probably won't be able to prove anything against him."

"Suppose he is caught and says he found the silver in a sack outside the window."

"Do you think anyone would believe him? Would you?"

"I suppose not," said Peter. He found it impossible to stop yawning.

When they got back to their dormitory, Snowball sat up in bed and said, "Where's you two bin?"

"We haven't been anywhere," said Stewart. "We've been in bed and asleep all night like good little boys."

"If you say so," said Snowball agreeably.

5

Proof, if proof were needed, that the Reverend Alvin Brind was not popular was afforded by the fact that when the news broke that he had been robbed, the universal reaction was hilarity.

Barker became a popular hero overnight. No one doubted that he was the burglar. It was also considered unlikely that anything could be proved against him. Indeed the ever reliable Annie reported that Brind had apparently said as much to the Inspector and the Sergeant from the Chelborough Force when they inspected the scene of the crime.

"And if he isn't keen for this chap to be pegged," said the Inspector, "I don't see why we should break our necks trying to help him." The Sergeant had agreed. They were having a cup of coffee in the kitchen at the time. This exchange also was overheard and reported.

In fact their housemaster not only seemed not to be regretting his losses, he appeared to be in unusually good form, more human and more forthcoming than usual.

"Oily Alvin," said Stewart. "Even grabbed my arm in a matey way and asked how the current number of the magazine was coming along."

"He's been better in class, too," said Peter. "Instead of dates and things he gave us a really interesting hour on Pepys' diary. He certainly seemed to know a lot about it. I expect it was the smut that appealed to him."

"I can't see what he's got to be so bloody cheerful about, all the same."

Peter said, "Mightn't it be because he had all that stuff insured and was glad of the chance to turn it into cash? He probably added in a lot of imaginary things, too, and doubled their value. The insurance company would assume that, being a clergyman, he was honest."

"I think you're right," said Stewart. "He's crooked enough for anything." But he was not happy. They had taken considerable risks. The fruit of success had turned sour. "I *know* he's up to something. You saw those packets of papers I took out of the right-hand drawer? Well, each bundle was six copies of the Mission account for the last three years. Sent by Father Elphinstone and intended, no doubt, for general distribution. So why did he hang onto them? The answer's in those diaries, I'm sure. If only we could read it."

Their first idea, that the shorthand was of the normal modern type, had been quickly disappointed. One of Lisa's friends, who had been studying shorthand in her spare time with an eye to a secretarial job, had produced a textbook of the Pitman school which had quickly demonstrated that the symbols used by modern stenographers bore little or no resemblance to the scribbles in the diaries.

It was on the fourth day, when Stewart's frustration had become extreme, that Peter had an idea. He said, "One of the things Brindy told us about Pepys' diary was that it wasn't written in a private cipher. It was in a system of shorthand invented by a man called Thomas Shelton." Stewart, who had been slouched in his chair, sat up suddenly. "Well, it occurred to me that if Brindy was nuts on Pepys he might have taught himself the same system."

"By God, so he might. That's brilliant, Peter. Where do we find out about it? Shelton?"

"I'll write to my uncle. He knows quite a lot about that sort of thing."

The Reverend Dolamore's answer arrived in a package three days later. He wrote, 'I am glad indeed, dear boy, that you are starting to take your historical studies more seriously. I am sure Mr. Brind will be pleased. I was, of course, aware of the facts you mention about Pepys' diary. The idea, which held the field for two hundred years, that it was in some sort of indecipherable code of his own, was dispelled by Lord Braybrooke. He discovered that it was written in a form of shorthand which was becoming popular at that time. The idea originated with the Reverend Timothy Bright, a most interesting man, who was nearly killed in the St.

Bartholomew's Day massacres in Paris in 1572, but managed to find refuge in the house of Sir Francis Walsingham, Queen Elizabeth's spy master. He was also a friend of Lord Burleigh and his system of secret writing was, no doubt, used by both of them in dealing with the plots against the Queen. It was refined and improved by the Thomas Shelton you mention and that was the version actually used by Pepys. It seems to have been roughly founded on the Greek 6 m μ ε 1 ο γ ρ δ φ 1 δ but very few specimens of this have survived – '

"Thank God for small mercies," said Stewart.

'It was subsequently taken up by Cicero and is said to have been based on five thousand arbitrary characters, later increased by Seneca to seven thousand, but it must have been a laborious and impracticable process, because it had been quite forgotten by the Middle Ages and no actual examples of it have ever been found.'

"Your uncle's enjoying himself, isn't he?" said Stewart.

"Well, it is his special subject," said Peter apologetically.

"Suppose we get back to Bright."

Skipping a couple of paragraphs dealing with China and Arabia, Peter read out, 'The most notable of Bright's books was a treatise on the art of secret writing. It was dedicated to the Queen. As you will see, there is an example of his system, which he called "Charactery" in the frontispiece of the book which I have enclosed with this letter. This is a life of Bright, which was printed at the beginning of this century and is rather a rare book, so I will ask you to take good care of it and let me have it back in due course.'

Stewart recapped the marmalade jar and moved it out of harm's way. Peter was studying the frontispiece. It consisted of eighteen closely printed columns of symbols, with a note explaining that it was St. Paul's Epistle to Titus, written in Charactery by Timothy Bright in 1586.

"Now we're getting somewhere," said Stewart. "All you've got to do is to compare what's here with the English version of the Epistle and the key is in your hands. Isn't it?"

"I'm afraid not," said Peter. "There are snags." He was turning the pages of the book as he spoke. "The first is that this isn't the system Pepys used. His one may have had some connection with Bright's Charactery, but actually it was quite a different system, which Shelton invented. He called it Tachygraphy."

"So what we really want is a text book of Tachygraphy."

"If such a thing exists."

"Ask your uncle."

The answer arrived three days later, also in a parcel. After expressing renewed satisfaction at Peter's interest in his historical studies, his uncle said, 'You are, of course, quite right. Pepys' diary was in Tachygraphy, not in Charactery. There are, I understand, two extant copies of Shelton's handbook which he called Zeiglographia. It was printed in 1650 and may have been the very work that Pepys studied from. One copy is in the Pepysian Library at Cambridge, the other in the British Museum. I could probably get you a reader's ticket in the holidays, though it might have to be in my name since you are still a minor. I will enquire about this next time I am in London.'

"Next holidays, for God's sake," said Stewart. "If it's going to be any use to us, we want the information right now. Next holidays will be too late."

Peter said, "Hold on. There's a postscript."

'I have managed to unearth one book from my library which contains an actual example of Tachygraphy. To tell you the truth, I'd quite forgotten that I had it. It is one of a set of volumes of Pepys' Official Correspondence on naval matters. It comprises the only fifty-six letters, out of a total of nine hundred and forty, which were written in this particular form of shorthand. I would suppose, having glanced at them, that this precaution was adopted because the subjects the letters dealt with were particularly confidential – such as the Prize Goods Scandal or peculation in the purchasing departments.'

"Is this going to help us?"

"We shall have to see," said Peter. "It might do. It's going to involve a lot of fiddling work." But Stewart could tell, from the gleam in his eye, that it was the sort of work he relished.

By that evening he was able to present a preliminary report.

He said, "There's one thing which really is helpful. In these letters proper names are written in clear, not in code. Have a look at letter x. 'Two thousand pounds $\theta < \odot 2$ Alderman Backwill'. In the translation this becomes 'Two thousand pounds *which is sent to* Alderman Backwill'.''

"Then you've got four words already.''

"Sort of. There are other places where θ can't mean 'which', but might mean 'who' or 'where'.''

"Tricky.''

"I can see that what I shall have to do is find a passage in Brindy's diary where the sense of what he's saying is fairly obvious. Then I'll fill in any known words from the Pepys letters and it shouldn't be too hard to guess the missing words, which will give us more symbols.''

"Right,'' said Stewart. "Then we must plan your work methodically. The best time will be from after tea until you go to bed. A straight run of five hours each day.''

"Always bearing in mind that a lot of that time I'm meant to be doing prep.''

"What are you at this week?''

"Latin construe. The *Aeneid*. Book four.''

"No problem. I'll get young Mowbray to do it for you. Nothing he likes better than turning Virgil's deathless hexameters into English prose. Devote yourself wholeheartedly to cryptography, my boy. *And* I'm ensuring that you're not interrupted.''

He had written out a notice, in large capital letters, 'DO NOT DISTURB. VISITORS UNWELCOME.' and this he now fixed to the outside of the door. It caused some comment, since boys spent much of their time drifting into each others' studies and gossiping. When Henry Bear queried it, Stewart explained that Peter was going in for a newspaper competition with a £500 prize. Mustn't be disturbed.

"Wish I could win a five-hundred-pound prize,'' said Bear, who never had any money. "Even a fifty-pound one would be helpful.''

That was on Tuesday. On Wednesday Peter worked until ten at night. On Thursday he worked until eleven. On Friday, when he proposed to continue until midnight, Stewart put his foot down. There was a red flush over Peter's cheekbones and his eyes seemed to be sunk further into his head than was at all healthy. He guessed that some unexpected snag had cropped up, but it was not going to be solved by Peter getting brainfever. So far he had refrained from any sort of interference. Now he said, "If you'll explain what the block is, I might be able to suggest a way round it, or over it, or through it. Dodging difficulties is one of the Ives' specialities."

Peter pushed away the untidy jumble of papers covered with hieroglyphics, ran a hand through his fair hair which was standing up like a halo and said, "I wish you could. Brindy told us that although Pepys wrote most of his diary in straight Tachygraphy, when he came to something indeli-cate – "

"Yes. I can see Brindy licking his lips at that point. I suppose he meant when Pepys was tumbling some wench."

"That sort of thing. Well, then he got much more secretive and used a super-private code of his own. It was a sort of numerical cypher, depending on abbreviations which he would understand, but other people wouldn't. As far as I can see, Brindy seems to have adopted much the same system in that sort of passage."

"Blow me down," said Stewart. "Don't tell me he's been having it off with one of the maids."

"No. The places where *he* gets dead secretive are where he's discussing money. It's maddening. I can translate a lot of the unimportant stuff now – the weather and house politics and things like that – which are no use to us, but as soon as he comes to money, which we do want to know about, I get lost in a maze of capital letters."

"Any particular letters?"

"A, B and S seem to be the favourites. P and D turn up occasionally. Since the topic is money I assume that 'A' could be accountant or actuary. 'B' could be banker or broker, or even barrister, in which case 'S' could be solicitor. Also there's one combination of letters which is constantly cropping up, 'I C R F'. It's obviously important, but I haven't been able to find it in any standard dictionary of abbreviations."

"Right now," said Stewart, "'B' stands for bed and that's where you're going. It'll all look a lot clearer in the morning."

Stewart was playing in the final of the Public Schools'

Racquets Championship. He objected, not unreasonably, to the tactics of his opponent, an unmannerly Harrovian, who kept grabbing hold of him. When he dragged himself back to consciousness he found it was Snowball who was shaking his arm. He said, "Something's wrong with Peter. Keeps talking. Think we ought to fetch matron?"

Stewart got out of bed and went across to Peter, who was rolling from side to side. There was enough light in the room to see that his eyes were half-open, but there was no sense in them. Then he said, in a conversational voice, "B. Must be something, mustn't it? B, B, B."

"Seems to have a bee in his bonnet," said Snowball. "What do you think we ought to do? If he rolls about much more he'll roll right out of bed."

Stewart, still half-asleep himself, was trying to think. He seemed to remember that it was dangerous to wake up someone who was having a nightmare. It could cause a disastrous shock. Or was that someone who was walking in his sleep? Whilst he was worrying about it Peter solved the problem for him by rolling to the edge of his bed and being sick. Then he sat up and said, "What the hell's happening?"

"You've had a nightmare and you've been sick. Don't bother, Snowball and I will look after it."

"I don't see why you should. I'll mop it up."

But Snowball had already departed.

"Relax," said Stewart. "Lie back. Take twelve deep breaths. That's right. Think beautiful thoughts."

By the time Snowball was back with a cloth and a bucket of water Peter was already asleep again. Looking down at his flushed face Stewart said, "Clearly it's time I took a hand in the game."

The next day Peter seemed to be his normal self. When he looked for his notes and papers Stewart said, "Not today, or tomorrow."

"I'm quite all right," said Peter. "Don't fuss."

"I'm not fussing," said Stewart. "I'm being realistic. A weekend off will do you all the good in the world. And it's no good looking for your stuff, I've locked it all up and I've got the key. Instead of stewing over those papers you're going to take some proper exercise. I've booked a racquets court for you and Bear this afternoon. You're neither of you any good, so you'll sweat like pigs."

"I thought we were in a hurry to get the answer."

"We are. And I propose to take certain steps in that direction myself."

Peter knew that further protests would be useless. Also the idea of a two-day holiday from the tantalising jigsaw in which he had buried himself had its attractions. He said, "I don't know what you think you can do, but carry on."

After lunch Stewart whistled up Bartlett, who seemed to have constituted himself his unofficial messenger-boy. He said, "Tell Dakin I want a word with him."

When Dakin came running, Stewart said, "I'm given to understand that your uncle is none other than the Lord Bishop of this diocese. Right?"

"That's right," said Dakin. He said it apologetically. It was not a relationship which had gained him any credit.

"Then listen carefully to what I'm going to say. Are you listening carefully?"

"Yes, Ives."

"Good. Tomorrow is the first Sunday out. I assume that you are planning to go home."

"Yes, Ives."

"Then when you've greeted your mother and told her how much you're enjoying yourself and all the normal lies, there's something I want you to say to her. Don't make it sound important. Just drop it in quite casually with other items, like what you had for breakfast and how many runs you made last Thursday. You follow me?"

"Yes, Ives."

"Now keep your eye on the ball, because here's where it gets important. Tell her that you've heard that I've got an extremely wealthy grandfather. Not just a millionaire, but a billionaire. And like all old buffers with too much money he's looking for a good cause to spend a lump of it on before he's carried off. Buying your ticket for Paradise is the technical name for it. So what I've asked you to find out, by dropping a tactful question to your mother, is whether the Bishop has any particular charity or charities which he favours. Now, have you got that?"

"Your grandfather wants to splash out some cash. Which charity is my uncle nuts on?"

"I think I put it a little more elegantly than that, but you have the gist of it. Report back here tomorrow evening at six."

"Right-ho," said Dakin and departed, happier than he had been since his arrival at the school.

Stewart wandered down to the racquets court to make sure that Peter was sweating properly. He trusted that the Bishop would not enquire too closely about his grandparents, one of whom was dead and the other as near bankrupt as made no difference. He hoped that Dakin would do his stuff. He wasn't much to look at, but if he were in the running for a scholarship he must have some brains. On Sunday, at six o'clock precisely, he justified Stewart's confidence in him. He said, "I think I've got what your grandfather wants, Ives."

"Good."

"The one thing my uncle's dead keen on is the Inner City Relief Fund – "

"Ah! You interest me strangely."

"He's – I forget the word – anyway he's the sort of head man of the fund."

"The Patron?"

"That's right. And he deals directly with the Prime Minister about it. Mummy says that if he plays his cards right he might even make Archbishop."

"Deservedly," said Stewart.

"Oh, and when he heard there might be some money coming his way he said it would be the second time School House had helped him. Mr. Brind has been supporting him for a good time. Some years ago he'd made something called a covenant. I didn't understand that bit and I don't think mummy did either. I expect you know about deeds of covenant."

"A seven-year covenant," said Stewart. "Yes indeed." The clouds were rolling away with a speed that was almost alarming. He had angled for a small fish and had caught a whale – or was it a shark? He said, "You've done excellently. I congratulate you." He fished out a fifty-pence coin and tossed it across the table. "Fill yourself up with buns and sausage rolls."

Dakin picked up the coin, looked at it for a moment, slung it back and took to his heels.

"Well, well," said Stewart softly. "A boy who values his principles above his stomach. Wonders will never cease. Must be the result of having a Bishop as an uncle."

Peter, coming in at this moment from the five-mile walk on which he had been despatched, said, "What are you sitting there mumbling about? You ought to be out in the fresh air, not slacking indoors."

"I have been far from idle. I have much to tell you. Sit down and give ear. In the long watches of the night, turning your problem over in my mind – "

"When you weren't snoring."

"Sages have ever been mocked. As I was saying, after mature reflection I decided that you had been looking in the wrong places. Since the topic was money, you had been thinking of bankers and accountants. Might I suggest a different interpretation? Bishops and Archdeacons. And, for good measure, Deans, Precentors and Succentors."

"Good God," said Peter. "Yes, I suppose it could be."

"As a clinching proof I have deciphered your mysterious 'I C R F'. It's the Inner City Relief Fund, of which our Bishop is the Patron and the moving spirit. Indeed, he has hopes that his efforts, well thought of by the Prime Minister, may move him up to Lambeth Palace."

"That's wonderful," said Peter. "We ought to be able to get home now. Let me have the papers – "

"Tomorrow," said Stewart firmly.

It took two more days, but with the thread in his hand Peter walked confidently through the labyrinth, turning corners which had baffled him before, selecting the right course when the road forked.

By bedtime on Tuesday the full picture had been painted. "There's a lot in the early diaries," he said, "about the question of house feeding against central catering. The change was made just before we arrived."

"You should talk to Bear about it," said Stewart. "The food

in School House was so bad that there was a riot. Some of the boys broke into the kitchen and helped themselves. They said it was that or starve."

"Brindy was obviously making a packet out of the old system. He fought tooth and nail to keep it. He even threatened to resign. But he thought better of it. It's clear, too, why he needed the money so badly. That's where Cathedral politics comes into it. First, there's talk about a chat with Redcliffe – "

"The Bishop's bum-boy?"

"That's the one. Then he moves up a step in the hierarchy and has tea with the Succentor, who tells him that Compton-Smith, the Precentor, is always threatening to retire and never doing it."

"Irritating for the Succentor. I suppose he had his eye on the senior job."

"They all seem to spend a lot of time working out who'd get what if someone else retired and Brindy is soon joining in the game with enthusiasm. You remember that letter to Redcliffe you saw. Well that was the first tickle. What he's got his eye on is a resident canonry. The Dean seems to have been stand-offish, but he realised that he might get round the Bishop by subscribing to his pet charity."

"More than the occasional subscription. According to Dakin he'd entered into a deed of covenant. It's a sort of tax wangle, isn't it?"

"That's right," said Peter. "My uncle gets people making them for his church. Small ones, in his case. If you do the thing properly, the charity gets back a lot of tax you haven't paid. But the thing is you've got to undertake to do it for a fixed period, *and you've got to keep the payments up*, or the whole thing falls to the ground. In the old days it had to be seven years. And that's what Brindy did. Undertook to pay five hundred pounds a year for seven years."

"Which, at that time, he could do out of his savings on housekeeping."

"Right. And when that stopped, he had to find the money from somewhere else. He hasn't got much capital of his own, I'd guess. At least, there's no sign of any dividends in his account books."

"So he helped himself out of the mission account. It must have seemed a pretty safe sort of swindle. No house knew what any other house had given. He was the only one who knew the real total."

Peter said, "Then all we've got to do is find out what that total was."

"And how do you suggest we do that?"

The two boys looked at each other. For the first time the enormity of what they were contemplating faced them squarely. Stewart said, "It's awkward, isn't it? Suppose we did ask the houses what they'd given each term, people would soon spot what we were up to. Someone would be bound to put two and two together. It would end in an official enquiry. And suppose we're quite wrong. We haven't got any actual proof. Suppose the money does come out of Brindy's own pocket. I can see us getting the sack for propagating a slanderous rumour and departing with our tails right down between our legs."

"It would be worse than that," said Peter. "We'd have to explain how we got the information. Housebreaking, reading people's private correspondence and after that no one would believe that it wasn't us who'd pinched the silver off the mantelpiece."

"I don't think it's as bad as that," said Stewart. "All we'd have to say would be that we'd talked to Father Elphinstone and suspected there was a shortfall somewhere. But I agree that we should only be vindicated if we were right. It's a problem. But there's usually a way round, if you really give your mind to it."

Unconsciously he was working his right wrist as though getting ready to meet a difficult service in the racquets court.

He said, "Do you remember Bear saying that he'd like to win a fifty-pound prize?"

"So what?"

"It gave me an idea."

"I hope it doesn't involve burgling someone else's study."

"Nothing so drastic. A little finesse should see us through. Gird up your loins for the decisive engagement. 'Now's the day and now's the hour. See the front 'o battle lour'."

"What on earth are those boys doing?" said the headmaster. He was walking across the quadrangle with Mr. Lathom, the Classics master.

Several pairs of boys were on their knees, apparently measuring something.

"I imagine that's the great competition, headmaster. The details were all in the school magazine. Perhaps you haven't seen the new copy yet."

"It was on my breakfast table this morning. I've got no further than an article – unsigned, but I presume it's by the editor – about a visit he and another boy paid to our London Mission. They seem to have extracted a lot of interesting information out of the missioner. I only wish more boys would follow their example. However, tell me about this competition. It must have a considerable pulling power if it's got boys crawling about on the gravel."

"It's called 'Know Your Own School'. There are about forty questions and there's a prize of fifty pounds for the first person to answer them all correctly. It's a race. The deadline is Tuesday evening, so they only have two days to ferret out the answers. You pay fifty pence for an entry ticket – they're on sale at the bookstore and the tuck shop. I'm told they're going like hot cakes."

"What sort of questions?"

"One of them was to give the distance in inches between the left-hand corner of the vestry wall and the right-hand corner of the war memorial."

"Yes, I see." There were now at least thirty pairs of amateur surveyors using tape measures, foot rules and pieces of string.

"Another was to give the Christian names of the staff. When I had been asked nine times for mine I concluded that the simplest course was to write them out and post them up on the notice board."

"I wonder if Miss Troop will be prepared to reveal hers. I've often wondered what the 'Y' stood for. But tell me – these questions are all factual?"

"All about the school, and all factual."

"I see. Then it is a contest of skill, not a gamble."

"There was a good deal of discussion about that point in the staffroom this morning. What one might call the Puritan Lobby was in good voice – "

"Led, no doubt, by Mr. Tuke."

"Your knowledge of your staff is encyclopaedic, headmaster. They were shouted down by the sporting element, who pointed out that since it was the object of education to prepare children for life, the sooner they found out that modern life consisted almost entirely of bingo and the pools the better for them."

The headmaster smiled faintly. He was himself a Puritan, but not an intolerant one. He said, "I imagine that the promoters of this – er – this contest have calculated the financial side carefully. Let me see. They would have to sell a hundred tickets to cover the prize money. That, you tell me, they will do."

"Easily, I'd guess. Even though many people are buying in pairs, one ticket for the two of them."

"Then there must have been certain overhead expenses. The printing of the entry forms."

"Since they were part of the magazine I imagine their cost would be absorbed in the general magazine budget."

"I see. Yes. Thought has been applied to this. Is it known who the promoter is?"

"I don't think there's any secret about it. Solutions have all to be handed in to the editor, Ives."

"Stewart Ives. Yes. A remarkable boy. Something of the F. E. Smith touch about him. Westminster Abbey or the Old Bailey. He has the makings of a financier."

"He's not in this for money. Any surplus has been promised to the Bishop for whatever charity he recommends."

The headmaster said, "Ah! That puts the whole thing on a different level." He sounded more cheerful. "Quite a

64

different level. If asked, I shall certainly vote in favour of it. Incidentally, I suppose the staff aren't allowed to enter."

"Boys and girls only, I understand."

"A pity. I shouldn't have minded having a shot at it myself. But thank you for your warning. I'll post my own Christian names on the notice board at once."

In the course of that morning Bear drifted into the Ives – Dolamore study. He said, "Some of those questions are real stinkers. How many headmasters of Chelborough since its foundation? Do you realise we've been going for nearly four hundred years."

"By the rules of the competition," said Ives severely, "the promoters are neither allowed to enter themselves nor are they allowed to give any assistance to competitors."

"Of course not. I wasn't asking for help. I was just making a comment."

"Then I will make a comment in return. Were you not aware that there is a history of the school in the library? Judging from the number of people I have seen heading in that direction you'll probably find yourself at the end of a long queue."

Bear grinned and said, "A queue is something I can deal with." He was back in ten minutes. He said, "You're quite right. The book had been more or less torn in two, but I got hold of the right half. Would you believe it, counting the present one we've had thirty-eight heads. One of them was in the job for fifty years, but the next one only stuck it for a year thus restoring, as you might say, the average. And talking of averages, I've had rather a bright idea. Question Thirty-Five – 'What is the highest score recorded as having been made in a cricket match at Chelborough? House games and lesser games are excluded.' It's a crafty question, because it looks as though it's meant to be confined to school matches."

"No comment," said Stewart.

"But it doesn't actually say so. I suppose you know that the school allows the pitch to be used in the summer holidays by the local cricket club. Tom Jennings prepares the pitch for them, for a consideration I imagine, and acts as one of the

65

umpires. I believe some pretty large totals have been notched up. I'm going to have a word with him."

When he had departed Peter said, "We hadn't thought about that one, had we? I suppose it's all right."

"Certainly. And the best of British luck to Henry."

"Of course, it won't stay exclusive for long. Anyone who wants to check on cricket scores will be bound to have a word with Jennings. Once Henry has put the idea into his head he'll tell all of them about holiday matches."

"'Facts are chiels that winna ding'," said Stewart, "'and downa be disputed'."

"I gather we've won the head's approval. Would you have guessed that his second name was Percival?"

Later that same day a deputation attended on the Reverend Brind. It was headed by Measures and was made up of the more influential middle-school boys. At the last moment Dakin had been press-ganged into it and carefully coached. They found their housemaster in his study. On the desk in front of him they were pleased to see an open copy of the School Magazine.

Measures was the spokesman. He said, "I can see you know about the competition, sir."

"I have just been studying it. Most ingenious."

"Yes sir. There were three questions we thought you might be willing to help us with."

"You are allowed to have help, then? The solution has not got to be all your own work?"

"Oh no, sir. Everyone's helping like anything."

"Well, then?"

"The first was your middle name. We know that the first name was 'Alvin'."

"The 'W' in my name stands for Washington. I was, I understand, named after the great American statesman. In the hope, no doubt, that it would make me as truthful as he was."

This was greeted with a polite murmur of laughter.

"And the next?"

"The date on which this became one of the official boarding-houses."

"I noticed the question. It is a tricky one. Originally the

whole of this building was part of the scholastic establishment. Some of these rooms were classrooms, others were used as accommodation for the visiting staff. I happen to know, however, that it was first separated off and used as a boarding-house in the autumn term of 1888."

This reply was greeted with enthusiasm. "You see, sir," explained Measures, "You've given us a swop."

"A swop?"

"I mean, sir, we can exchange it with boys in other houses for their dates."

"I see. Good. And that's all?"

"There's one other, but it shouldn't be difficult. Question Twenty-Five. How much did each house subscribe for the school mission in each term last year?"

"I'm not so happy about that. It's a financial question and these matters are usually regarded as confidential. Have other housemasters been willing to divulge these figures?"

"Oh yes, sir. We've already got York House, Firbank, Old House and Westbury."

When Mr. Brind still seemed to be hesitating someone kicked Dakin on the ankle. He said, "You know, sir, that the profit is going to one of my uncle's charities. I expect he'll choose the Inner City Relief Fund. I'm sure he'd be glad to know that you'd helped us."

"Yes. I see," said Brind. The way in which he said it seemed to imply that he saw a great deal more than they did. He unlocked the drawer of his desk and extracted a red covered account book.

"The figures for this house," he said slowly, "were for the spring term – fifty-five pounds. For the summer term – fifty-seven. And for the autumn term – fifty-three."

Pencils were scribbling busily.

"Is there anything more?"

"No sir. That's exactly what we wanted."

After they had departed, Brind got to his feet and moved across to the window and stared out of it. It had started to rain.

"Exactly what they wanted," he repeated softly. "Well, well."

*

"I've got it," said Bear, bursting into the study. Had there been more space he would have performed a war dance.

"Calm down, Henry," said Stewart. "What have you got?"

"The answer to Question Thirty-Five. The only true and correct answer. Two years ago the Chelborough Club played a visiting team that called themselves the Rabbits. 'They weren't no rabbits at cricket,' said Jennings. 'Top-class club players most of 'em. I well remember the score, because they'd rattled up four hundred and forty-seven with one ball to go. I was wondering whether they'd top four-fifty when the batsman – had a beard nearly as long as Grace's – ran half way down the pitch and hit the ball slap into the pavilion.' Four hundred and fifty-three runs. That's the right answer, no argument.' "

"And I expect Jennings will have passed it on to dozens of other earnest enquirers."

"Certainly not. I've promised him ten per cent of the prize money if he keeps his mouth shut."

"I'm surprised at you," said Stewart. "What a demoralising effect money can have. Have you got all the other answers?"

"Not yet. But I'll have them by this evening. We're doing a trade with a syndicate in Brooke House. We were able to sell them some good stuff we'd got from Brindy."

"Well, well," said Stewart. "So Alvin has been bearded in his den, has he and forced to reveal all. We are indeed approaching the finale."

"So now we know," said Stewart.

"Now we know," agreed Peter.

Neither boy sounded happy.

It was Wednesday evening. The competition result had been announced and the first prize, amid howls of 'favouritism', had been awarded to Bear as the only competitor to have the correct answer to Question Thirty-Five.

In answer to Question Twenty-Five, most of the other boarding-houses had returned totals comparable to School House. The Day Boys, where the contribution came directly out of the pockets of their parents, had topped the list. The girls, who were uninterested in slum boys, were last. The total for the year was one thousand four hundred and seventy-five pounds.

"Which means," said Stewart, "that Brindy pinched four hundred pounds."

"Yes," said Peter.

The two boys looked at each other. What had started as a game had degenerated suddenly into real life. After a long and uncomfortable pause Stewart said, "Well, what are you going to do about it?"

"What am *I* going to do about it?"

"It's your battle. I'm just your Chief of Staff. If you want to stop now, there's no compelling reason for going on."

"You mean, just sit back and do nothing?"

"If that's what you want."

Peter thought about this for a full minute, his face getting redder as he did so.

Then he said, "No. I'm damned if I do. That four hundred pounds which Brindy pocketed was meant for a lot of East End kids. We can't just let that go."

"You're forgetting two things," said Stewart coolly. "The first is that the four hundred pounds isn't going into Brindy's pocket. It's simply been diverted, via the Inner City Relief Fund, to a lot of different kids."

"All the same – "

"The second and more important thing is that we didn't go into this to blacken Brindy's character. The object of the exercise was to make him think twice about blackening *your* character and taking away your scholarship."

"You may be right," said Peter. "But it's still bloody awkward. Do you mean that I've got to form up in front of him and say, 'Either you give me a good report, or I tell on you to the authorities'? I couldn't do it."

"Nothing would be gained by such crudeness. No. A little subtlety is called for. You introduce the topic as though it was quite unimportant. You say, 'We thought, when we visited the Mission last holidays, that Father Elphinstone was getting rather past it. He was quite confused about figures. Do you know he was complaining that last year he only had £1,075 from us? What he clearly meant was

£1,475. If he gets confused like that about simple arithmetic one wonders whether he's really up to the job'."

"Hold on," said Peter, who was scribbling wildly. "I want to get this down. Father Elphinstone – can't add up – too old for job. Right?"

"Then you brush the whole thing lightly aside. Say, 'That wasn't what I wanted to talk about. It's my scholarship. If it's going to be taken away, I shall have to leave. I really don't know what I'd do. Perhaps Father Elphinstone would take me on as an assistant. He certainly needs a younger man to help him'. Brindy's no fool. By that time he'll have understood exactly what you're getting at."

"I wish you could do it. You'd be so much better at it than me."

"Your bird. You've got to shoot it."

At this point young Bartlett poked his head round the door.

"Your manners leave much to be desired," said Stewart. "Did no one ever tell you that it is usual to knock before entering?"

"Sorry, Ives. But it was urgent. Brindy – I mean Mr. Brind – wants to see Dolamore right away."

"You may set his mind at rest. Dolamore will be with him anon."

Bartlett grinned and removed himself. Peter had picked up the paper on which he had been scribbling and was muttering to himself. "Father Elphinstone – simple arithmetic – my scholarship."

"Don't deliver it as a recitation," said Stewart. "If it is to be convincing it must sound impromptu. And try not to look as though you were on a visit to the dentist."

After Peter had left he sat looking out of the window. Dusk was closing in and someone had turned on the lights in the chapel. They shone out through the memorial window which honoured the Chelburians who had fallen in two World Wars. At the last armistice day service the Reverend Alvin Brind had preached a sermon which had touched the hearts of all in the crowded chapel.

'Good Lord what is man?' he quoted to himself from his favourite poet. 'For as simple he looks, Do but try to develop his hooks and his crooks, with his depths and his shallows, his good and his evil, All in all he's a problem must puzzle the Devil.'

As minute succeeded minute, adding up slowly to ten, fifteen and then to twenty minutes, he wondered what could be happening. One thing was clear, Peter had not been slung out on his neck. It was nearly half an hour before he heard him coming back. He tried to detect from his manner of walking whether he was despondent or triumphant.

When he came in and sat down his expression gave nothing away.

"Well," said Stewart. "Did you manage to deliver your message?"

"Not exactly. No."

"Then what did you say?"

"So far as I can remember I said 'yes' twice and on two other occasions I gave a sort of gulp. Something you might transcribe as 'uh-huh'."

"Explain yourself."

"Well, Brindy seemed to be in a surprisingly genial mood. He invited me to sit down and started to talk about my scholarship. Here it comes, I thought. He's breaking it to me gently. Quite wrong. He was saying what a remarkable turn for the better my work had taken recently. He'd had two letters from my uncle, reporting my interest in Pepys and his diary and the shorthand and so on."

"Interesting."

"He said that this autumnal flowering of intellect at puberty was by no means unusual. I was clearly a late developer and was now starting to demonstrate my true abilities. He added that he'd had a similar report from Lathom, who'd told him that my Latin construe had suddenly shown signs of definite improvement. That was where I inserted my first uh-huh."

"A justifiable comment. Did you get the impression that he guessed, perhaps, that the translation was not all your own unaided work?"

"There was a glint in his eye, which seemed to indicate some reservations, but I was too interested in what came next to worry about that. This bit was on a very matey, man-to-mǎn sort of basis. He didn't actually pat me on the back, but the general impression was that we were two old friends discussing topics of mutual interest. What he was going to tell me, he said, was highly confidential and I was to keep it to myself for the moment. He didn't mind me passing it on to you, as he had every confidence in your discretion."

"Indeed! And what did you say?"

"That was where I got in my first 'yes'. Then he said, 'This chance of commending your work, as I certainly shall do when your scholarship comes up for review, has been particularly timely, as it is the last opportunity I shall have. At the end of this term I am handing over School House to Mr. Lampier and my history teaching to Mr. Westall. Following the retirement of the Precentor – none too soon, in my view – there has been a reshuffling of cathedral posts and I have been offered the Succentorship. It was not quite what I anticipated, but I have accepted it. No doubt it will be a first step to higher things'. Here I interpolated a second and rather hearty 'yes'."

"And then?"

"Then he got a bit serious and said, 'I shall be very much occupied with making the necessary preparations for this change, so I may not have much chance to speak to you again. We have had our differences in the past, but I think we can regard the account as closed'. I can't remember if I said 'yes' or 'uh-huh', but he must have got the impression that I agreed with him, because he shook me warmly by the hand and I slid off."

"What an old snake," said Stewart. He started to laugh quietly. "The account closed, a balance struck, a red line drawn under it. You get what you want. He gets what he wants." He thought about it. "A success, not a victory, wouldn't you say?"

Peter said, "Uh-huh."

PART TWO

IN-FIGHTING

There are two kinds of dealers involved in the illegal art trade. One might be the proprietor of a small Chelsea antique shop or Third Avenue junk shop, a flea-market *brocanteur*; the other a hazy figure who maintains no gallery and operates from his home. . . . Once set up in the trade, there is an almost constant flow of art coming from churches and châteaux all over Europe. Uninsured, unphotographed and often unmentioned in the press, these stolen objects make up a lucrative business. With the quantity of freight being shipped today there is no problem with transport. The objects pass so easily that the process can scarcely be called smuggling.

Bonnie Burnham. *The Art Crisis*

1

Number Twelve Priory Crescent North was the sixth door that Peter had knocked on that morning. At two there had been no answer. At three of the others his reception had been discouraging.

The door on this occasion was opened by a cheerful-looking woman not much more than thirty, Peter guessed. His street directory had told him it would be a Mrs. Carstairs. She proved more agreeable than the other five. She neither blocked the entrance nor jammed the door with her foot, but came right out of the house, examined Peter and must have decided that she liked what she saw.

"I'm sure you're selling something," she said. "But as long as it's not double glazing or insurance."

"Neither," said Peter. "I'm selling knowledge." He indicated the heavy canvas bag which he had put down on the step.

"An encyclopaedia, is it?"

"Not just an encyclopaedia. The *New Omnium Encyclopaedia*. The most up-to-date of all of them."

"Perhaps I could have a look at it."

"Easier if we took it inside."

Mrs. Carstairs thought about this and then said, "I must agree that you don't look like someone who's going to rob me or rape me, and in any case, there's only two pounds fifty in the whole house and that's for the laundry, so come in."

Following her in Peter noticed a school cap and a school hat hanging in the hall. He guessed that, with her husband away at work and the children at school, Mrs. Carstairs was simply glad of company and that this was why she had so recklessly invited him into her house.

Or not so recklessly, perhaps. The window of the sitting-room was wide-open and he could see an elderly man in the next garden assaulting the weeds with a hoe. He had a sour look on his face, as though he hated the weeds and blamed them for daring to be there. Peter decided that he would skip Number Fourteen.

He extracted a number of the volumes of the Encyclopaedia from the bag and displayed them on the table. They were attractive-looking books with cleverly designed covers.

"The set consists of ten volumes," said Peter. "Just over forty thousand articles, eight million words and two thousand five hundred illustrations."

"My goodness. That's certainly a lot of words. Would you care for a cup of coffee?"

"I'd love one."

The omens seemed favourable. So far, in a fortnight of effort, he had achieved only one actual sale, to an eccentric old lady who lived in a house full of cats and parrots. In addition there had been a number of expressions of interest which had not, so far, ripened into cash. Was this going to be his second real sale?

When the coffee arrived he explained the financial arrangements. "You choose one volume," he said, "and pay for that. The normal cover price is five pounds, but if you're buying a set you get it for four pounds fifty. You sign a form agreeing to order the other nine volumes, but that obligation can be cancelled at any time within thirty days. It gives you an opportunity to look through the volume you've got and make your mind up about the others."

"That sounds fair. I think I'd like the G – H volume. I've always been interested in hawks."

"An excellent choice," said Peter, sliding the contract form onto the table. This was the bit that always made him feel like a confidence trickster.

"I told you I hadn't got any money in the house. Would a cheque do?"

"Of course."

Some minutes later, as he was walking away down the pavement, Peter was doing some mental arithmetic. The Sales Manager of the Omnium Encyclopaedia Company had told him that some of their representatives made well over ten thousand pounds a year. His commission was fifteen per cent of the sales that he made. A set cost forty-five pounds – fifteen per cent of that was six pounds seventy-five. To make ten thousand he would have to sell – couldn't do it in his head – it must be about one thousand five hundred sets a year. He had a long way to go. Perhaps his technique would improve as he went along.

By three o'clock that afternoon, he had reached the end house in Priory Crescent South. It was rather larger than the others, had more garden and a wider frontage. The door was opened by an elderly man with a shock of grey hair and a pair of half-moon glasses. He peered over them at Peter, said, "Are you a government snooper, a public opinion pollster, or a salesman?"

"A salesman, I hope."

The man looked at the bag and said, "I suppose it's books. An encyclopaedia?"

"The *New Omnium*."

"Never heard of it. But come in. I'm interested in encyclopaedias. I've already got a few."

He led the way into a room at the back of the house. The windows were wide-open and the afternoon sun streaming in lit up the backs of the books which packed the shelves. Peter spotted the eleventh and last English edition of the *Encyclopaedia Britannica*, the twelve-volume 'Everyman' version, the *Dictionary of National Biography* with all its decennial supplements and the *Grand Dictionnaire Universel* of Pierre Larousse. Other shelves seemed to be full of works on mathematics and physics, many of them by foreign authors. He noticed Wittgenstein's *Lectures on the Foundations of Mathematics* and Laplace's *Essai sur les Probabilités*.

Whilst he was making this rapid survey of the shelves the old gentleman had picked up the volume P – R and was studying it. From where he sat Peter could not see the entry he was reading. Judging by the twitching of his lips it seemed to be causing him some amusement. After a minute he got up, walked across to one of the shelves, selected a book, returned with it to the table and continued his reading.

From time to time he broke off to make a note in minute handwriting on the pad beside him. Finally he said, "You were not, I take it, personally involved in the compilation of this interesting work?"

"No, indeed," said Peter. "I'm just a salesman."

"But you must have formed some opinion of the object you were offering for sale. I mean, if it was a vacuum cleaner you would have ascertained that it cleaned carpets."

"I suppose I should. Yes."

"That it extracted dirt, rather than spewing it forth." The old man closed the volume. He said, "In a sense, that is what this volume is doing. Spewing forth rubbish. I have been reading the article on quantum physics. It appears to have been copied almost verbatim from the article in the *Oxford Textbook of Physics*, with a few arbitrary alterations and additions, inserted no doubt to avoid a charge of plagiarism. Unfortunately these additions obscure rather than clarify the body of the article into which they have been inserted as arbitrarily as a cook sprinkles currants into a plum duff. There is a reference to the Schrödinger theory which the compiler seems to confuse with the Heisenberg uncertainty principle, without bothering to explain either of them."

The old man closed the book and steered it gently across the table towards Peter.

"If the other articles in your encyclopaedia are on the same lines, you are peddling what are not even second-class, but barely third-class goods. I must leave it to your conscience whether you can continue to do so. Good evening."

Peter was still blushing when he walked away down the pavement. It was true that the one article he had read, on French architecture, which was something he did know a little about, had seemed to him to be short and full of platitudes, but it had not occurred to him that the whole compilation might be a confidence trick. He quickened his pace. If he was going to do what he had in mind there was no time to lose.

When Mrs. Carstairs opened the door, he could see that she was worried. She said, "Oh, it's you is it? I ought to tell you that I 'phoned my husband at work and he wasn't very pleased."

"Don't worry," said Peter. "Here's your cheque. Tear it up and it can go into the wastepaper-basket with your contract." He had got this out of his bag and was tearing it up as he spoke.

"But – "

"Please forget this morning. Believe me, if I'd realised then what a rotten encyclopaedia it was I wouldn't have tried to sell it to you. Anyway, thank you for the coffee."

As he walked off down the path, Mrs. Carstairs stood quite still, looking after him until he had turned the corner.

"What did you say to the Encyclopaedia people?" said Lisa.

"Nothing much. I just gave them back all the samples and papers and said I'd decided the job wasn't for me. They said something about I'd agreed to give a month's notice, so I said they could keep the six pounds seventy-five they owed me, for the one sale I had made, in lieu of notice and took myself off."

"So you've worked for a fortnight for nothing at all."

"I'm afraid so," said Peter sadly.

"What you want is a drink."

"I can think of something I'd rather have first."

"O.K.," said Lisa agreeably.

Half an hour later they were having the drink as well.

They were in a two-room flat at the top of a gaunt Victorian pile in Shepherd's Bush. His uncle, who had died a year after Peter left Chelborough, had made him his residuary legatee. This had sounded exciting when the solicitors had told him. It had added up in cash to just over three thousand pounds. He had used much of this in a payment of illegal key-money to secure his tiny pad. His engagement to Lisa had been announced to her mother on the day that he had moved in.

When she had got her breath back, Mrs. Shilling had said, "I can't prevent you going to bed with that beautiful young man, but if you think I'm going to agree to your marrying him, think again. Of course, you can marry without my consent. You're both of age. But I don't suppose he'll want to marry against my wishes or to live on your money."

"Not only," said Lisa coldly, "has he refused to touch a penny of my money, but he has also made it clear that he won't marry me until he's got a good enough job to keep both of us."

"Very proper," said Mrs. Shilling. "I imagine you're going to have to wait quite a long time."

The second part of this comment was made to herself, not to her daughter. It looked like being an accurate prediction. It was not an easy time for a young man without professional or technical qualifications to get a job. Peter's first idea, that he could live on government bounty whilst looking round for an opening, had been scotched by a new regulation which imposed a compulsory period of a year between leaving school and applying for social security. This was, no doubt, designed to effect a cosmetic improvement in the unemployment figures. Just exactly what a school leaver without parental support was supposed to live on in this period was not clear. If a few of them died of starvation this would, of course, further diminish the numbers of the unemployed.

It was Lisa who had suggested a solution. Peter still had some of his father's money left. With this he had paid the fees at International House and had got the PSA Preparatory Certificate, which entitled him to instruct foreigners in English. A number of his pupils, as he slowly built up his class, had turned out to be anti-Khomeni exiles.

The older ones were serious-minded men who seemed to know, in their heart of hearts, that they were never going to get back to Iran and that a grasp of English represented their only hope of employment. The younger ones were more active. They spent their spare time parading the streets with placards and leaflets describing the horrors of totalitarian Iran. So many men and women tortured and maimed; so many killed.

Peter used to dispute with one of the most intelligent, a thin boy called Mohammed Jemal. "You are wasting your time," he said. "The Ayatollah Khomeni will pay no attention to your posturing and shouting." To which Jemal had replied, "You do not understand. We have friends and relations who are suffering. We are the lucky ones, who have escaped. What we are doing now may seem trivial, but wait. A time will come." There was a flint-like look in his eyes that killed argument.

Having discovered, by trial and error, that he was a competent instructor it had occurred to him next to apply to a well-known firm of scholastic agents for a job. He knew that it was no good trying for a post in a school. The state schools required a Teaching Diploma and the better private schools were looking for men with university degrees. But there were other possibilities.

"There's Nigel," said the young man who interviewed him. "He's had to leave his preparatory school because he simply can't cope. I don't mean that he's an imbecile. Far from it. He's dyslexic, but that was a handicap the school was prepared to cope with. The trouble is that his brain seems to move so much more slowly than the average child's. He wants very careful handling. It's a good family. House in Kensington. Father in the City. Mother what you might call a society figure. It's a resident job and the pay's good."

Peter wondered what it was about Nigel that had left such an attractive job available to a late-comer like himself. Was he, perhaps, one of those children who indulged in tantrums and spat at his instructor? In fact Nigel had turned out to be a docile child, who took to Peter at once. In a month he had made quite remarkable progress and his father was delighted.

At the end of the month Nigel's mother returned from an extended visit to the South of France. On the first afternoon that she was back she despatched Nigel on a walk with one of the maids and commanding Peter's presence in the drawing-room made it clear to him that certain additional duties, or delights, were in store for him. When Peter had declined her invitation she had immediately complained to her husband that he had tried to rape her. Her husband, who had a clear idea of his wife's proclivities, had told Peter that he must pack up and go. He did so apologetically and pressed on him a cheque for his next month's salary.

When he told Lisa about this she said, "You were too soft with him. You should have stuck him up for three months' salary. A solatium for your wounded feelings."

"It wasn't my feelings that were wounded," said Peter. "It was his. Poor chap. I really felt sorry for him. Fancy being married to a bitch who could try to seduce the hired help

81

on the first afternoon back from a trip where she had been having it off with God knows who on the Riviera."

"You can't afford to be high-minded. That's reserved for people with six-figure incomes. What are you going to try next?"

The encyclopaedia had come next.

On his return that evening, sitting together on the edge of Peter's bed, they had knocked back the better part of a bottle of Spanish wine before Lisa said, "It does look as if it's going to be quite a long time before we can go to my mother and say, 'Here is the latest young capitalist. Let the banns be read'."

Peter said, "It's the fault of our bloody silly Victorian relic which pretends to be an educational system. I remember Stewart saying to me – it was when we were coming back from that visit to Southwark – is anything you are being taught at school going to fit you for survival in the battle of life? And try as I would, I really couldn't think of anything."

"What sort of things do you think you should have been taught?"

"Well, for a start, we might have been allowed to take the PSA foreign language certificate. It would have been more use than any 'O' and 'A' levels and would have saved me from having to sit around for three months, to say nothing of spending a further chunk of my non-existent capital on their fees."

"As long as you're not suggesting that you should have been taught to pick locks and steal cars."

"No. I don't see much future in that. But we might perhaps have been taught shorthand and typing. Girls seem to pick it up and they get jobs easily enough. You've had – how many – three since you left school? Your present one sounds the best of the lot."

"It's interesting," agreed Lisa. "And well paid. Actually I don't have to do much typing, but I sometimes think – "

She was interrupted by the electric buzzer which had sounded three times. This was an indication that there was something in the post for the top flat. When Peter came back he was carrying three letters. One was a circular, marked Urgent. (Do you want the chance of winning fifty thousand pounds?) The second was a local election broadsheet. Both went into the wastepaper-basket unopened. The third looked more interesting. Peter did not often get private communications.

'Dear Peter,

If you are not overwhelmed with employers queuing eagerly for your services, perhaps you would be prepared to consider a little idea I had in mind. If so, come round to the above address any time in the early evening. We work late in this *atelier*.'

The address was Starfax Ltd., 4 Bolingbroke Mews, Wilton Place, Knightsbridge. Peter did not need to look at the signature. He had recognised the spidery handwriting as soon as he opened the envelope.

A single note from a flute, or perhaps from a clarinet, had interrupted the rhythm of the tympani and the strings to announce the start of a new movement.

Lisa said, "Of course you must go. But don't let Stewart talk you into anything stupid."

2

Six cottages stood shoulder to shoulder along one side of Bolingbroke Mews, fronting a row of what had once been stables and were now garages. Peter observed that five of the cottages were asserting their identity defiantly, by different coloured plaster frontages, by elaborate chromium fittings on the windows and fanciful knockers on the doors, by tubs of flowers beside the steps and bronze lanterns on the door posts.

Number Four was adorned only by the plate on the door which said 'Starfax Ltd. Registered Office. Knock and Enter'. When Peter had done this he found himself in a small front-room which already contained two people. One of them, a young man with carefully styled hair and a cheerful face was scribbling busily. The other, who seemed to be about the same age, had his back to the room and was studying what looked like a street directory.

The scribbler got up and said, "If there was another chair, I'd ask you to sit down. Have you come to see the boss?"

"Mr. Ives did ask me to look in one evening."

"Then I guess you must be his old school chum, Peter. Right? I'm Ron. That chap with his back to us pretending to work is my brother, Len."

When the second man swung his chair round, Peter recognised him. He said, "Oh, we've met before."

"That's right," said Len. "Last time we met I was teaching the boss how to steal cars. We've progressed since then. Now we're strictly legitimate."

"Roughly legitimate," said Ron.

At this moment the clatter of a typewriter, which was being bashed in the next room, knocked off and Stewart appeared. Peter had kept in touch with him in a desultory way since they had left Chelborough, but they had not seen each other for nearly a year.

Stewart had cultivated an aggressive moustache and this combined with an obviously expensive suit to give him an air of maturity. Peter wondered whether he had grown up inside as well as outside. He seemed genuinely pleased to see him. He said, "Getting to know the staff? They've introduced themselves? Excellent. Come into my *sanctum sanctorum*."

The inner room was larger than the outer one, but not much. There were two desks facing each other and a long table along the wall which held a row of wire baskets, seemingly full of incoming and outgoing mail.

Peter said, "Was that you performing on that typewriter?"

"It was. It took me a month to learn and it was bloody hard work. You'll have to do the same."

"Hold your horses," said Peter. "Do I take it you're offering me a job?"

"Of course. I always promised myself that as soon as Starfax really got going I'd cut you in on it. Do you like our premises?"

"It's a beautiful little house. It must be worth a packet. How did you get hold of it? Is it all yours?"

"It belonged to my great-aunt, who gave it to my aunt, who gave it to me. The ground floor is our office and I live above it. Customers are impressed by the address and even more impressed if they drop in to see one, as sometimes happens."

"And what is Starfax doing exactly?"

"At the moment, believe it or not, it's earning me quite a lot of money. Quite sufficient for me to add to my team of part-time assistants and employ a whole time deputy. That's the job I'm offering you."

"For old times' sake, or because you really want one?"

"Because I want one. But if you've already latched onto an interesting and remunerative post – personal assistant to a millionaire, or something of that sort – "

"Nothing like that. In fact my last job, which I've just chucked in was a stumer."

He told him about the encyclopaedias.

"In that case," said Stewart, "my offer would seem to have come at the *moment critique*. I'm sure you'll find the job

I have in mind for you interesting. And well suited to your capabilities."

They were back in their study, three years ago. It was a sort of game. Stewart would indicate that he had some scheme in mind and would talk all round it. If, in the end, he forced you to ask him directly what it was, he had won a point and you had lost one.

Peter decided that it would be quicker to surrender. He said, "What does Starfax do?"

"Well, I imagine you've read the columns in the papers. 'You and your Stars'. That sort of thing."

"I've seen them. I don't bother to read them."

"Why not?"

"They don't seem to mean much, as far as I'm concerned."

"Exactly. They're impersonal. The millions of people born between certain dates are labelled with a so-called sign of the zodiac and given the same advice. And pretty woolly advice at that. 'If you have certain plans in mind, now is a good time to put them into operation.' 'You'll find it easy to get started, but don't jump to conclusions.' I mean, what's the use of that sort of thing?"

"No use at all."

"Now Starfax is quite different. We start at the other end. We invite people to consult us."

"And do they?"

"Certainly. Our advertisements are discreet, but well placed. At the moment we're dealing with between fifty and sixty replies a week. We make people a simple offer. If they will let us have the day and year of their birth, together with the exact hour, if they happen to know it – which a lot of people seem to do – and will enclose the preliminary fee of five pounds, we will take a look at them. If we feel for any reason that we are unable to help them, we will return the five pounds. That enables us to weed out the duds and the practical jokers from the genuine enquirers."

"How do you know the difference?"

"Instinct mainly. We're very rarely wrong. If we can accept them, we write back and tell them so. As soon as they have sent us forty-five pounds – that makes up the full fee of fifty pounds

– we will get to work on their case. Incidentally this gets rid of a few more duds that we may have missed on the first trawl. Very few people are prepared to pursue a joke enquiry at the cost of fifty pounds."

"When you say, get to work on them, what exactly do you mean?"

"That's where my staff of external investigators come in. They're all in jobs which put them into contact with members of the public. Ron is a free-lance journalist who specialises in business topics. He is also a part-time opinion pollster. Len is, among other things, a typewriter mechanic. That gives him the *entrée* to almost any office. Even if he gets slung out he'll probably have time to chat up the secretaries and typists. Their cousin, Les, moves in a different stratum of society. He's a bookmaker's assistant, runner and debt-collector. He was also, at one time, a good boxer in the light-heavyweight class. Those are our regulars. We've got a number of occasional helpers who happen to be well placed. One of them's a female traffic warden in Kensington. And there's an Indian dentist. You'd be surprised how chatty people get when they're in the torture chamber."

"That's all very well. But suppose it occurs to someone to blow the gaff. You'd look pretty silly if one of the popular newspapers came out with 'Starfax a Fraud'."

"It's a chance we have to take," said Stewart. "But it's not as risky as you think. Ron, Len and Les are solid. And the others aren't given the whole picture. All *they're* told is that we want to know if the applicant exists before we waste our analytic expertise on them. The extra information they always seem to bring is incidental. We don't ask for it."

"O.K.," said Peter. "You've got people who can get round and ask questions. But what, exactly, are they supposed to be finding out?"

"First, of course, as I said, whether the people exist. We've been given a name and an address. If either of these is phoney – it is sometimes – then we drop them. The forty-five pounds goes straight back, with a cold missive saying we can't deal with people who aren't candid with us. And although you might not believe this, in about half of these cases they apologise and say they were using a pseudonym or an accommodation address because they were a bit shy of their families – or friends – finding out what they were up to and they send the forty-five pounds back again, along with correct particulars. In this game once someone's truly hooked he's almost impossible to shake off."

Peter thought about it. Like all Stewart's schemes it was outrageous and fantastic, but there was a wild logic somewhere at the heart of it. He said, "What am I supposed to do?"

"Help me with the letters."

"Answer them, you mean?"

"Of course. If you can manage four or five a day that would be splendid."

"But what am I supposed to say?"

"In most cases you'll have a report from our field staff to work on. One thing they always try to discover is what the correspondent really wants to do. Give you an example. One man was a solicitor's clerk who went in for amateur theatricals. What he was longing to do, as Len found out, was to sing. We told him that he was destined to be an opera star so he joined the local operatic group and was a great success. Took the leading part in the *Desert Song*. All he'd needed, you see, was self-confidence. And the voice of the stars gave him plenty of that. He was so pleased that he told all the other members of the company about us and we got half a dozen new clients. I remember we told one of them he was a born comic. He started telling funny stories on every possible occasion and became such a menace that they turned him out of the company. That wasn't one of our successes. You have to take the rough with the smooth in this job."

"You want me to start straight away?"

"The sooner the better."

"You realise I'll have to write my answers in longhand?"

"And I'll have to type them out. So the quicker you learn to type the better. I've still got the Instruction Manual that I used. It seems as good as any of them. Take it home with that typewriter and get stuck in."

When Peter reached his flat he found Lisa waiting for him. She said, "What have you been up to now? It must have been an effort lugging that typewriter up three flights of stairs."

"It nearly killed me," said Peter. "And I'm devilish hungry. Do you think you could knock up some scrambled eggs or something?"

"I could do you eggs and corned beef. And you can have half a tin of sardines for starters."

Over this impromptu meal Peter tried to explain his new job. "Stewart's paying me four hundred pounds a month to begin with. It'll go up as I get into it. He can afford it, you know. His turnover must be nearly ten thousand pounds a month and that's increasing by leaps and bounds. If it gets beyond the two of us, he did wonder whether you'd care to be roped in. After all, you can type."

"I wouldn't want to give up my present job. It's the most interesting I've had."

"Something to do with pictures, you said."

"Pictures and panels and tapestries. Mostly they come from France and we sell them here and abroad. A lot of them go to South America. Anyway, I don't see Starfax lasting. Sooner or later someone will blow the gaff. It's on a par with the crazy sort of things Stewart went in for at school."

"Crazy maybe. But they got me an extra year at Chelborough, remember?"

"And might have got both of you the sack. It's clear why he went in for it. He enjoyed pitting his wits against old Brindy. Also, of course, he did it for love of you. And for God's sake stop looking embarrassed. Aren't we allowed to refer to one male person loving another without being supposed to imply that they sleep together? All right, then. What was I saying?"

"You were saying that Stewart goes in for these mad schemes because he loves excitement and me."

"Exactly. That business of burgling Brindy's study. Surely he could have got the information he wanted without going as far as that?"

"I don't quite see how," said Peter doubtfully. "And I've got to admit that it affected me, too. I don't just mean that I was excited. Most of the time I was in a blue funk. But there were moments when all my senses seemed to be functioning exceptionally well. Something to do with adrenalin, no doubt. When we were in his study I suddenly realised that Brindy was asleep just above us and I found I was able to look right through the ceiling and through the mattress and I saw him quite clearly lying in bed with his thin legs sticking out of his nightshirt."

"Did he really wear a nightshirt?"

"That bit was imagination."

Much later that night Lisa said, "One day he'll get involved in something too big for him and he'll get hurt."

Peter knew she was talking about Stewart.

By the end of the week he had got into the swing of his work. He found that a few platitudes went a long way. 'One of your friends will start making unreasonable demands on you. Be firm.' 'There are bargains to be picked up if you keep your eyes open.' This was based on a tip from Len that the woman concerned spent a lot of her time at local auctions. 'There is a busy period ahead of you, so take every opportunity to rest and relax.' This suited almost all the applicants, male or female.

Typing went ahead too, but proved more difficult to master than prophecy. "You must tackle it properly," said Lisa. "It's no good hunting and pecking. Put a handkerchief over the keyboard and bash on with it. It doesn't matter if you make mistakes. All you've got to do is remember the letters for the four fingers on each hand. Don't worry about the thumb. Keep that for the space bar. Now then – the left hand – "

"QAZ: WSX: EDC: RFV: TGB."

"Ten out of ten."

"It's easy enough to recite them, when you give yourself time to think. It's when you have to hammer them out that I panic."

"Practice makes perfect. Let's try some Xs and Zs. 'My ex-cousin plays the sax in the jazz band'."

Peter groaned.

On Friday evening he revolted. He said, "I got my first pay today. We're a pair of capitalists. Do you realise that between us we earn well over one thousand pounds a month?"

"Less tax."

"A trifle of PAYE."

"And it's not capital. It's income."

"Don't be such a filthy realist. We're going to celebrate. As secretary to the head man you must have become an expert at booking tables. Book us one at the most expensive restaurant you can think of."

Lisa said, 'Wow', and got busy on the telephone. She chose a very well-known and expensive restaurant in Jermyn Street that one of her previous employers had sometimes taken her to. The head waiter remembered her, showed them to their table himself and proffered the massive bill of fare as though it were a sacred missal.

"We're only pretending to be rich," said Lisa. "So let's do it thoroughly. We'll kick off with smoked salmon."

"And to drink," said Peter, consulting the equally impressive wine list, "I suggest champagne to start with and then a bottle of Château Loudenne. It's just down the road from Lambrécie."

They had a superb meal. Peter had no doubt about what he wanted to do afterwards, but the food and wine were too much for him and he fell asleep before he could undo a single button of Lisa's pyjamas.

On the Monday of the following week Stewart pushed a letter across to him. It was on expensive cream-laid paper and the address was Hertford Street.

"Fringe of Mayfair," he said. "Rather an exclusive part of London. And he sounds a bit of a nob. We'd better send Len to look into it." The signature at the bottom, in an aggressive scrawl, was 'H. L. Meyer'.

"Don't bother about Len," said Peter. "I can find out all we need to know. That happens to be Lisa's current employer."

"How strange are the workings of providence," said Stewart.

When Lisa came home that evening Peter showed her the letter.

'Gentlemen,' it said, 'I am in receipt of your communication accepting me as one of your clients and demanding a further forty-five pounds. I enclose my cheque for this amount. I have little doubt that you are charlatans, but am prepared to take a long chance on it. If you can provide me with definite *and* helpful information I shall not be ungrateful.'

She said, "Absolutely typical. He accepts your offer, but is careful to insult you at the same time."

"What sort of man is he?"

"I can give you some background because when I was offered the job I made a few enquiries from a friend who seems to be able to find things out. The truth was that the pay was so good that I thought I was taking the first step into white slavery. Five minutes with Harry Meyer dispelled *that* idea. He's not interested in girls. Only in pictures. And in money, of course. He's Belgian by birth. His father, who got out of Belgium in 1939 just ahead of Hitler, brought him over with him. Papa somehow managed to get himself naturalised, so it seems that Harry has dual nationality, which is no doubt very useful to him. He's certainly got plenty of contacts in Belgium and France."

"Fine. But what sort of person is he?"

"He's a physical fitness freak. He's got his own gym and swimming-bath in his private house. He must be over fifty, but he likes to behave as if he was a super-fit thirty. Bounces about on his toes. Prefers to work standing up. That sort of thing. Also he's a bully. He doesn't bully me, because my mother has already bought two or three pictures from him and plans to buy more. But he takes it out of his assistant, a nice middle-aged pansy called Colin Chaytor, who does a bit of painting on the side. And when I say he's a pansy I don't mean he behaves like one, just that he looks like one. Long hair and floppy bow ties and a squeaky voice. Actually I believe he's quite happily married. When his wife turned up at the office the other day it was obvious she was the driving end of the axis."

Peter thought about all this. It was interesting, but didn't give him quite what he wanted. He said, "Meyer is interested in pictures and money, *bien entendu*. But is he interested in anything else? Has he got private ambitions to perform brain surgery or conduct an orchestra?"

"All I can tell you is that when he can get away from the office he goes racing. And he's got a credit account with the Tote. I know that, because his settlement statements come in monthly."

"Yes. That might be useful. He wouldn't spend a lot of money on betting unless he thought himself a judge of horse flesh. I'll throw a fly and see if he bites."

The next morning he composed a letter. He gave a lot of thought to it. He had no premonition that he was dropping a stone into the water, the ripples from which would spread to unimaginable shores. But he realised that the occasion was important.

'Thank you for your letter. Though expressed in somewhat rough terms it denotes a measure of confidence in our ability to help you, which will not, we hope, prove ill-founded. The hour and date of your birth are most important. In your case particularly so. In the early hours of September 23rd the sun was leaving the house of Virgo and commencing its descent through Libra. It is generally accepted that persons who happen to be born on this day and at this hour will have an interest in the pictorial and graphic arts. What an uninstructed investigator might have failed to note is the pre-eminence at that juncture of the star Denebola in Leo. It is not, of course, to be confused with Deneb in the Swan. Although its meaning derives from the Arabic *dhanab-al-asad*, the tail of the lion, it has from earliest times been associated also with the horse, an animal held by the Arabs in equal regard with the king of beasts. In your case this suggests something more than a generalised interest in horses. It should lead you to a study of them as serious and scholarly as the curriculum of any student from our ancient universities.'

He signed the letter 'Starfactor', a name used also by Stewart. In case it became necessary at a later date to differentiate their letters Peter signed at the left-hand and Stewart at the right-hand bottom corner.

When Peter handed this letter to Stewart to type he said, "Good stuff, don't you think?"

"Excellent," said Stewart. "You are rapidly becoming as big a charlatan as I am."

"You mean you don't believe in it?"

"If I did I couldn't write the convincing nonsense that I do."

"Well, I'm glad of that. I had an uneasy feeling that an

Intelligence might be at work up there, waiting to pounce on anyone who made fun of it."

Stewart said, "Don't misunderstand me. I don't disbelieve in the existence of a First Cause. There must, indeed, have been an Intelligence to start things off." When he settled back comfortably in his chair Peter suspected that a homily was pending. When Stewart lit a cigarette he was sure of it.

"What I absolutely refuse to believe is that this supra-normal unbelievably intelligent Intelligence can have the faintest reason for fiddling round with the conjunction of certain astral bodies, or that such conjunctions can possibly affect human lives and characters on this planet. If you think that the relative position of stars and planets does have such an influence, then you must suppose it to be permanently accurate. Right? However, because of the influence exerted by Precession – which is, as I expect you know, the westward movement of the equinoxes on the ecliptic – "

"Of course, of course."

" – the signs of the zodiac do *not* now agree with the constellations. For example, the first point of Aries is now in the constellation of Pisces. And if that doesn't convince you – "

"Oh, I'm sure you're right."

" – Then consider one further point. Suppose you had been born on September the fourteenth 1752. A happy member of the class of Virgo. Quite suddenly you learn that, as a result of the Calendar Act passed that year September the fourteenth has become September the twenty-fifth! You are now a Libran! Your whole character has been changed, by Act of Parliament."

"Point taken," said Peter. "Astrology is nonsense, but a lot of people believe in it."

"Long may they continue to do so," said Stewart devoutly.

There was a surprising convert at hand. The answer to Peter's letter to Meyer arrived two days later.

'I hasten to congratulate you,' it said, 'not only on the accuracy of your prediction, but on the tactful way in which it was presented. Noticing that there was a horse called Oxford Scholar taking part in the Levy Board Apprentice

Handicap at Catterick Bridge with the reasonable price tag of eight to one, I placed two hundred and fifty on it with considerable confidence. A confidence well justified when it came in first, two lengths ahead of the favourite. I feel that our relationship must not be allowed to rest solely on the letters so far exchanged. It promises well for the future. I should be delighted if Starfax would pay me a visit at some convenient time so that we could discuss the possibilities of a fruitful collaboration."

Peter, when he showed this to Stewart, was laughing. Stewart looked serious. He said, "Certainly we will accept his invitation. But we must not allow ourselves to be manoeuvred into becoming permanent tipsters to this picture-dealer. Also it's clear that I shall have to go. If you went you would be hard put to it to conceal your connection with his secretary."

Peter said, "All right." It sounded logical, but he knew Stewart well enough to realise that he was not going to pass up a promising opening of this sort if he could manage to get in on the act.

"We'll suggest a date ten days ahead. We don't want to sound too eager."

3

Harry Meyer came bouncing down the stairs at his Hertford Street house. It had belonged at one time to the unfortunate financier, Clarence Hatry, who had installed the gymnasium and the swimming-bath, but had used them rarely. Meyer used them every day. He also kept a careful record of his weight. One hundred and eighty six pounds on the scales and very little of it fat. His bald head gleamed from a morning of exertions on the parallel bars and the ropes followed by a fast ten lengths of the bath.

His office was a room inside the front door on the right. Apart from it there was nothing to suggest to a visitor that he was not in the private residence of a wealthy man. "I do not keep a shop," Meyer used to say. "Nor do I maintain a picture gallery. If you want that sort of thing, go to Bond Street."

In the office Lisa was typing and Mr. Chaytor was turning over the pages of the superb catalogue 'The Genius of Venice' which had been produced by the Royal Academy of Arts for their 1983 Exhibition. He was running the tips of his fingers over the reproduction of Titian's *Tarquin and Lucretia* as though he could bring the fingers to life by stroking them.

"Looking at the dirty pictures?" cried Meyer. "You're a naughty old man. Did you know that? A filthy old man."

Mr. Chaytor sniggered and shut the catalogue.

"Makes me wonder what you get up to when your wife's away. Chase the tarts in Maddox Street, is that it? Or wouldn't you know what to do with a tart if you caught one? I could always give you a few simple lessons. Tarts and how to masticate them."

Mr. Chaytor looked apologetically at Lisa, as though indicating that such matters ought not to be discussed in the presence of a lady. Lisa disregarded the look. She knew that if she said anything on Mr. Chaytor's behalf it would only provoke Meyer to more outrageous assaults. If he allowed himself to be bullied that was his affair, she thought.

She said, "This form arrived about an hour ago, by hand, from the Ministry of Culture. As far as I can see it's in order. It's been signed by the Secretary-General. And this time, I'm glad to say, they haven't forgotten to stamp it."

She hoped Meyer would deal with it quickly. She was beginning to think about lunch.

"Red tape," said Meyer. "They strangle you with it. Like Laocöön and his sons, eh. What picture is this?"

"*Family Friends.* A cat and a dog sitting side by side in front of the fire. By Beatrice Oldfield."

"Ah, yes. One of Beatrice's domestic masterpieces. Odd, is it not, how they appeal to the businessmen and magnificos of South America. A reaction, do you think, from their excessively macho life style?"

This was accompanied by a broad smile shot at Mr. Chaytor.

"Now, what is it we have to do next? Some further formalities no doubt."

He knew quite well what had to be done next, but liked to pose occasionally as a helpless citizen enmeshed by bureaucracy.

"We need a photograph," she said patiently. "We send this form and the photograph to the Ministry of Economics. Then, with luck, we get our export permit."

"Really. That seems so simple. You don't think we ought to involve a *third* ministry somehow? We mustn't make things too easy."

At this point the telephone on the desk rang and Mr. Chaytor, who was closest to it, picked up the receiver.

He said, "What?" and then "Oh!" and again "Oh!" in tones of such horror and despair that Meyer leaned across, twitched the instrument out of his hand and said, "Who is that?" He listened for ten seconds and then interrupted the speaker at the other end.

He said, "Just listen to me, my dear, and listen carefully. I realise you may now have to miss the two o'clock train from the Gare du Nord, but there's normally a later one, around five o'clock for the seven thirty boat. You'll probably have to book seats as the boat-trains are crowded at this time of year, but spread a little money around and you should manage it all right."

As she listened to him Lisa was seeing a different man. The bouncing, posturing bully was gone. This was someone altogether more formidable.

"I will see Mrs. Westmacott myself, right away, and will explain what has happened. I'm sure she will understand. And I will go with her personally to meet the boat-train at Victoria. You should be there by half past nine. I'll check the exact time. By the way, what did you tell the two girls?"

"You said you'd been involved in a taxi accident? Excellent. You kept your head." His voice became colder and harder. "Don't panic. Continue to keep your head. Understood?"

He replaced the receiver and said, "That's not *advice*, Chaytor. As far as you're concerned it's an *order*. Stay here and refrain from worrying. Go home at your usual time. Your wife will be with you long before midnight."

Lisa said, "You're not forgetting that a gentleman called Starfactor is coming to see you at five o'clock."

"I had not forgotten it. What I now have to do happens to be more important than chatting to this astrological magician. Either put him off until a later date or, if he is up in the stratosphere and you are unable to contact him, you and Chaytor will have to entertain him."

When Meyer had swept out and the turbulence of his parting had subsided, Lisa said to Mr. Chaytor, who was sitting miserably silent and staring at the telephone, "Why don't you come along with me and have some lunch?"

"Oh, I don't think I could – "

"Of course you could. You'll feel better when you've had something to eat."

"Ought we to leave the office empty?"

"Why not? This is a private house, not a shop. We'll go to that new sandwich bar in Ham Yard. I'll stand you one of their pastrami specials."

It was not an easy meal. Lisa knew that it was no use

98

asking what catastrophe had overtaken Gertrude Chaytor. Either she would be told, or she wouldn't. This restricted the conversation to general topics. She would start a hare and Mr. Chaytor would make a feeble effort to chase it, before lapsing once more into dumb misery.

By three o'clock that afternoon she had had enough. All attempts to make Mr. Chaytor go home had been met with: "Oh, I think I ought to stay here. There might be some message." She got up and went out into the hall. The room opposite the office was Meyer's own sanctum, in which he entertained important visitors. Meyer usually locked it when he went out, but on this occasion, in the flurry of his departure, he had omitted to do so. Lisa knew that there was a telephone there, with a separate outside line.

She dialled the Starfax office and was relieved to hear Stewart's bland voice.

"Of course. I'll come round at once," he said. "We can't have Mr. Chaytor cutting his throat. Messy and unproductive. I will think up a few light-hearted reminiscences. Perhaps a limerick or two. You think not? Well, I will do my best. At least you will have a companion in misery."

As Lisa was making for the door her eye fell on the press which stood in the alcove between the two windows. It was an oddly shaped piece of furniture, broader than it was high, and she had often wondered what her employer kept in it. This seemed the moment to satisfy her curiosity. It was divided inside she found into a number of vertical slots clearly designed to hold pictures or prints. She eased out one of the canvases. It was a group of rather modern-looking shepherds, staring up into the sky, with their mouths wide open. She remembered Peter describing a picture like that, but she had forgotten the exact occasion. She made a mental note to ask him about it. The sound of feet on the steps outside made her slide the picture quickly back into its slot, but it was only the afternoon post.

Mr. Chaytor was sitting exactly as she had left him. As she walked in he said, for the hundredth time, "If only I *knew* what had happened."

*

When Gertrude Chaytor had arrived at Dover Marine at midday on the previous day the Passport Officer had welcomed her with a smile. She was a familiar figure, in her nurse's uniform, carrying a suitcase and a green umbrella carefully rolled. She was shepherding two small girls and a boy.

"Off to France again, Missus," he said. "And who have we got this time?"

"Robin Pearce – take off your cap Robin. That's right. And Jessica and Mavis Pearce."

The two small girls bobbed a curtsy. As the Passport Officer remarked later to his confrère on the Customs, "She's the best type of old-fashioned nanny that Mrs. Chaytor. She looks after their manners. And no fooling round when *she's* in charge of them neither."

"Pretty expensive, I imagine," said the Customs Officer.

He was wrong about this. Not only did Mrs. Chaytor fill all her clients with confidence, but her fees were not exorbitant. Over the past few years her personal escort service had become so popular that she was able to pick and choose.

She installed the children on a bench at the stern of the boat, sheltered from the wind, and said, "The sea will be quite calm." She spoke with such authority that they felt confident that the sea would do as it was told.

By six o'clock that evening she had handed over her charges to the French Countess with whom they were to spend their holiday and was free to contemplate her own programme. She was staying, as she usually did, at a small hotel in the Rue Jacob. On the following day she was due to pick up Mrs. Westmacott's two daughters and escort them home. Seats had been booked on the train which left the Gare du Nord at two o'clock. She had arranged with their hostess to meet them at the barrier at a quarter to two. She did not want them any earlier than that. It was her experience that children on their way home were more exuberant and less submissive than on the way out.

Also this would fit in very well with the other meeting which had been fixed for half past one at the Café Continental, less than five minutes' walk from the station down the Boulevard de Magenta. The man she was meeting would be prompt to

100

the minute and it was her intention that no time should be wasted on this occasion either.

Since her hotel had no restaurant, her evening meal would be taken out. She had no objection to this. She had ample funds and a wide experience of Parisian eating places. She had chosen the Tartuffe, at the southern end of the Pont de Sully and had walked there in the pleasant sunshine of an early autumn evening; along the Quai des Grands Augustins and the Quai de Montebello, noticing on the other side of the river the squat shape of the Palais de Justice and the towers of Notre Dame. The streets were not crowded. It was the quiet time between the outflow from the offices and the influx of evening pleasure seekers.

Thinking about it afterwards Mrs. Chaytor was not sure whether she knew that she was being followed. It was easy to be wise after the event. Certainly she had noticed nothing until she left her hotel that evening. Her mind had been on her charges and on her own arrangements. At this more tranquil moment she did have time to examine other people. There was a thin young man with a coffee-coloured face coming down the pavement on the other side of the road. Paris was full of such people. It was either him or another like him that she saw when she turned into the restaurant.

She had given no thought to the matter then, or on the following morning when she paid her customary visit to the Louvre, buying two copies of their catalogue. She would give one each to the Westmacott girls to read on the way home. At half past twelve she walked back to her hotel, settled the bill, recovered her overnight case and her umbrella and hailed a taxi. She reached the Café Continental at a few minutes after one o'clock. She was, as she liked to be, in good time.

The Café was in two sections, the front half spilling out onto the pavement, the rear half under a glass canopy to which patrons could retreat when it rained. Mrs. Chaytor chose one of the tables in the covered portion. It was empty. When the sun shone most patrons preferred to sit outside. She ordered and paid for a *café au lait* and settled down to watch the passing scene.

It was at this point that she first consciously noted the

presence of the thin brown-faced youngster; and she would not have remarked on it if a flicker of memory had not told her that she had seen him, or someone very like him, the night before. He passed the Café twice. First, a few minutes after she arrived, ten minutes later on the opposite pavement. Even this did not register with her as unusual. The street was full of window-shoppers – many of them foreigners making last minute purchases before they caught the boat-train. The matter was put out of her mind by the man who appeared.

This time he had not sent one of his subordinates, but had come in person. It was, she realised, a considerable compliment. Very few people had met Agazadeh Zaman, in public or in private, since his arrival in Paris ten years before. Only a handful of people knew the address of his flat and those who did know it knew that he changed it every six months.

He walked in, bowed slightly to Mrs. Chaytor, as though asking whether he might share her table and, when she smiled and nodded, sat down beside her. He ordered for himself a *café cognac* and offered Mrs. Chaytor a further cup of coffee, which she declined.

He then opened the document case which he was carrying, extracted a rolled-up paper, some twenty-four inches long and handed it over to Mrs. Chaytor. Her overnight case was already open on the ground beside her. She put the roll into it and snapped the lid shut. She then opened her own capacious handbag, took out a stout envelope of the type used for registered letters and handed it to Zaman who slid it into his inner pocket.

The double transaction was carried out so smoothly and quickly and so entirely without fuss, that only a close observer would have noticed anything at all. Mrs. Chaytor finished her coffee and got to her feet.

She said, "I have a rendezvous with my charges at the station in five minutes' time."

"Then I will not detain you," said Zaman showing his teeth in a grimace. Mrs. Chaytor picked her way through the tables on the pavement, most of which were now occupied by folk taking their pre-lunch aperitifs. She walked away without looking back.

As soon as she had left the thin young man sauntered up to the Café and threw something, with an overarm swing, in the direction of Zaman. He saw it coming, whipped up the light iron table and held it in front of him. The object struck the table and rolled off it towards the pavement. By the time it stopped rolling Zaman was flat on his face at the back of the empty rear section.

The shock wave of the explosion threw Mrs. Chaytor, already thirty yards away, onto her face. Six of the people who were seated in front of the Café, and two who happened to be passing, were killed. Ten others were wounded. The thin young man, who had taken to his heels as soon as he had thrown the bomb, escaped unhurt; as did Zaman.

Lisa had made three abortive attempts to make Mr. Chaytor go home; or, if not home, to go anywhere rather than remain crouched in his chair in front of the telephone, jumping every time it sounded off. When Stewart arrived he accomplished this seemingly impossible task by picking up the stamped and addressed envelopes on the desk and saying, "Be a good chap and put these in the post. We'll stand by if there are any messages."

Mr. Chaytor looked surprised, but scrambled to his feet and said, "Yes, all right. I'll do that."

Lisa said, "It's very kind of you. Those two on top have to go by registered post." And, when he had departed, "There's always a queue at the registered letter counter. That should give us a breathing space."

"Excellent. There are a number of matters I wanted to discuss with you before I see your boss."

"Before we talk about anything," said Lisa, "There's something I want to show you." She led the way into the room across the passage and took out the picture she had found there. "I'm sure Peter told me about a painting like this. Does it ring any bells with you?"

"A peal of bells," said Stewart. The excitement in his voice was carefully masked, but Lisa had known him long enough to be able to detect it. "Let us probe further."

He drew out two other canvases from adjacent slots and laid

them on the table beside the one he had already examined. One of them was a conventional picture of the Holy Family in the stable with the babe. The other, more modern in conception, showed three bearded men, each bearing a casket.

"What are they?" breathed Lisa. "Do hurry up."

Fatima in Bluebeard's chamber. She had taken post at the window to give warning of anyone approaching the house.

"These," said Stewart, "are the component parts of a triptych painted by Niccolò Frumenti and two of his pupils, and stolen more than three years ago from the church of St. Brieuc des Caves near Sassencourt by two Iranian thugs. Their presence in the private cabinet of Mr. Meyer raises a number of interesting questions – "

"Put them back, for God's sake. And let's shut this thing up and talk about them next door."

When they were back in the office Stewart said, "It seems to me, correct me if I am wrong, that you are scared of your boss."

"I wasn't until today. Until then I'd thought of him as clever, rather self-satisfied and a bit eccentric – "

"Eccentric?"

"Well – he hadn't made the slightest suggestion of a pass at me – "

"Eccentric indeed. But go on."

"Well, this morning, when he was talking on the telephone and coping with whatever it was had happened to Mrs. Chaytor, suddenly he seemed to be quite a different sort of person."

"I see. And what exactly *had* happened to Mrs. Chaytor?"

"I've no idea. Except that she was on a two-day trip to Paris. I didn't even know that she was involved in Meyer's business."

"Do you mean to say that you've been here, with him, for three hours and haven't got him to tell you all about it?"

"I didn't feel I could ask him. Could you?"

"I could. And I will. Let me read in the crystal ball. Some time this afternoon, or early this evening, his wife will telephone him and will tell him that everything is all right. She will be speaking in her normal wife-to-husband voice and will order him to stop fussing and go home. He will be deeply relieved. That is where we take him in hand. We tell him that he must not on any account get home before his wife does. Sitting in an empty house will upset him all over again. Solution, to come out and have a celebratory drink. We'll go to one of the pubs in Shepherd Market that our boys use and have a real rave-up. I shouldn't imagine that Chaytor is a hardened drinker."

"I'd guess not."

"Then very soon alcohol will combine with relief to loosen his tongue and we shall have the whole story."

"Stewart," said Lisa.

"Adsum."

"Tell me, just *why* are you so interested in Mr. Chaytor? In fact, why are you so interested in what goes on here? As I understood it, it was Peter's case. He wrote the letter that hooked Meyer – "

"True. What I felt was that a situation was developing which might merit the attention of both of us."

"What you mean," said Lisa severely, "is that you couldn't resist the temptation to poke your nose in. Isn't that correct?"

The return of Mr. Chaytor saved Stewart from having to answer this. Half an hour later the expected telephone call came. The voice of Mrs. Chaytor boomed reassuringly down the line. A very short time after this saw them ensconced in the saloon bar of The Running Footman, one of Shepherd Market's most cheerful taverns.

Stewart was sorry to find that Mr. Chaytor preferred to drink beer. The trouble was that an inexperienced drinker, imbibing more pints than he was accustomed to, would probably be sick before he was intoxicated. A glass or two of whisky would have produced the required effect more quickly and more neatly.

Ron and Len were there, with their cousin Les Britton the bookmaker's muscle-man. It had, thought Stewart, as he made his way through the crowd round the bar, the makings of a good party.

The most prominent man in the crowd, with the loudest voice and the reddest face, was haranguing two or three people who might have been his friends, or might simply have found themselves next to him at the bar. As Stewart squeezed past him, he half turned and caught sight of Mr. Chaytor. The sight seemed to upset him.

"Bugger me," he said, "I thought this was a saloon bar, not a Pixie's Paradise."

One of the men by the bar said, "What are you talking about?" and three or four heads swung round.

"Look what they've let in. Do my eyes deceive me, or is it a fairy?"

He had spoken loudly enough to embrace everyone in the bar, but if he had intended to raise a general laugh he was disappointed. Stewart put down the drinks he had collected, swung round and said, "Who are you talking about?"

The crowd seemed to have drawn back, in the way crowds do when trouble is brewing and there was a clear space between Stewart and the red-faced man. From behind Mr. Chaytor, Ron, Len and cousin Leslie, a powerful phalanx, advanced towards the point where Stewart was standing.

Stewart said, "It's a simple question. You called someone a fairy. Who were you talking about?"

"I made a private comment."

"You made it loud enough for everyone in the bar to hear. So let's all have the answer."

"I – I refuse to be cross-examined."

"Are you going to refuse a punch on the hooter?" said Les, who was now within swinging distance of the red-faced man.

"Speak up," said Ron. "Don't keep the audience waiting."

The red-faced man seemed to have shrunk. He looked round for support, found none and said, "I'm not looking for trouble."

"Then apologise," said Stewart. "And be quick about it."

"If anything I said was taken in the wrong way, I'm sorry."

"Not a very good apology. But it will have to do. And now, if you really want to avoid trouble, I advise you to slip off home. No, don't bother about your drink. We'll finish it for you."

"Good advice, chummy," said Les. "New teeth cost a mint of money these days."

The red-faced man was already sidling towards the door. As he went out the conversation in the bar resumed. Stewart picked up the drinks. The Starfax party returned to their table. The incident was over. Les said, "Pity he scarpered. I'd got my eye on just the spot in his lovely grey waistcoat that I was going to plant a swinger."

From that point it was a very good party and might have gone on until closing time if Mr. Chaytor hadn't caught sight of the clock over the bar. He said, in a sudden panic, "It can't be as late as that."

"Pub clocks are always fast," said Len.

"But I must be off. I can't let my wife get home and find no one there. Really I can't."

Stewart looked at him judgmatically. He said, "That's right, Colin. You must be there when your wife gets back. I'll run you home."

"Please don't bother. I can manage."

"At this time of night?"

"There are plenty of trains to Staines. Then I get a bus out to Stanwell. They run quite late."

"Why take a chance on it? I've got my car here."

"Well, if you insist. It's very kind of you."

"I do insist," said Stewart.

4

"Bloody lucky I did take him home," said Stewart to Peter next morning. "I don't believe he'd have got a bus from Staines at that time of night and if he'd tried to walk to Stanwell, as like as not, he'd have ended up in the George VI Reservoir. I don't think he'd any idea how much he'd drunk."

"Where and what is Stanwell?"

"It's tucked away in the south-west corner of Heathrow." Stewart demonstrated on a plan of the airport and its surroundings. "Before the airport was built it must have been rather a charming little place, with a manor and a park. Now the Chaytor homestead is the only remaining inhabited house in it. Some nice stuff in it too. Old china and good reproduction antique furniture. More his taste than his wife's I should guess."

"From which we conclude that Meyer pays him well."

"Handsomely, I'd think. And he does some painting on his own, too. There's a studio at the back of the house. Nice northern light across the airport. He had it built on a year or two ago. I thought he was a little bashful about the studio, but I was allowed to poke my nose into it. Oils, water colours, acrylic paints, the lot."

"A versatile performer."

"Certainly. And, as I discovered from our talk, versatile in more fields than painting."

"Explain."

"Well, when we'd settled down in the living-room, he opened his heart to me. It wasn't just the drink. I think it was the first time anyone had stood up for him in public and he was overflowing with gratitude. I don't mean that he told me anything personal. But interesting, all the same. You remember those three triptych paintings?"

"Vividly."

"They were stolen over three years ago. Right? Then do you realise that Meyer's only got to hang onto them for another two years and they could be sold openly in France? And a year or two later in England or America."

"How so?"

"It's a useful gadget known as the Statute of Limitations. After a certain period the person in possession of stolen material can no longer be charged with stealing it. A different period for different countries. France is the shortest. Five years. Seven years here and in America, and ten in Italy."

"You mean when that time's up he can offer it openly for sale with no fear of prosecution?"

"Right. But that's not all. There's something else he explained to me. If you buy a picture at a public auction, which Meyer often does, through an outfit called Pikorx, then that gives you another let-out. If the police get interested they might pursue the auctioneers. But clearly they're only agents, selling for the real owner. And anyway, how were they to know that the stuff had been stolen? Particularly if it's a fairly obscure painting or tapestry lifted from some continental church or museum. The theft may never have been officially notified here at all."

"But if it *is* notified, then the police, who are not entirely stupid, are surely going to ask the auctioneers who their principal was?"

"Easy. He was a Monsieur Le Blanc, with an address in Paris. If our police pursue their enquiries in France – which they probably won't as it's expensive and they seem uninterested in recovering stuff stolen abroad – they will find that Monsieur Le Blanc and his address are both fictitious. And that, you may be quite sure, is the end of the matter."

"Then how does Mrs. Chaytor come into it?"

"Easy. She's the carrier. Can you imagine anyone less likely to be suspected than a woman who's shepherding a gaggle of kids? A woman who's been backward and forward so many times that the officials on both sides of the Channel probably know her by her Christian name."

"Rather elaborate, don't you think?"

"What do you mean?"

"I should have thought that anyone could have brought in the small stuff. The sort you were talking about, that hasn't been notified here. Suppose he was stopped, he'd say, 'Oh, I picked that up for a few francs from one of the stalls on the South Bank. Pretty isn't it?' End of Customs Officer's interest."

"Right. If you're talking about the small stuff. But what about the important pictures? The ones on the Interpol File and the International Art Registry List."

"Yes, I suppose they might use Mrs. Chaytor for those. It's feasible."

"*And* to take back the considerable sums in cash needed to pay those two thugs and any of Meyer's other connections in France. The men who do the actual stealing."

Peter could see Stewart's eyes lighting up with excitement as the scroll was unrolled before him, bright with the primary colours of danger and device, ruse and counter-ruse; a boy's enchanted landscape, with mountains to climb, forests to explore, lakes to swim across.

Time to bring him down to earth.

He said, "Let's stop theorising and stick to the facts we know. And here's a question to start with. Just *why* should Chaytor have picked on that impossible place to set up house? And if he's spent a lot of money on building an annexe for his studio he must be intending to stay there. Less than a mile from the main Heathrow runway! For God's sake! No one would go there unless he had some very good reason for it. Everyone else seems to have been driven out."

"Of course there was a reason for it. When those pictures reach England – the important ones, I mean – they've got to go out again. The only real markets would be the States or South America. So what could be more convenient than a private back door to Heathrow Airport?"

"I hope you realise," said Peter coldly, "that you're talking nonsense. If you looked carefully at that plan you'd see that once Chaytor had climbed the fence at the end of his garden he'd find himself among the airport sewage-works and filter beds. All right? Having picked his way cautiously through those he next has to cross an extensive area which is used by various firms to park their lorries. If he crossed this unchallenged he would find himself in the main airport. Which, mark you, he could have got into *without the slightest difficulty*, on foot or in a car, by one of the public entrances. The checks and controls at Heathrow only start when you get into the Terminal Building and head for the aircraft."

"Perhaps he was planning to pass the picture to one of those lorry drivers."

"Most unlikely. If the idea was to get it sent over to the States as part of Messrs. XYZ's consignment of Scotch whisky, the handover would have been done in private. Not in front of the interested gaze of a dozen other lorry drivers."

"All right," said Stewart crossly. "All right. Point taken. You're supposed to be the brains of this combination. Suppose you devote some of your famous intellectual power to solving your own conundrum."

"I've got a feeling that there *is* an answer and if we could find it we should be nearer to understanding just what is going on. Always supposing that it's any of our business."

"Everything about our clients is our business. Time devoted to investigating it must not be grudged."

Peter sighed. He realised that what Stewart really meant was that he had got onto the track of a promising mystery and was unwilling to let it go. "All right," he said, "but business first. Here's a letter from the man who conducts the astrology column in the *Brighton and South Coast Times*. He's complaining that I've been copying his predictions."

"Have you?"

"I might have picked up one or two of his favourite expressions."

"No problem. Write to him and point out that what he is passing on to his readers is the Voice of the Stars. The copyright in these statements belongs to the Stars, not to him. If he's planning to sue anyone for breach of copyright he'd better watch out to see that Virgo and Taurus don't sue *him*."

Some days later Lisa said to Peter, "You've got a chance of getting into mummy's good books."

"A sound move, if it can be done."

"She's accepted an invitation to spend two or three days at Lambrécie. Important local characters will be there. I gather that late September is the traditional time for this sort of jamboree. It's the week before the grape-picking starts. The last row of vines has been weeded, the gear overhauled, the casks scrubbed. A moment for feasting and merriment."

"It sounds perfect. But where do I come into it?"

"You're to go with her."

"Why on earth?"

"Maybe she feels she's getting a bit old for unaccompanied foreign travel. Or perhaps she wants to get to know her future son-in-law better."

"She'll pay the fare for me?"

"Of course. First-class travel and all found."

Peter said, "Fair enough. When do we start?"

"My dear Constantia," said Joseph Wellborn, "how kind it was of you to leave your comfortable Highgate mansion and risk the discomforts of my rustic dwelling."

"Don't try that stuff on me," said Mrs. Shilling. She had long ago taken her younger brother's measure. He, let the truth be known, had been slightly scared of her since their nursery days. "You know perfectly well that you've got a gorgeous place here. Far too good for you, actually."

"You see," said Joseph to the portly gentleman alongside of him, "being a sister she feels able to proffer an insult when she is hardly inside the front door. Allow me to introduce you. His Excellency, Alfred Bruneau, Deputy Mayor of Bordeaux. Next year he will occupy the mayoral chair and will be too proud to visit us."

Monsieur Bruneau smiled politely and introduced his wife, who had been hovering in the background.

"We are honoured also to have with us for the weekend

Professor Philibert-Lucot, whose work on the chemistry of the saccharomyces is the bible of all wine-growers. And – I forget my manners – I should of course have introduced her first, Madame Philibert-Lucot."

The Professor was tall and thin. His wife was twelve inches shorter than him and comfortably rotund.

"She is the Broad and I'm the High," Peter quoted to himself. "We *are* the University." He managed to keep a straight face as the introduction proceeded. Fortunately the Professor's idea of conversation was a monologue, so he was not forced to reveal his ignorance of the history of the grape, delivered some inches above his head. When the Professor paused for a moment Joseph interrupted to indicate a brown-haired, brown-eyed man who had been standing unobtrusively in the background. He reminded Peter of the Kent cricketer Underwood and turned out to be Commissaire Paul Meurice of the Brigade Criminelle of the Bordeaux Police Judiciaire.

The Professor, deprived of his audience, turned to Mrs. Shilling and said, "You have survived your lengthy journey well, Madame. In the heat of September it must have proved fatiguing."

"I was much helped by my young friend."

"We had the pleasure of his company here a few years ago," said Mr. Wellborn. "He arrived – on a bicycle!"

"Ah, the young," said Madame Bruneau.

"This time, as you hear, he has been escorting my sister. He has one great advantage as a courier. He speaks excellent French."

"Not surprisingly," said Mrs. Shilling drily, "since he is a de Clissac and was brought up in France."

"Indeed," said the Professor, now bending forward so that his head came down to Peter's level. "What branch of the de Clissacs is that?"

Fortunately Peter knew more about his family history than he did about oenology. He said, "It is the cadet branch: From Alexandre de Clissac – " and was soon deep in one of those genealogical discussions dear to the French upper classes.

When he could get away he made for the turret bedroom which had, once again, been allotted to him. He found it being dusted and tidied by Laure Gobard. Laure was sixteen and was a junior member of the family which comprised most of the château staff. Her father, Michel-Ange and her uncle Hervé were gardeners by day and guards, in turn, by night. Her other uncle, Georges, operated a fishing-boat and ferry service from the Port de Goulée, half a mile from the château, where the Chenal de Guy ran out to the Gironde. Her grandmother, the matriarch of the family, known to all as Gran'mère Marthe, ran the kitchen and master-minded the meals for which the Château was famous.

On his previous visit Peter had passed some of his most relaxed hours in the kitchen with the Gobard family. He now sat down on the bed, told Laure to stop fussing round and sit down beside him, which she did with no reluctance at all. He said, "You can give me all the gossip."

Her father and her uncle, she said, were doing less and less gardening and more and more guarding. This was because of all the stories in the press about the picture.

"Which picture?" said Peter. "There are lots of pictures here."

"It is the big one in the salon. The one that the patron has said he will sell to America for billions of francs. There has been much trouble about that; letters to the papers – "

"If you're talking about the *Madonna of the Swans* I can understand that there would indeed be trouble."

"There have been men from the newspapers all over the place. Not just our local papers. Men from Paris. From other countries, too. They even questioned me, but since I knew nothing there was nothing I could tell them."

"Frustrating."

"The only one who is enjoying the excitement is darling Bruno. He is on patrol every night and is given extra meat and dog biscuits to sustain him. One evening he caught a newspaper reporter and ate his camera."

"An omnivorous beast," said Peter.

The member of the family who seemed to have been least disturbed by these excitements was 'Gran'mère'. The dinner that evening was a salute to classic French cookery. *Barquettes à La Normande*, followed by a Coulibiac of fresh salmon, followed by a magnificient *Poularde à La Derby*: a fat pullet which had passed a life of tranquillity and good feeding and now graced the table roasted and stuffed with *foie gras* and truffles. Peter's small appetite was soon defeated, but the official guests dealt manfully with the heaped plates placed before them. To drink they were given a Lambrécie of the great 1961 vintage; but Peter noticed that, when other wines were offered to supplement it, their host had avoided the *premiers crus* and had tabled Château Frombrauge and Château Batailley, neither of them calculated to diminish his own product.

Owing to the predominance of men at table he was seated next to the Commissaire, who congratulated him on his grasp of French. "Your accent is perfect," he said. "Metropolitan, of course, not provincial. It is only your choice of certain words which indicates that you learned French young. When you wished to indicate that something was sensational you said 'fantastique'. That is a schoolboy expression. A young man nowadays would almost certainly say 'épique'. It is only in minor matters that one detects that your adult life has been passed in England."

"You are too kind," said Peter. "Let us talk about crime."

"Not a topic for such a gathering. But if you would care to visit me at my headquarters. It is on the Quai de La Monnaie. You will know it by the tricolour outside."

"There is nothing I should like more," said Peter truthfully.

"The day after tomorrow then. The early afternoon will be the best time."

When the ladies had withdrawn the conversation turned, inevitably, to the Titian *Madonna of the Swans*. "Its fame comes partly from its provenance," explained Mr. Wellborn. "As you no doubt know it is one of a trio of pictures painted by Titian when he was in Venice. There is the *Madonna of the Quarries* in the Uffizi and the *Madonna of Victory* in the Louvre. Some critics maintain that this one is the finest of the three."

The Mayor said, "Then the price you have been offered by this American gallery – fifty million francs according to the press – may be an under payment."

"It is not solely a question of money. I inherited all my important paintings from my father and he from his father, who made his collection in France. It has come to be considered part of the French national heritage."

"Correctly so," said the Mayor. "If I might presume to say so."

"On the other hand," said the Professor judgmatically, "fifty million francs is a considerable sum of money."

"There is much I could do with the money here," agreed Mr. Wellborn. "A picture as celebrated as this one is an expensive thing to house. When an insurance company was asked to cover it, they demanded an annual premium which would quickly have bankrupted me. So I am forced to protect it myself. I have installed the most up-to-date alarm system. Whilst it is in operation I would defy any intruder to set foot in the house without being detected. You will appreciate that such a system is not cheap. Also my vineyard badly needs clearing and replanting. The existing root-stocks are old and becoming feeble. If I do so, it will be – how long would you say, Professor?"

"Three years, perhaps four, before the new grapes started to approach their prime. You could make a wine of sorts before that time, but you might not care to market it under the label of your château."

"Exactly. I should not attempt to do so. And that would mean that during that time I should be forced to live on the income produced by this new capital."

The tones in which he said this incited general sympathy, but Peter was able to withhold his. He could not help reflecting that he would be very happy to live for a year or two on the income produced by five million pounds.

The room which Peter was shown into on the Wednesday afternoon did not look like his idea of the office of the senior detective officer of the City of Bordeaux and the Department of the Gironde. It was no more than fifteen feet square and was painted in olive-green and drab brown, the accepted colours of French bureaucracy. The only hint of officialdom was the long row of filing cabinets against the northern wall. The Commissaire's modest desk stood with its back to the

116

windows and was faced by two chairs, one padded and easy, one hard and upright.

"You observe the distinction," said Meurice. "One is for people I wish to cajole, the other for people I wish to cross-examine."

"And which of them would you like me to sit on?" said Peter. He had not supposed that a busy policeman would have invited an unimportant foreigner to his office to gossip.

"Oh, the easy one, please. You are not a suspected criminal." This was accompanied by a warm smile which wrinkled up the eyes. "But it is true that you might be able to help us." Then, after a brief pause, "And we might be able to help you. Let me explain. Some years ago you were involved, though not closely, with two men at Sassencourt. You recollect it? Yes, but I perceive that you are surprised that I should know about it."

"I am, rather."

"Because you arrived at your hotel that night too late to sign the register and left it somewhat precipitately the following evening, without having corrected this small irregularity."

"When I thought about it afterwards I was very glad that had happened. I would not have wished either of those two men to know my name or my address in England."

"Understandably. The information, however, came to me quite simply. The officer who drove you to the ship – he has been commended for his initiative – slipped back on board when you were, I believe, purchasing something to eat. Yes? Since it was a French ship he was able to persuade the Passport Officer to make a note of all English travellers. There were not more than a dozen. From the information given to him, he had no difficulty in identifying you. He had then only to question his sister at the hotel, add what you had told her to the account you had given him in the car and we had a clear picture of what had occurred."

"He didn't seem very interested in what I had to tell him," said Peter. The recollection still rankled.

"He was exercising professional discretion. This did not stop him from using his brains and submitting a report – which came to me as I was at that time in charge of our Normandy office. He concluded his report by pointing out that the activities of this pair of Iranians must have been motivated by a fear that you were in a position to identify them. Shall we see if they were right?"

The Commissaire opened one of the folders on his desk, extracted two photographs and slid them across. Peter looked at them and said, in a choked voice, "That one, yes. I came face to face with him in a good light. The other I hardly saw. I only heard his voice. But it seemed to me, from the way he spoke, that he was the leader."

"You may be right. In my view there is little to choose between them. The one you saw is Mahmoud Rasim. The other is Nasser Goraji. Both are Iranian and both started their careers as police-officers under the late Shah."

"Under the Shah?"

"Indeed. Very zealous officers. Their speciality was obtaining confessions. So highly did he think of them that he sent them on a special mission to France, to track down and deal appropriately with his enemies here. By which he meant the adherents of the Ayatollah Khomeni then resident near Paris. One must suppose that they kept their ears very close to the ground, since they had switched their allegiance even before the Shah was deposed. They started working for Agazadeh Zaman, who is a remarkable man. The Ayatollah's chancellor of the exchequer in exile, you might call him. A very different character to those two apes. Just as hard, just as ruthless, but infinitely more dangerous because he is a dreamer and an idealist. When the Ayatollah's régime was first set up in Iran he could have had any post in the new government that he chose to demand. He refused such promotion. He realised that he was more valuable to his master if he stopped here, in France."

"Valuable in what way?"

"Oh, in many ways. He had obtained some influence in political circles and had friends among the senior bureaucrats who, in our country, really run the government."

"In ours also," said Peter sadly.

"But his main function was as a collector of money. You may be assured that any Iranian working in this country pays a regular contribution. Such money is channelled through

Zaman. But the big money comes from other sources. Much of it from the arms firms. Iran needed ground-to-air missiles, air-defence radar, heavy artillery shells, yes. But the arms salesmen needed the orders and they are in cut-throat competition. Nobel Kemi in Sweden, Muiden Chemie in Holland, Forcit and Kemira in Finland, Rio Tinto in Italy, our own SNPE and your Nobel company. The final decision as to who gets any particular order rests with Zaman. When you consider the stupendous profits these firms make you can imagine the sums they are prepared to pay to be at the head of the queue. And when I say stupendous, please do not imagine that I am exaggerating. Before our recent elections one of our companies, Luchaire, shipped more than a hundred million dollars' worth of artillery shells to Iran on faked end-user certificates which alleged that they were going to Brazil and Thailand. There's nothing confidential about what I'm telling you. It was, naturally, featured in all the opposition papers. What wasn't featured quite so prominently was the fact that after the election an attempted investigation into these transactions was quietly buried by the new Defence Minister."

As Peter listened he realised, more from the tone of voice than the words, that what Meurice was telling him was distasteful to him; that he was a policeman first, but also a patriot.

He said, in a tone of voice that was deliberately provocative, "Are you telling me then, that the reason France has been buttering up Iran lately is not – as we all thought – because she wants to save herself from trouble by terrorists like Georges Abdullah, but simply because she wanted to keep the Gulf War going and make a lot of money out of it?"

Meurice, who was too experienced to be provoked, said, with a smile, "Oh, both reasons, no doubt. Two motives, the same result." He added, "You may have asked yourself – I have seen you asking yourself – why I should have invited you down here to give you a politico-economic lecture. The reason, as I indicated, is that we may, at some point, need your help. The farmer, André Renouf, who was unlucky enough to intercept Rasim and Goraji was in hospital for three months

119

before he died. The doctors who attended him have stated without qualification that his death was the direct result of the injuries he had received. They are prepared to give evidence to this effect when – as I hope may be the case – these men are put on trial. It will not now be a charge of assault or even of theft. It will be a charge of murder and it will be your testimony that links them to the affair. You saw one of them outside the church. You heard the other discussing it with the *curé*."

Peter listened to this with a hollow feeling in the pit of his stomach. He said, "You mean that I should have to stand up in court here and put the finger on these two apes?"

"You sound alarmed. It would not be as dangerous as you are thinking. No doubt the money that Zaman handles would enable him to hire and pay thugs in any country in Europe, but his main organisation is here, in France. Once you had given your evidence and were safely back in England why should he mount a personal vendetta against you? There would be no profit in it for him. He might even be glad to be rid of these two heavy-handed subordinates. Such men outlive their usefulness."

"I hope you're right," said Peter.

"I would, however, suggest that if this situation should arise you should avoid visiting this country for a year or so. Memories are short. Other interests intervene. Meanwhile my advice to you is to stay clear of all these people. They are professionals. You are an amateur. Yes?"

"Yes."

"Amateurs play games for fun. Professionals play only to win. You understand what I am saying?"

"Yes," said Peter unhappily. "I do understand exactly what you are saying."

PART THREE

THE KILLING GROUNDS

The young are attracted by violence. They see in it an instrument of liberation and progress. And it is true that violence is a form of strength and that one can try to employ it. But it contains the seeds of corruption. It affects all who use it and it degrades the objective which you are seeking to attain. There is no possible argument about this. It is sufficient merely to stand here and listen, in your mind, to the cry uttered by a man or woman at the moment when they were no more than a step away from the door of the extermination chamber and you will be turned away, for ever, from the idea of finding in violence the least spark of light or the least element of justice.

(From an address given by Giscard d'Estaing at the site of the Nazi death camp at Buchenwald)

1

On the day after Peter's visit to Commissaire Paul Meurice in Bordeaux, Stewart set out to discover something about Pikorx Ltd. The name was so repulsive that he felt it must conceal secrets worth investigation.

Ron, who had paid a preliminary visit, had reported, "It's a dump. Just one room, upstairs, in Poynters Alley. That's a dirty little street between Mincing Lane and Mark Lane. There are quite a few sale-rooms thereabouts, but this is definitely not a high-class outfit. When I was there, around midday, the door was padlocked and there was a notice 'Auctions 3 p.m. Mondays, Wednesdays and Fridays'. If you looked in on one of those you might find out something useful. It seems a long shot to me."

It seemed a long shot to Stewart, but he was feeling restless. Starfax, he realised, had nearly run its course. As a novelty it had made him a surprising amount of money, but the graph of its profits was sinking. There had been a number of sardonic comments in the press from well-established astrological rivals. It would be sense to get out while the going was good. In fact, closing down would be surprisingly easy. There were none of the complications which arose when a normal business folded. Staff to pay off, premises to dispose of, debts and redundancy payments. None of that in his case. He would have to do something about Peter, but his part-time assistants would expect no more than a handsome parting bonus. Tax payments were up-to-date and the company's account was in very comfortable credit. If he did decide to stop – all he would have to do was to sign off existing clients and decline to take on any more. Inside a month Starfax could fold its tents and steal away as quietly as any of Longfellow's Arabs. The thought was a pleasing one. Stewart was by nature peripatetic.

He was thinking about this as he made his way to Fenchurch Street station and descended one of the alleys which led down to the river. It was after half past two when he arrived at the premises of Pikorx. There were signs of life. Quite a few people had arrived and were sauntering round the room examining the paintings. There were some forty of these, hanging from pieces of back-boarding nailed to two of the walls. He noticed a fair-haired youth who was accompanied as he moved by a little court of admirers. Max Berry, someone whispered to him. There was a man with a red beard whom he thought he recognised as a kerbstone artist who had obtained a temporary celebrity status by holding a private exhibition on the pavement of Chelsea Embankment. Most of the paintings, he thought, were by amateurs and he guessed that their perpetrators were among the crowd, hoping to sell them to their friends. Three of the pictures were different. They were antiques. Two of them were of stations of the cross, the flogging and the crown of thorns, done in the unemotional, almost anatomical manner of the eighteenth century. The third was the picture of a man wearing the red biretta of a cardinal bishop. Stewart got the impression that the original of this picture might have been larger and have been cut down to show only the head and shoulders. He wondered if this had been done to remove some legend by which it could be identified.

A rapping called his attention to the auctioneer on the rostrum at the far end of the room, a small man with a mop of white hair. He had a noticeable squint. When he went into action this was useful as he seemed able to keep his eyes on different bidders without moving his head.

Business went forward smoothly. The amateur paintings either went for small sums to friends of the artist or were withdrawn. Better prices were paid for Max Berry's misty riverscapes, a long way after Whistler, and for some pictures in the pop-art manner from the kerb artist, but it was only when the three antiques were put up that the bidding became brisk. The dealers opened their mouths for the first time and Mr. Chaytor, who had slipped quietly into the back of the crowd, accepted battle.

All three of the pictures ultimately went to him.

"It was a complete racket," said Stewart to Peter. "Chaytor knew he could bid as high as he liked. The auctioneer – his name, believe it or not, is Crankling – was in it too, I imagine. Meyer, I'm sure, had already bought the pictures from the men who stole them on the Continent and had paid them the agreed price. Probably not a great deal. So if they were knocked down to him now for five times as much, what did he care? He was only paying himself. And the fact that one of them – the portrait – apparently now cost him £4,000 at auction would be a very useful bargaining point when he sold it to a Midland boot manufacturer who liked a little art about the home."

"Very smooth," said Peter. He had already told Stewart about his talk with Commissaire Meurice. Somehow the interval of two days and a few hundred miles had weakened the impact of the Commissaire's warning. If Peter had been worried by it, Stewart was not. He said, "I think that idea of muscle being for sale here is greatly exaggerated. I'll have a word with Les. He knows all the hard boys. Anyway, we aren't interfering with this racket. We're simply investigating it. No harm in that, is there? As long as we keep our distance."

"I suppose not," said Peter. "As long as we do that."

"And we've found out a lot of the answers. We now know – "

"Or suspect."

"All right. We suspect that Meyer's in touch with a number of petty thieves who lift paintings from country churches and small-town museums. He buys them for about a tenth of what they're really worth, pushes them through Pikorx and sells them for something more like their real value, to customers in this country. All profit on these transactions goes to him. Right?"

"Yes. I think that's right."

"That's the small stuff. The important paintings are lifted by the two Iranians. The reason they do it – this must be right, surely – is that in these cases, although Meyer takes a handsome commission, the bulk of the profit goes to Zaman and is channelled by him to Iran. The pictures are either stored by Meyer until the relevant period is over and he can put them up openly for sale, or they are sold at once to a dealer in South America."

"Why South America?"

"Because, once a picture lands up in South America, the authorities refuse to answer questions about it, or to investigate who it belongs to. Result – as far as its owner's concerned, it's gone for good. Chaytor told me all about it."

"Why was he so forthcoming?"

"To tell you the truth, I did wonder. He's invited me twice to that house of his and I've met him once for lunch up here. That was the only time that I had him alone, without his wife and on that occasion I did get the impression that he was trying to tell me something, but was afraid to do so."

"Afraid because of his wife being implicated?"

"That's what I thought at first. Now I'm not so sure. I think he's in it, too. It may be his wife who brings the important pictures back from France, but I think that he's involved in the next step."

"Their export to South America?"

"Yes. And it can't be easy. To start with, they'd probably go by air and you can bet your bottom dollar that packages to South America are closely scrutinised."

"Could he send them openly? Apply for a licence – "

"For a picture important enough to be on the Interpol List?"

"I suppose not. Perhaps, if we keep our eyes open, this time we may find out how it's done."

Stewart looked at him suspiciously. He said, "This time? What do you mean? You're keeping something back aren't you?"

"I thought you might be interested in something I read in *France Libre*. I bought it at the airport."

The report was written in the style of sarcastic indignation at which French journalists excel. 'Le Mans', it said, 'stands in the mind of most Frenchmen for one thing only. Motor racing. Probably they visualise the inhabitants spending their time either speeding round the famous twenty-four hour circuit or collecting the autographs of the heroes who do so. Such a notion overlooks the plain truth, that Le Mans has a cultural life of its own. One of the centres of culture being the Musée de Pierre Roland, tucked away in a quiet corner between the cathedral and the Quinconce des Jacobins. A museum little visited by the public maybe, but which holds, as a gift from its founder one of the country's most notable treasures. The earliest of Rembrandt's self-portraits, painted at least two years before the *Portrait as a Young Man*, now in the National Gallery in London. We say that the museum holds it. Had they taken reasonable precautions, they might still do so. Unfortunately there were no night guards and an inadequate alarm system. A thoughtful arrangement which no doubt appealed to the two men who entered the museum over the roof of an adjacent building, broke a window in the main gallery and abstracted the painting with no trouble at all.' The article concluded by expressing, in no unmeasured terms, its opinion of people who took so little care of the country's national treasures.

Stewart read the report carefully. Some of the expressions in it had to be translated for him. His grasp of French was a long way short of Peter's fluency. Finally he said, "You know what this means, don't you? If we're right about what's going on here, Gertrude Chaytor will soon be on the move. I'd like to know if and when that happens."

"Lisa will know."

"How?"

"By watching Chaytor. The moment his wife takes off – particularly in view of what happened last time – he'll be wetting his pants."

"Right. And we go round and mop up."

"You can go. If you think it will serve any useful purpose. I've got a lot of letters to write."

It was five days later when the call came. Lisa said, "Mrs. Chaytor went off this morning. It must have been an impromptu arrangement. Normally she escorts two or three children in both directions. This time all she can manage is one boy to be taken across."

"Interesting," said Stewart. "Expect me around four o'clock."

When he got to Hertford Street he found Colin Chaytor in

127

the anticipated mood of nervous desperation. He said, "I told Gertrude, this *must* be the last time."

"Why?" said Stewart. "It seemed to me she was onto a very good racket."

"What do you mean?"

"Escorting rich kids. I imagine she gets well paid."

"Oh, that. Yes."

"Or is the trade falling off? I gather it was only one boy out, this time, and no one back."

Chaytor did not ask Stewart how he had come by this information. Instead he said, "It's not just the children. It's something else – "

Unfortunately, at that moment Lisa came back. She said, "If you'd like to hang about here, Mr. Chaytor, please do. I imagine you've told your wife to telephone here when she gets back."

"It's very good of you."

"Then I'll leave you and Stewart in charge. I've got a date I can't skip – with my hairdresser. She's so booked up since she was patronised by royalty that you have to go down on your knees to get a booking a month ahead. Meyer's in Belgium, so the shop is all yours."

"What happens," said Stewart, "if an Eastern potentate rings up and wants to spend some of his ill-gotten millions on a picture?"

"Offer him the *Mona Lisa*."

2

Since, this time, she had with her only the one boy, a polite and biddable viscount, and realised that she might be pressed for time, Mrs. Chaytor decided to use the hovercraft crossing from Dover. She was in Paris by midday and had completed the handover of her charge before one o'clock. She then made her way, on foot, up the Boulevard de Magenta, passing the western end of the Gare du Nord. She noticed that the Café Continental was back in business, though looking sadly battered. She was heading for the maze of small streets that lay to the north of the station, on the other side of the Boulevard de La Chapelle.

She had been warned that she might be followed and had been told to take no notice of it. 'Carry on as normal,' Harry Meyer had told her cheerfully. She hoped that he knew what he was doing.

The Café d'Afrique, which she found in the Rue Jessaint, was a smaller and quieter place than her previous rendez-vous. There was a single line of half a dozen tables on the pavement, none of them occupied. She stumbled down two steps into the dark interior where she found a bald man, with his sleeves rolled up, leaning over the 'zinc', and two workmen drinking pernod and arguing with him. The discussion, a political one, was accompanied by thumpings on the bar and other gestures of dissent and defiance. She succeeded, finally, in attracting the bald man's attention and he served her with a cup of lukewarm coffee, which she paid for.

Her appointment was for two o'clock and when this hour had come and gone she began to get worried. On previous occasions her contacts had been punctual to the minute and she had been instructed that if they failed to arrive she should take herself off as quickly as possible and return home without making any further attempt to get in touch.

She decided to give it exactly five minutes. At four minutes past, when she was gathering her things together, the street door opened. But it was only a small and grubby boy. He came into the café, looked round, and sauntered over towards Mrs. Chaytor. He seemed fascinated by her coloured umbrella which was propped against the table and stared at it and at its owner with bland impertinence.

The proprietor, spotting him, said, "*Défilez, goujon,*" before continuing his discussion which had ascended to a climax of fury. The boy took no notice of the insult, but sidled up to Mrs. Chaytor and said what she guessed to be, "Are you waiting for someone?"

She nodded. The boy dipped a hand into the pocket of his baggy ankle-length trousers and produced an envelope. He said, with a grin, "There is nothing to pay, ma mère," and sidled out followed by a glare from the proprietor.

The paper in the envelope said, 'Leave without haste and make your way to the Gare du Nord. Opposite the steps which lead down to the Métro you will notice a line of four *guichets*. They deal with such matters as, reservations, group tickets and refunds. They are not much patronised. The *guichet* on the left will be shut. Approach it at *exactly* half past two. This is important. Time yourself by the clock above the Métro steps. Knock on the *guichet* window. When the man, who will be waiting inside, opens it, do what he says.' The note was typewritten and was unsigned. She folded it, put it in her handbag, finished the coffee and made for the door. None of the three men spared her a glance. The street outside seemed to be empty.

Mrs. Chaytor was a woman who usually managed to control her nerves, but she was conscious that her mouth was dry. She said to herself, 'Don't hurry. You've time to spare. Spend a few minutes buying yourself a paper at the bookstall. Don't keep looking at your watch. There are plenty of clocks in the station."

She located the *guichet* which had been described in the note. At two twenty-nine, she started to stroll towards it. When she knocked the interior blind shot up as though she had touched a spring. There was a speak-through attachment in the glass of the window. A man whom she could only see indistinctly said, "Go to the door on your left. It will be unlocked." The blind shot down as quickly as it had gone up.

The door was marked, 'Personnel SNCF'. She turned the handle, pushed the door open and went through, pulling it shut behind her. Now that she had a clear view of the sallow youth who was waiting inside she realised one thing. He was terrified almost out of his wits. His hand was shaking so badly that he bungled the job of refastening the bolts on the inside of the door. She pushed him aside and finished the job for him. "Well," she said sharply. "What now?"

"Through there." He was pointing to a door on the other side of the room. "Quickly, quickly."

"It would save time, young man," said Mrs. Chaytor, in her most schoolmistress-like French, "if you pulled yourself together and gave me proper instructions."

The youth gulped and said, speaking a little more calmly, "You go through there, along the passage and down the stairs. At the bottom you will find a door which you can open."

"Very well. And then?"

"That is all I know. Now, please, please go."

He was almost on his knees. Mrs. Chaytor moved off with deliberate slowness. When she reached the door at the foot of the stairs she found that it was both locked and bolted, but as the key and the bolts were both on her side she opened it without difficulty and stepped out. She was in an alley, between one side of the station and a windowless block that looked like a warehouse. While she was wondering what to do next, a closed car slid up beside her.

She recognised the driver, a stout and jolly-looking man who had acted as go-between on previous occasions. Everyone addressed him as Jojo. She had never discovered his real name. When she started to get in beside him he held up one fat hand and gestured her into the back. After she had climbed in and shut the door she discovered that the windows were curtained. Jojo drove off, gathering speed as he cleared the mouth of the alleyway.

This was a part of Paris that Mrs. Chaytor knew well, a district favoured by traffickers in cheap jewellery and knick-knackery. With time to kill when waiting for her charges, she had often strolled through it, window-shopping and occasionally making a small purchase. When the car checked before crossing a main road, she knew that it was the Boulevard de La Chapelle. The immediate right fork which they took was clearly the Rue de La Goutte d'Or where some of the better shops were to be found. The next main crossing was over the Boulevard Barbès. After this she was at a loss. The car was taking first right and first left turnings at random. All she could tell was that it seemed to be heading west. Then, as it turned a corner, the curtains swung slightly apart and she caught a glimpse of white monuments and gravestones. This could only be the Cimetière de Montmartre and she now knew where she was. A right turn as they reached the north-west corner of the cemetery wall, followed by a left turn, would take them into the Rue Lamarck. It was an area which had lately been redeveloped, she remembered, with blocks of newish and rather expensive flats.

The car came to a halt. Jojo said, speaking more sharply than he had ever done before, "Do not get out until I tell you. When you move, move fast, but don't run."

It was evident that he was keeping his eye on passers-by on the pavement. She could hear their footsteps approaching and receding. She sat with one hand on the door-catch.

"Now," said Jojo.

She pulled the door open and moved quickly across the pavement and into the entrance hall of the flats opposite. Jojo was on her heels, but she had time to notice the number, thirty-four. A porter was standing beside the lift. Jojo ignored him. He hustled Mrs. Chaytor into the lift and slammed the gate shut. When it stopped at the fourth floor he held the gate open for a few seconds, examining the passageway to left and right, before he allowed her to get out. Then he walked across, pressed the bell and spoke into the entryphone. As the door opened Mrs. Chaytor noticed how ponderously it moved and saw that a sheet of steel had been bolted across the inside.

She was in a fortress.

There were two young men in the passage. One of them shook hands with Jojo, the other ushered Mrs. Chaytor along the passage and into a room, adequately but unimaginatively furnished, with a long window which filled the outer wall. It would have given more light had its bottom half not been covered by a mesh screen. The man who had been sitting on the couch in front of the window, rose to greet her. The young man grabbed her umbrella and suitcase and hurried out of the room.

When Commissaire Paul Meurice had described Agazadeh Zaman to Peter as a dangerous man, he had spoken the truth. He was a fanatic who had camouflaged himself behind a façade of mediocrity. His black hair, originally curling and rampant had been subdued by careful barbering. His skin was no browner than that of any Frenchman who had spent his summer on the Riviera. His suit of charcoal grey cloth was well, but not too well, cut. Passing him in the street you would have placed him at once as one of the legion of middle-class bureaucrats and businessmen who kept the wheels of government and finance turning in that crowded strip which lies along the north bank of the river between the stations of Concorde and Châtelet; men who lunched in the Rue de Montpensier and returned every evening to their families in the outer suburbs.

This impression would not have survived five minutes of conversation, but Zaman talked very little and never to strangers. Mrs. Chaytor only knew that she respected him and feared him; feelings which were increased by his invariable politeness.

He waved her to a seat and said, "I trust you have not been put out by our last minute change of plan."

She said, "Well, it was a little disconcerting."

"But necessary." Although he spoke impeccable French, when dealing with Mrs. Chaytor he preferred to converse in English. He knew that her French, though serviceable, came from the schoolroom.

"On the last occasion, and on this, you were followed by a young man whom we believe to be called Mohammed Jemal. He is one of a group of dissidents from our country who have

133

been given sanctuary in yours. They spend much of their time parading the streets with banners calling for the overthrow of the Ayatollah. If that was all they did they would hardly be worthy of notice. Unfortunately one or two of them are more active. Jemal is one such. His primary objective in following you was, I surmise, to find me. And, if he could, to kill me."

Mrs. Chaytor noticed that he said this without emphasis or bravado. He had lived under the threat of assassination for so long that it had become a way of life, to be accepted without emotion.

"Our manoeuvre at the Gare du Nord has had two excellent results. He has lost your trail. We are still on his. So, having failed in his primary task, he will be all the keener to succeed in the other one; which is, I feel certain, to deprive you of the exceedingly valuable picture you will be carrying and our country of the large sum of money it will fetch through the efforts of the good Mr. Meyer. And of your husband, too, of course."

Mrs. Chaytor said, "Yes." She was aware of the important part that her husband played in these matters.

"On this occasion the picture is too old and too fragile to be rolled in your umbrella. It will be in that suitcase." He indicated the case which was standing at the end of the couch and which had caught her eye as soon as she came into the room. It was not her suitcase, but it was very like it. It was the same size and made of the same stuff. There were labels on it not unlike those on hers.

"It has a compartment in the lid which I would defy anyone to find, even in the unlikely event of such a regular traveller as yourself being suspected. I will show you the trick of it. It is this case upon which young Jemal's attention will assuredly be fixed. He will have no opportunity to steal it whilst you are on the train or the boat for we will see that you are well, and moreover openly, escorted until you reach London. In any event, it is no doubt on the final stage of your journey that he will be planning to act. I assume that he knows your house and the surrounding area well. Explain to me exactly how you reach it."

134

"On one of the suburban line trains from Waterloo to Staines. Then a bus to Stanwell. Then a walk to our house."

"How far?"

"Less than half a mile."

"But not, I understand, along a well-lit street."

"Unhappily, no. It's a side road. There's no lighting on it, or in the place where we live. We are, now, its only remaining inhabitants."

"Excellent. It is surely there that he will plan to relieve you of your suitcase. As an additional incentive he will have noticed that the last of the team that was guarding you on your journey was left behind in London. You follow what I am saying?"

Mrs. Chaytor understood exactly what Zaman was saying and liked none of it.

"Don't be alarmed. The withdrawal of your escort will be more apparent than real. We are planning this campaign on a large and careful scale. Two of my best men are leaving by air. Rest assured they will deal with Jemal."

When he stopped speaking the words 'deal with' seemed to hang in the air. Mrs. Chaytor said abruptly, "You mean they will kill him?"

"Certainly. And if you cherish any soft feelings towards him perhaps you will recollect that he has already been responsible for the deaths of a number of French citizens."

"Then why not report him to the authorities here?"

"I considered it, of course. But I had to reject it. To bring the crime home to him, I should have been forced to come out into the open and give evidence. It would be the end of my usefulness. My services to our leader are too valuable to take such a chance. Of course, if you were prepared to give evidence yourself – "

"I couldn't possibly identify him," said Mrs. Chaytor hastily. "Why, I hardly saw him – "

With a contraction of the lips that might, in a less reserved man, have been described as a smile, Zaman said, "You will see, then, that my way is best. All the necessary steps will be taken in England. We will leave the whole matter as a puzzle to be unravelled by your celebrated Scotland Yard. Right? Then,

135

all we have to do now is to transfer your personal effects to this case and send you on your way."

"Yes," said Mrs. Chaytor. She hoped that her legs would support her when she stood up. "That's all." But to herself she said, with total conviction, 'Never again. Never again.' She repeated this in time with the beating of her heart, which had started to play tricks with her, slowing at one time to a heavy irregular thudding, then doubling in speed and racing.

Once she was seated in the train, speeding smoothly towards Amiens and Boulogne and had taken several deep breaths, she felt her heart steadying. She told herself, in the firm voice she had so often used with her young charges, 'Stop being silly. Everything will come out all right if you do exactly what you've been told.'

She had no difficulty in spotting her guardian for this part of the journey, a tall Iranian with a pock-marked face who had seated himself where he could keep an eye on her and on her case in the rack above. When he left the carriage at Amiens and moved to the corridor one of his compatriots, who had been standing there, immediately took his place. This one was shorter and stouter, but looked equally wide awake. Both of them followed her as she made her way onto the boat. They did not embark with her, but she noted that one of the stewards, a dark boy, was unusually attentive. He found a seat for her in the lounge and visited her more than once with offers of refreshment and of help, which she did not need.

At Dover the Customs Officer, an old friend, waved her through with a smile and without troubling her to open her case. Everything seemed to be going easily and smoothly.

It was while the train was running through the fields and orchards of Kent that doubts began to creep in.

Zaman was clever, no doubt about that. And an excellent organiser. But had he, on this occasion, misread the minds of his opponents? Were his precautions all being taken in the wrong place? Those two men of his, who were to guard her on the last stage of her journey, had crossed, that evening, by plane. Presumably Jemal had done the same. There was an hourly shuttle service between de Gaulle and Gatwick.

But why should it be supposed that Jemal was operating on his own? Zaman had mentioned that there were a number of activists. The walk from the bus to her house looked like being a battlefield, with her in the middle.

These fears travelled with her to Victoria. She considered the possibility of cloakrooming the case, but realised that this action would certainly be observed. The objective of her assailants would then be switched to the cloakroom ticket in her pocket rather than the bag in her hand. There was no comfort in that idea.

Dusk had fallen by the time her suburban train crawled into Staines. Fortunately the bus terminus was directly opposite the station exit. She went out with the crowd and made her way to the waiting-room. There were several people there waiting for the Windsor and the Chertsey buses. It was nearly an hour before her bus arrived. By that time only three other passengers remained: a middle-aged woman with two talkative children. She hoped that they would come all the way with her, but they got off at the reservoir turning, leaving her alone with the conductor.

He seemed inclined to conversation. It appeared that he was a vegetarian, a teetotaller and a member of the Staines Regatta Committee. She expressed suitable interest in all these activities. She wondered whether she could possibly ask him to walk with her from the bus terminus to her house, but decided that this offer would certainly be misconstrued and equally certainly rejected.

When the bus finally drew up she dismounted slowly, picked up her case and started off. She had not gone far before an urgent shout stopped her. Looking round she saw that the conductor was holding out her umbrella.

"Likely you'll need this," he said, "before you get home."

She had been too worried to pay much attention to the weather, but now she noticed for the first time that the stars had been covered and the wind was rising.

On the left of the road there was a dry ditch with steep sides. On the right it was open ground until about half-way, where there was the entrance to a farmhouse, so long empty that the 'For Sale' boards were almost illegible. No help there. Indeed, the entrance would be a very likely place for an ambush.

Drawing on her considerable stock of resolution, Mrs. Chaytor put these thoughts aside and strode out. In the event of attack she had decided to drop the case and bolt. Let them have the picture. It would give her a chance of escape.

She had almost reached the farmgate when she heard the sound behind her and swung round. It was a car and it was coming fast. She jumped for the farmgate, found it padlocked and threw herself at the top bar.

The car stopped with a jerk and a voice said, in tones of surprise, "Mrs. Chaytor? Well met. Sling that case on board and jump in." It was Stewart. Her husband was already out on the road. He took the case and handed it to Peter who was in the back of the car. He said, "You should have taken a taxi from Staines, my love. How often have I told you? Five minutes later and you would have been soaked to the skin."

The first heavy drops of rain were hitting them.

"Autumn storm. Quick come, quick go," said Stewart. The windscreen wipers were working overtime as he drove forward through a screen of rain. "I'll park as close to the door as possible. You go first, Colin, with the key and get the door open. Then we'll all jump for it. Right?"

Five minutes later they were sitting in front of a newly kindled fire, sampling Mr. Chaytor's whisky. Even Mrs. Chaytor, normally abstemious, was gulping down her share with the rest. Her husband, who had been in the kitchen to fetch the glasses said, "You were last out of the house this morning, my love. Did you leave the kitchen window open?"

"Certainly not."

"Well, it's wide open now."

"Burglars," said Stewart comfortably. "Better go and see if they've taken anything."

When he came back Mr. Chaytor was looking puzzled. "As far as I can see," he said, "they haven't taken anything. On the other hand the catch of the window had certainly been forced and there are muddy footmarks on the kitchen floor. Red mud from the back garden and it's still wet."

"That solves the mystery," said Stewart. "It was a burglar. He heard us coming and bunked."

Peter and Mr. Chaytor nodded agreement. Mrs. Chaytor kept her thoughts to herself. So Jemal had broken in and had been waiting for her, expecting the house to be empty. Zaman's men, if indeed they were outside, would have been in no position to interfere. She would have been at his mercy.

"You're shivering," said her husband. "Have another drop of whisky and I'll get some soup on the boil."

"I'd better refix the window," said Stewart.

Peter, left alone with Mrs. Chaytor, looked at her curiously. It was clear to him that she had been badly frightened, but far from clear by what. Was it the attempted burglary? No. She had been frightened before that. Then was it something that had happened in France? That was more probable.

Stewart, standing at the open kitchen window, was thinking on the same lines. He did not entirely believe his own burglar theory. And what had Mrs. Chaytor been up to? As he drove up she had not simply been standing in the entrance to the farm. He had the impression that she had been starting to climb the gate.

The rain had nearly stopped and the moon reappeared for a moment among the racing black clouds which were the tail end of the downpour.

It was whilst he was staring out of the window that the scream came.

It was from somewhere beyond the end of the garden, a shriek of pain and outrage, cut off sharply. It had been loud enough to fetch Peter and Mr. Chaytor from the front room. They stood staring out into the night. The moon was playing hide-and-seek among the clouds. When it shone out they could see as far as the garden fence, but not much beyond.

The cry was not repeated.

"A rabbit chased by a stoat," suggested Peter.

"That wasn't an animal," said Stewart. "It was human."

Mr. Chaytor nodded agreement. They stood for a minute peering out and listening, but all they could hear was the wind whipping through the branches of the trees.

"Have you got a torch?" said Stewart.

Peter said, "You're not going out, are you?"

"Must see what's happening."

Typical, thought Peter. "Why should we?" he said.

"It's none of our business," agreed Mr. Chaytor. But when he had produced a torch the three of them set out together, with Stewart leading, and climbed the railed fence at the bottom of the garden.

A hundred yards beyond it they reached the filter beds. These covered an area as large as a football field and were surrounded by a three-strand barbed-wire fence. They were divided, by one central and a number of transverse walkways, into rectangular boxes with steep sides, full of the partly treated sewage of the airport. An overlay of some green chemical which floated on the top of each box masked the smell.

"It came from somewhere in there," said Stewart. The top line of wire was slack enough at that point to be pressed down and stepped over.

"For God's sake," said Mr. Chaytor, "be careful how you go. Some friends of ours lost a dog there last year. He slipped in and couldn't get out. Poor beast."

The centre walkway was wide enough to be used with some confidence. When they were half-way along it, Stewart said, "We've gone too far. It was over on the left, back there. Watch your step."

This was one of the side turnings, easy enough in daylight, tricky by the light of a single torch. They advanced cautiously until they reached the boundary wire on the left.

"It came from near here," said Stewart. He swung the torch. Away to the right something was hanging on the barbed-wire. From where they stood it looked like a bundle of rags. As they edged closer they could see two feet sticking up into the air. A scarecrow had been turned on its head and lashed to the wire.

Stewart swung the torch down and they saw a face, slimed with green, the eyes open and staring.

"Jesus Christ," said Peter. "It's young Jemal."

3

"We did think at first," said Superintendent O'Keefe, "that it might have been mugging and robbery. Rather an unpleasant sort of mugging, you might say. He'd been drowned. Held head down in that muck. Not very nice."

His fatherly manner and matter-of-fact way of speaking robbed the words of some, but not much, of their brutality.

It was five o'clock in the morning. His audience was Mr. Chaytor, Stewart and Peter. They were seated in the living-room before a dying fire. In the last few hours a large number of people had appeared and disappeared. Most of them had tramped through the house. A photographic team, with flash-lights; finger-print men who seemed able to work in the dark; a police doctor, followed by a well-known pathologist who had been treated by everyone with great deference and had looked as neat and as wide awake as if he had been in his Harley Street consulting-room.

Statements had been taken from everyone and a follow-up team had appeared and erected a tent over the spot where Jemal had hung. A pathetic catafalque, thought Peter.

The police doctor had sent Mrs. Chaytor to bed and had given her a sleeping-pill before he left.

"However, when we got that boy's prints on the computer at Central and found out he was – " the superintendent consulted his note-pad, "an Iranian called Mohammed Awali Jemal, a member of a militant section of his compatriots, why then we changed our minds somewhat."

"If you already had his finger-prints on record," said Stewart, "does that mean that he had had previous convictions?"

"Some form, yes sir. He'd been up twice for brawling in the streets. The second occasion was more serious. People got hurt. Rather a violent young man. Well, you know how these groups fight among themselves. Hate each other, sometimes more than they hate their real enemies. And this had the look of a revenge killing."

"You said mugging *and* robbery."

"Did I?" O'Keefe looked surprised. "I suppose I thought that because there wasn't much in the young man's pockets. If he had had a wallet or anything like that it was gone. Only thing we found, in his watch-pocket, was a damp piece of cardboard which might tell us something when our back-room boys have worked it over. They do wonderful things with screens and cameras. You say you knew him, sir?"

This was shot, without warning, at Peter who had been slumped in his chair. Now he sat up and tried to pull himself together.

"I wouldn't say I knew him well. It was when I was doing a stint of teaching foreigners English. Quite a few of the Iranian dissidents came to me. Jemal was one of them."

"What did you make of him?"

"I thought he was a very earnest young man, wholly devoted to the anti-Khomeni faction. And prepared, unlike most of the others, to take active steps."

"Active steps?" said the superintendent thoughtfully. "Yes. You didn't know, perhaps, that a young man of his description is wanted in France in connection with an outrage in the Boulevard de Magenta?"

"I read about it," said Stewart. "A bomb was thrown. Do you mean that was Jemal?"

"It might have been, sir. There is no certainty. If it is true, it provides another possible explanation of what happened here last night."

"You mean that French agents – "

"Agents of some sort. The Special Branch, who deal with such matters, will be informed later today. After they have breakfasted. They are gentlemen of regular habits who do not appreciate being deprived of their sleep. Speaking of which, I will now leave you to yours."

After he had gone, Chaytor put another log on the fire. So little of the night was left that it seemed scarcely worthwhile

142

going to bed. It was Stewart who raised the matter that was in all their minds.

He said, gently, "Don't you think, Colin, that this might be a moment to clear up some of the points which have been puzzling us all?"

"If I can," said Chaytor. It was the hour for confession. "What points had you got in mind?"

"We all saw your wife when the headlights caught her. She was trying to get over that gate. Ergo, she thought she was being pursued. Presumably by Jemal. Now why should she think that?"

To help him along, Peter said, "We really do know a lot about it already. And what we don't know we've guessed. She was acting as a courier, yes? To bring back one of the really valuable pictures, the ones that Goraji and Rasim stole for Agazadeh Zaman."

"You know about them?"

"I was given a run-down by Commissaire Paul Meurice when I was in Bordeaux."

"If you know that, you know the whole story."

"Most of it," said Stewart. "Some things are still a bit puzzling. One question first. Why did these pictures have to come to England at all? Couldn't Zaman have arranged for them to be sold in France?"

"Yes. If he wished to get a tenth of what they were worth. Or even less. The only man who could realise anything approaching their real value was Meyer. He had the contacts you see, in São Paulo in Brazil and Bahia Blanca in the Argentine. South America is the best market for truly valuable paintings. Local industrialists and war criminals with money, who have taken refuge there. They are attracted by a form of property which is easily transportable and increases in value every year. Meyer has been dealing in this market for many years."

"Right," said Stewart. "So your wife brought them over and Meyer sold them in South America. One final point, then. These were well-known paintings, on what I believe they call the Interpol list. Once they got to South America, no doubt they would be safe enough. The authorities there are, I understand, notably tolerant. But they had to get through the controls at this end. How did Meyer manage that?"

"He had various methods," said Chaytor. After this there was a long silence. When it was clear that this was all he was going to offer them, Peter said, "Do you think we might have a look at the one she's just brought with her? I suppose it's in that case."

They thought that he was going to refuse, but after a moment of hesitation Chaytor shrugged his shoulders and said, "Why not? I shouldn't mind having another look at it myself before it disappears."

He lifted the case onto the table, opened the lid and gripped the catch between thumb and forefinger, turning it first in one direction, then in the other. When the false lid folded down all they could see was a single piece of white cardboard, exactly fitting the interior. Chaytor fiddled this out using the blade of his pen-knife and there was the picture. It was firmly held by transparent corner pieces, on the thicker cardboard which backed it. Chaytor took it out and held it, tilted, on the table.

Whilst they had been talking morning had been coming back into the sky.

Chaytor said to Peter, "If you'll switch out the light, we shall be able to see it better."

The brown shadows and half-tones of the background and the silver and drab green of the coat concentrated the eye on the face; the face of a young man, confident in his power and sure of his destiny.

"The greatest of the Dutch masters," said Chaytor reverently. "Lesser than Velazquez and Titian, but excelling them in humanity. It's hard to realise, isn't it, that Rembrandt was barely out of his teens when he painted this?"

Stewart was rubbing one finger gently over the picture. The three centuries and a half since it had been painted had hardened the surface of the paint and produced a faint spider's web of cracks, almost invisible at a distance. He said, "Lucky it's been carefully handled. It would never have done to have rolled this one up in an umbrella."

Peter was the only one who said nothing. He was revolted at the thought that a thing of such beauty should be destined

144

to adorn the *estancia* of some ex-Nazi thug or the penthouse flat of a Brazilian millionaire.

He kept these thoughts to himself.

Seeming to sense his reserve, Chaytor said, "You realise that there was nothing criminal in what we were doing. We were breaking a lot of administrative rules, that's all. If we'd been found out, no doubt we'd have been fined. The pictures confiscated, perhaps."

Peter realised that Chaytor was talking to reassure himself. He still said nothing.

They were half-way home in Stewart's car before he broke his silence. He said, "He didn't tell us much we didn't know. And the one thing we did want to know, he didn't tell us."

Stewart grunted. He was concentrating on his driving. The mist was still lying in patches in the hollows. For most of the time they were in the clear, then, without much warning, they were travelling in a white obscurity through which they crawled cautiously forward, feeling their way.

As had happened before when he had lost a night's sleep, Peter's brain was working with particular clarity. All the remaining questions were concentrated into a single question. If one could see the links one could see the answer. It would not come by thinking about it. It needed a spur from outside.

A red tail-light showed suddenly. Stewart braked in good time and for a whole unpleasant minute they were stationary, wondering if a less cautious driver would ram them from behind. Then the lorry in front of them moved on and they were out in the early morning sunlight.

Stewart said, "All clear ahead now."

"I hope so," said Peter.

4

"Well, I've been offered a job on this paper," said Ron. "It's run by a character I was at school with."

"What sort of paper?" said Peter. He was alone in the Starfax office. Stewart was off on some ploy of his own.

"It's a marketing magazine. A freebie. Most of it's advertisements. With bits between to fill up the gaps. Blocks, they call them. Well, I did one or two of those, when they were. hard up for something to put in. They seem to have gone down O.K. Now I've been offered a full-time job."

"Grab it," said Peter, "with both hands. I've got a feeling this lark may not last much longer."

"The skipper certainly seems to leave most of it to you nowadays."

This had become the pattern. As Stewart lost interest in his brainchild, Peter became more and more involved. He had a touch which endeared him to his correspondents, particularly the female ones. Some of them, he was alarmed to discover, were already elevating him to the status of guru. One lady had, without demur, paid four fees of fifty pounds to obtain the advice of the stars on matters which should more suitably have been put to her doctor. Another was, he suspected, feeling her way to an offer of marriage. Whether with himself or the stars only time would show.

"I'll be off, then," said Ron.

One result of the swing in their responsibilities had been to bring Peter into closer contact with their three regular assistants. They had quickly ceased to be puppets and had acquired three-dimensional personalities. Ronald and Leonard Terry had both been educated at the Sir John Summerfold School, near the Oval cricket ground and could, when it suited them, speak the classless middle-English of the television age. After leaving school they had taken different paths. Leonard was the boy who was clever with his hands. Ronald preferred to save his hands and use his brain. Both of them, he noticed, had regulated their accents and their modes of speech to accord with the company they kept; Len, with his clipped participles and unexpected diphthongs sometimes sounded almost like a stage cockney, whilst Ron could have passed for a modern product of the London School of Economics. He wondered, incidentally, how they spoke when they were at home together. Perhaps they didn't talk to each other. Some brothers didn't.

Peter was thinking about this when the telephone rang. It was Lisa and she sounded worried.

She said, "We've had a man round here – in fact he's been round twice – asking for Meyer. He seemed quite upset when I couldn't produce him and admitted I wasn't certain where he was. Not the perfect secretary, he evidently thought."

"What sort of man?"

"I guess he was a policeman."

"Did he have a name?"

"It sounded like O'Keefe."

"Then he is certainly a policeman. A Detective Superintendent no less."

"I had a feeling he might be someone important."

"According to Les, he's one of the coming men at the Yard. Said to be excellent at putting on a fatherly act. But watch out for it, Les said. It's only an act. Really he's a very tough customer."

"I got that impression, too."

"So what did he want with Meyer?"

"He didn't say. He just wanted to know where he was and how soon he could see him. All I could tell him was that he'd been going to Brussels first and would be away for a day or two. Had he left an address or a telephone number? Neither, I said. This seemed very strange to him and I think he thought I was stalling. That was when the fatherly manner slipped a bit."

"Don't panic," said Peter. "He can't arrest you for not knowing where your boss is."

*

147

Meyer had indeed been to Brussels, but he was no longer there. On the Monday afternoon he had had an appointment with the manager of the Banque Liégeoise, where he had been received with the deference due to a man who had, for some years, maintained a very large current account. He was ushered straight into the Manager's sanctum and offered a cigar. The Manager took one too and they were lit with appropriate ceremony.

When he was comfortably settled and had agreed that the government was scandalously incompetent (much better leave things to businessmen), that the state of the nation was what might have been expected and the weather deplorable, Meyer cautiously opened the real business he had come to discuss.

"As you must know," he said, "I have, in the past, found in South America, a ready market for my clients' paintings."

Monsieur Blaineau did know it and said that it showed a commendable spirit of enterprise.

"I now have a chance," continued Meyer, "to operate in a reverse direction. It has come to my knowledge privately that a South American businessman – you will, I am sure, excuse me for not mentioning his name – is prepared to sell one of the few remaining portraits by Goya which is still in private hands. He has, I fancy, little idea of its real value. If I can buy it at the price offered I have a purchaser in New York who would pay – well, a great deal more than I had given."

"It is always an agreeable state of affairs," said the Manager, "when one can sell for more than one buys. I imagine such opportunities do not often occur."

"Very rarely. And when they do they have to be grasped swiftly, but carefully. There is an additional complication. For various reasons the vendor has stipulated that the money must be paid to him either in local currency or in some form which is freely transferable into local currency."

"South American currency of some description," said the Manager thoughtfully.

"Correct. But there is a further complication. The paramount requirement in this case is secrecy. I have, I need hardly say, every confidence in you and in the few persons in your organisation who would be cognisant of the transaction at this end."

"You are very kind."

"But this confidence does not necessarily extend to the people who would be handling the matter if it were to be conducted on a normal bank-to-bank basis. Too many busy-bodies would be asking themselves why is Mr. Meyer, the well-known picture dealer, exporting such a very large sum of money to South America? And it would be a large sum. It would, temporarily, amount to almost the whole of my balance with you. You appreciate my uneasiness."

"I do indeed," said Monsieur Blaineau, who was himself exhibiting the sort of uneasiness which a bank manager feels when a large sum, held on current account, and therefore paying no interest and earning a comfortable income for the bank, is threatened with removal. "But tell me, how would you obviate this difficulty?"

"There is only one way. I have a courier who operates from Paris. He would have to take the money across personally."

"In Belgian francs?"

"They would have to be exchanged, either here or on arrival, into the appropriate currency."

"Cruzeiros or pesos."

"Or australs."

"Certainly, if you require the money in the Argentine."

"It is not a question," said Meyer sharply, "of where I require it. The person who will dictate that is my vendor. If he plans to retire in the Argentine when he gets his money, then naturally he will require it in the currency of that country."

Monsieur Blaineau said, "I quite follow that." He was trying to sound as broad-minded as a bank manager can when a favoured customer is suggesting to him what amounts to the closing of his account. He said, "You will, of course, have considered the various steps which have to be taken in connection with a transfer in cash."

Meyer regarded the fingernails of his left hand for nearly half a minute before he said, "Tell me frankly, Monsieur Blaineau, do you feel competent to advise me on this trans-action?"

"It is a little out of my field. But there are experts whom I can consult, without, of course, mentioning any names."

"How quickly?"

"I could have an answer for you by tomorrow."

"Good. Tomorrow I shall be in Paris. I have a small apartment in the Rue Oberkampf in the eleventh arrondissement. I have written down the telephone number for you." He handed him a piece of paper. "Please do not leave it lying about. Only a few people know of my Paris *pied-à-terre* and the fewer the better. I will expect a call from you around midday. Agreed?"

"Certainly. And have no fears. As is necessary in my profession I have an excellent memory for figures." He extracted one of the long cedar-wood matches which had been used for their cigars and set fire to the paper, depositing the ashes in the tray on his table.

"It is a pleasure to do business with a man of such discretion," said Meyer, with a smile which nearly reached his eyes.

He caught the evening Brabant Express and was in Paris in time for dinner. He doubted whether Monsieur Blaineau would be able to give him any useful advice or help, but he had achieved his real objective, which was to prepare the manager for the removal of his personal fortune from the Belgian bank to a Parisian one.

Next morning he paid two visits. The first was to the Paris office of Messrs. Mauger & Finch, whose London office looked after most of his travel arrangements. He had a word with young Mr. Finch. His return reservation to London had been made for that day. Since he had decided to spend a second night in Paris he now wished it to be rescheduled for a Wednesday morning flight. This was achieved, without difficulty, on the telephone. Having paid the small extra charge involved, Meyer said, "There was one other thing. An agent of mine, who is resident here, may shortly have to make a trip on my behalf to South America. He will have business to conduct either in São Paulo or in Bahia Blanca. One of the difficulties is that I shall not know until the last moment which of the two will be his destination."

"No problem if it is São Paulo. Both Air France and British

150

Airways have flights twice daily to Rio. From there he would catch the local shuttle to São Paulo."

"And Bahia Blanca?"

"That needs a little more thought. Aero-Argentina runs a direct flight daily from Geneva. It leaves at the rather awkward hour of two o'clock in the morning and I have never known it to be fully booked. However, if your agent is resident in Paris, it means that he will have to go first to Geneva. Nothing difficult about that, of course. Only some additional expense – "

"The expense is of no importance. What matters is the timing. It will not be certain until the last moment when he will have to leave. But when that moment comes, it is essential that he should leave at once. Flying to Geneva might waste an entire day and that could be fatal to the particular piece of business which he will be called upon to transact. You will excuse me if I do not go into details – "

"Certainly."

"I take it there are no direct flights from Paris?"

"Occasional charter flights, of course. But no scheduled service."

"I hardly think," said Meyer with a smile, "that important though this matter is it would warrant chartering a trans-Atlantic aircraft – "

"Might I, then, make a suggestion." Mr. Finch was scrabbling through the heap of timetables and information booklets on the table, like a terrier who has scented a promising bone. "I am fairly certain – no – yes, here it is. A.C.S.C., which is the Chilean national line, has recently inaugurated a daily flight to Santiago. It's first and only stop is Buenos Aires. It leaves at twelve o'clock in the morning – a much more civilised hour – and with the clock in its favour it reaches Buenos Aires at four thirty. Bahia Blanca is not much more than three hundred miles south west of Buenos Aires and there is a local service daily – a return service in fact – so your agent could be in Bahia Blanca early in the evening. How would that do?"

"It would do excellently. And I am much obliged to you. If his negotiations are successful, my man may have to proceed from South America to New York. In the first instance, therefore, I would propose to book him a single ticket. How much would that cost?"

Mr. Finch, having played a complicated tune on his desk calculator, said, "The South American exchanges tend to fluctuate, but it should not cost you much more than four hundred and fifty pounds. Tourist class, I assume."

"Then I will deposit with you now the sum of six hundred pounds. That should cover all contingencies. Then all that will be necessary will be a telephone call from me to you, stating which booking I need. It will be a person-to-person call. You do understand that the prime requisite is confidentiality."

Mr. Finch said that he understood perfectly.

Meyer's second call that morning was at the Banque de La Guyane. Here again he was ushered straight into the office of the General Manager.

Meyer had met the man before and knew something of his career. He had started as a junior secretary in the Chilean Embassy at Madrid, had become involved in Intelligence work and had shown such enthusiasm for it that the Spanish government had ordered his expulsion on twenty-four hours' notice. He had then joined the Banque de La Guyane, first at Georgetown, subsequently in Paris.

No cigars this time. Straight down to business.

Five minutes conversation convinced Meyer that Mr. Agostino was going to be much more useful to him than Monsieur Blaineau. He seemed to be a broad-minded man, with both feet firmly on the ground.

Meyer said, "When I was in Brussels I warned the manager of the Banque Liégeoise that I was contemplating a purchase in South America which would necessitate withdrawing the balance which he holds for me on current account."

"A large sum?"

"The equivalent in Belgian francs of a little more than £700,000. How long would it take to move this money into your hands?"

Trying to look neither gratified nor surprised the manager said, "By expedited inter-bank transfer, twenty-four hours. Longer, of course, if a weekend or a Bank holiday intervened."

"Good. The next point is perhaps not quite so simple. My vendor has indicated that he requires the money in the form of bearer scrip."

"Hoffman-Laroche, perhaps?"

"We thought of them, of course. But I am dealing with a man who looks well ahead. Odd things sometimes happen in the pharmaceutical industry. No. In the end we settled on N.T.T."

"Nippon Telephone & Telegraph. Yes. He could hardly do better."

"You must understand that the two essentials in this transaction are expedition and secrecy. Tell me, once the money from Brussels is in your hands how long would it take you to complete the purchase of the scrip?"

"No delay in the actual purchase. The order and confirmation would go by fax. The purchase money would be paid by inter-bank transfer. The only difficulty is that, being a bearer security, the scrip itself will have to come from Switzerland."

"And that would take how long?"

"A week or more."

"Yes," said Meyer. "That does present a difficulty."

"If speed is essential, might I suggest an alternative form of bearer security? A certified draft on this bank. It would be cashable on sight anywhere in South America."

"And I could have that at once?"

"But certainly. The money to back it would be in your account. There would be no difficulty and no delay."

"Do you know," said Meyer slowly, "I think that's an excellent idea? And so simple. I can't imagine why I didn't think of it for myself."

Having concluded both pieces of business in such a satisfactory manner he stood himself an expensive lunch at the Taillevent and was only marginally upset, on returning to his apartment, to receive a telephone call from Lisa warning him of the impending visit of Detective Superintendent O'Keefe.

"Did he say what he wanted to talk about?"

"Not in so many words," said Lisa. "But I gather it's to do with that young Iranian they found outside Colin's cottage."

"In that case," said Meyer cheerfully, "since I know

absolutely nothing about it, there's nothing I can tell him."

He had plans for that evening. They involved a visit to a Turkish bath in the fourteenth arrondissement. There, on payment of a sum considerably in excess of the normal fee, he would be given the use of a private bathroom and would be looked after by a young sailor from Toulon. The thought of that suntanned and muscular body was already exciting him.

5

"I realise that you're a busy man," said Detective Superintendent O'Keefe. "It's good of you to see me."

Meyer, who also thought it was good of him, nodded.

"I needn't waste time telling you about the unfortunate business out at Stanwell last Monday. Mr. Chaytor is, I believe, your – what is the correct description?"

"My assistant."

"Your assistant. Yes. I see. He has been with you for some time?"

"For twenty years."

"Indeed." The Superintendent paused. He seemed to be in two minds as to how to proceed. Then, starting to speak more briskly, he said, "We know a good deal about both the parties who were involved in this unpleasant affair. Not everything, of course. But enough to be able to arrive at certain preliminary conclusions. Mohammed Jemal was a young and active member of the Iranian Freedom Group. It is thought that he may have been the perpetrator of a recent bomb outrage in Paris. As to the two other men, they would appear to be professional thugs, Nasser Goraji and Mahmoud Rasim by name, who work for the pro-Khomeni faction in France. Our colleagues in the Special Branch duly noted their arrival at Heathrow on Monday."

Meyer said, with indignation that was only partly assumed, "Surely, Superintendent, if they knew the sort of people they were, they should either have detained them or sent them back?"

"Difficult. They were travelling on what appeared to be perfectly genuine passports. Moreover, they were armed with a letter from an official in the French Foreign Ministry stating that they were accredited to the Syrian Embassy, with whom they had urgent business to conduct. Detaining them would have led to a diplomatic incident at least. In any event, they were not here long. They were on a flight which arrived at half-past six on that Monday evening and they were observed returning to Paris by the nine o'clock plane the next morning."

"Having met and disposed of Jemal."

"So one would assume."

"It's obvious. They were sent over to kill him and they killed him."

"No doubt. But why did they select the neighbourhood of your assistant's house?"

Meyer had been expecting this one and was ready for it. He said, "I don't find that difficult. It is practically on the back doorstep of Heathrow Airport. Probably they all came over on the same plane. The two thugs followed Jemal, happened, by chance, to catch up with him at or near Stanwell and carried out the assassination."

"The—o—retically," said the Superintendent, spreading the word out to its fullest length, "that is a possible solution. But, in fact, it's quite untrue."

"Oh. What makes you say that?"

"I say it because it does not fit in, in any way, with the rest of our information."

As he said this, Meyer realised that the Superintendent was dealing out facts in a carefully predetermined order, as an expert bridge player might lay his cards on the table. He realised, also for the first time, that he would have to be careful when playing his own cards.

"For instance," continued the Superintendent, "we know that Goraji and Rasim were met at the airport by a car hired for them by the Embassy. It took them to Stanwell Moor, which is a small village on the other side of the B 379. Here they left it, instructing it to wait. They said they might be away for some hours. They were back by eleven o'clock and were driven to a small hotel in Egham where they, and the driver, spent the night. Next morning he took them back to catch their flight to Paris. That information came from the car-hire firm. I see no reason to doubt it."

"Nothing there contradicts the idea I put forward."

"Agreed. The contradiction comes from the known movements of Jemal. He was seen in London in the late afternoon and no doubt approached Stanwell, in the normal way, by train and bus. That is still to be confirmed. But what we do know is that, when he arrived, he broke into Mr. Chaytor's house, which was empty at the time, and made himself comfortable in the kitchen."

"How can you possibly – ?"

"How can we be sure of it? We are on very firm ground." The Superintendent smiled slightly. "In every sense of the word. You may remember the weather that night. It was dry and clear until about half past nine. Then there was a sudden downpour. It lasted for not much more than half an hour. But a very important half hour, since it enabled us to work out, with great precision, what Jemal had done. He was wearing the very narrow shoe which such people often affect. The prints which he left, both before and after the storm, were quite clear."

He was speaking slowly and Meyer was now paying close attention. He was not sure how it affected him, but had an uneasy feeling that there were snags ahead.

"He broke into Mr. Chaytor's house some time before the rain started. When he left it, in a hurry, it was raining hard. He ran up the path, beside the garden, back to the main road. At that point his prints are joined and trampled on by two much heavier pairs. Goraji and Rasim, we assume. Two professionals would not have taken long to master a boy."

"That seems clear," said Meyer.

"Yes. But what is far from clear is why Jemal waited in the house at all. Who was he waiting for? It can't have been Mr. Chaytor and his friends, since he ran away as soon as they arrived."

"I suppose you will say that he was waiting for Mrs. Chaytor."

"Exactly. She came through Customs at Dover at five o'clock. Train and bus would have got her to the house at half past nine. You know why she went to France, of course."

"No," said Meyer sharply. "Why should I know?"

"Mr. Chaytor has worked for you for twenty years. Did

he never mention that his wife escorted children to and from France?"

"Oh, that, yes. I thought you meant – "

"Yes, Mr. Meyer, what did you think I meant?"

"What I was going to say was that I knew about Mrs. Chaytor's trips to France, but wasn't particularly interested in them."

"Is that right? I rather gathered that there was one occasion at least on which you were not only interested, but took a very active part."

"Was there? I had forgotten."

"It was not all that long ago. Mind you, my information is second-hand and may be quite incorrect. The story, as I had it from one of Mr. Chaytor's friends, was that he was getting very upset about his wife missing her train at the Gare du Nord. And that you took charge in quite an admirable way."

"It was not an event of great importance," said Meyer with a smile. "Now that you mention it, I do recall it."

"Do you know what had caused the delay?"

"I gather that the taxi which was taking Mrs. Chaytor to the Gare du Nord was involved in an accident."

"A serious accident?"

"Not really. It seems that the driver's attention was distracted and he collided with a private car."

"One can hardly blame him for being distracted. After all, it's not every day that a bomb goes off in your immediate vicinity."

"A bomb?"

"Thrown into a café in the Boulevard de Magenta. Quite close to the station."

Meyer was thinking fast. He said, "I'm afraid you've got this wrong. A bomb was thrown. I read about it in the paper. But that was some time after Mrs. Chaytor's accident. That was nothing to do with it."

"It only shows how careful one must be."

"What do you mean?" said Meyer sharply.

"In accepting information at second hand."

"Oh, yes. Of course."

"But there are still things about Mrs. Chaytor's part in this killing which I find it difficult to understand. I am trying to build up a picture, but some of the parts refuse to fit. For instance, it might help me if I understood more clearly what part Mr. Chaytor plays in your organisation. You described him as your assistant. What does that involve?"

"I can tell you about that," said Meyer. (If this bloody man didn't dodge about so much I might get some idea what he's really after.) "Colin Chaytor is a painter. Not, perhaps, of the first class, but a very competent professional. He has also made a study of French and Italian art. This enables him to advise me about the pictures I buy."

"He does a little more than simply advise you. Doesn't he bid for the pictures, at auction?"

"Yes he does." (What are we getting to now?)

"At Pikorx. You know about them, of course."

"Yes, I know about them."

"I felt you must do. Since you formed the company and hold all the shares; some of them in the names of nominees."

Meyer drew a deep breath. This man was dangerous. He said, "What put that idea into your head?"

"Our Company Fraud Department. They're not often wrong about things like that."

Meyer decided that the time had come to lose his temper. He said, "Look here, Inspector – Superintendent. I've been very patient with you. I've answered questions on matters which seem to me to have no connection with the crime you're meant to be investigating. This boy Jemal had no connection with me, nor I with him. Now – if you don't mind – "

He got to his feet. O'Keefe made no sign of complying. Instead he felt in his inner pocket and pulled out a piece of white card. "This is a photocopy," he said. "The original was badly stained, but our people brought it up. You recognise it?"

"Of course. It's my professional card."

"And if you have no connection with Jemal, nor him with you, what was it doing in his pocket?"

Meyer took a second deep breath. He said, "Many people have these cards. Potential customers, agents, art lovers – "

"And into which category would you place Jemal?"

As he said this, the Superintendent got to his feet. He was

159

a lot taller than Meyer and broader. Standing there, face to face, he appeared for the first time to be menacing.

"I am sorry, Mr. Meyer. But I am afraid you are not being entirely frank with me. You would be well advised to consider your position." Before Meyer could reply, the Superintendent had swung round, made for the door and let himself out, closing it behind him. Meyer heard his feet rapping on the tiles in the hall, then heard the front door open and shut. He sat without movement for a whole minute, then put out his hand, felt for the telephone, pulled it towards him and dialled a number.

At the last moment, he seemed to change his mind and cut off the call before it could start ringing.

The number Meyer had started to dial was the Starfax office. If he had persisted, he would have found both Starfactors at their desks. Peter was typing a letter. Stewart was reading the Michaelmas term issue of the Chelburian which had arrived that morning.

"An improvement on the last few numbers," he said. "The new editor has a glimmering notion of how to write."

Peter said, "Uh?" He was attempting to compose a letter to a madman.

"An interesting section of School Notes, too."

"Grow up," said Peter. "You left school three years ago."

Stewart ignored this. He said, "I see that Dakin has won a scholarship at Oriel. I always said that kid would go far."

"Actually, you called him a spotty drip."

"I revised my opinion later. And what do you think of this? 'All Chelburians will have been pleased to learn that the Reverend Alvin Brind, formerly our Chaplain, has now been offered one of the senior positions in the Cathedral hierarchy as Precentor. Among his other assignations will be oversight of the Cathedral choir. He said, "My long experience of working with boys of all ages at Chelborough will be of great assistance to me in carrying out this duty." He is remembered here as an inspiring preacher and a great teacher of history.'"

"He'll end up as a Bishop," said Peter. "Now, please – "

160

"One more item. A sad one this time. Do you remember little Mr. Pleydell?"

"He taught art. Lived in a cottage in Dene Lane and rode to school on a very old bicycle."

"Correct. On this occasion he fell off his bicycle in front of a lorry."

"How unpleasant. Did it – ?"

"No. The lorry stopped in time. He had died of heart failure."

"An artistic finish," said Peter. "Now, if you don't mind, I must get on with this letter. Damn." It was the telephone on his desk. A one-sided conversation ensued. Peter said, "Oh, hello darling. No, never too busy to hear from you." Then, "Oh" a number of times and "Why on earth?" And finally, "Well, I suppose I'll have to."

Stewart said, "I take it that was Lisa. What's she trying to talk you into now?"

"I've been invited to tea by her mother. Today."

"Accept at once," said Stewart. "You'll get a good tea and insinuate yourself even further into her good books."

"I'm not sure. She's a tough old girl. I still can't make out if she approves of me or not."

"Give her that lovely smile of yours and she'll fall flat on her back."

When Peter had gone, Stewart resumed his study of the Chelburian. There was a picture of Precentor-elect Brind with the Bishop. Both men looked pleased with themselves. He was deep in a study of the season's cricket results when Ronald Terry came in. His new style of dressing reflected his elevation to a post in the City. He said, "Really I came in to say goodbye. I don't think I shall be much use to you now."

"A busy journalist."

"It's a bit more than that. I've been offered a job in a company called Inter-Continental Marketing. Not a large outfit, but it seems to be doing very well. Doubled its turnover last year."

"Marketing," said Stewart thoughtfully. "I've heard one or two people talking about it lately."

"It's the in-thing."

"What exactly do you do?"

"We sell other people's products for them."

"Advertising, you mean."

"Much more than that. All forms of promotion. Briefing their reps, free offers, packaging, presentation – "

"Good luck to you," said Stewart, "and thanks for all your help in the past."

After Ron had left he sat for a long time, occasionally turning over the pages of the magazine, but no longer really reading it. When it became too dark to read, he did not turn on the light, but sat there, thinking.

Quite apart from the defection of Ron there were a number of reasons for supposing that the time was at hand for Starfax to close. The only real obstacle was Peter. Those futile jobs which he had tried since leaving school! How could he throw him back onto that dead-end market? Moreover, Peter was clearly enjoying his Starfax work and had a talent for it. An impossibly difficult decision.

It was nearly eight o'clock when Peter came back. He was surprised to find Stewart sitting in the dark. He switched on the light and said, "What on earth are you doing?"

"Thinking," said Stewart. "And stop smirking. I do think sometimes. How did it go?"

"Very friendly. It's an astonishing set-up. One of those mansions with four storeys and a basement, in Fitzjohn's Avenue. I imagine you could run it very comfortably with a fatigue-proof staff of six. All she's got is one old girl who's almost dying on her feet."

"A *grande dame* without the cash to support it."

"I don't think it's lack of money. According to Lisa she's rolling in it. The fact is you can't get people nowadays who are prepared to struggle up and down four flights of stairs bearing burdens. When the ancient retainer brought in the tea I thought she was going to drop it, silver teapot, silver tea-set, crumpets, cucumber sandwiches, chocolate cake and all."

"So what did she want? Apart from stuffing you with food."

"She offered me a job."

"Helping to carry things up and down stairs?"

162

"No. The offer came from her brother, Joseph. He wants someone to act as secretary-cum-companion-cum-resident policeman."

"Which would mean living in France."

"It would have done. If I'd accepted it. Which I didn't, of course."

"Why?"

If there was a very faint undertone of disappointment Peter missed it.

He said, "Mainly because I don't particularly like Joseph – who seems to have got himself into some sort of mess, incidentally. Also because I'm enjoying what I'm doing here."

"Good on you," said Stewart. "And am I going to need you! What else did you find to talk about? You can't have taken three hours to eat even that tea and turn down the job."

"As a matter of fact, I didn't. I stopped off, on the way home, at the Marylebone Public Library. It's got one of the best reference sections in London."

"With what object?"

"I was looking for a lady called Beatrice Oldfield. Lisa tells me that one more of her domestic masterpieces will shortly be winging its way to South America. This one is called *Farmyard Friends*. It depicts a cat, a goat and a collie dog eating out of the same trough."

"It sounds just the thing for a Gestapo fugitive in Rio."

"So I thought I would find out a little more about Beatrice. She proved curiously elusive. I started with Vasari's *Lives of the Painters* – two volumes – and worked my way through to the *Teach Yourself History of Painting* in ten volumes. No luck. Since I gathered that she was late Victorian I had high hopes of Muther's *History of Modern Painting*, which was published in 1907, incidentally. Still no luck."

"Are you telling me," said Stewart, who was beginning to sound interested, "that Beatrice doesn't exist?"

"I began to think so. But I found her in the end. In a work devoted to the Pre-Raphaelite movement. Not actually an account of her, but a statement that 'although the movement was a revolt against the grand style and arrogance of the

163

Romantics it was equally an assault on the demure symbolism of such postcard-artists as Beatrice Oldfield and Valerie Mellows, very few, if any, of whose products survived, or deserved to survive, the attack.' When you consider that *Farmyard Friends* is the *fifth* forgotten masterpiece to be despatched to South America in the past two years – well, it makes you think."

"Possible, but improbable," agreed Stewart. "What do you propose to do about it?"

"Discuss it with Lisa, as soon as I get home. If she will help, I think this final knot can be untied."

"It's no good going home now, you won't find her there. I meant to tell you. She telephoned and left a message. She's been invited out to supper."

"Did she say who by?"

"By her boss."

"By Meyer?"

"Correct. She added two things. First, that she is perfectly capable of looking after herself. Second, that there is the remains of a steak and kidney pudding in the fridge that you can heat up."

"I'm sure she's capable of looking after herself. Anyway, like all physical fitness freaks, Meyer's probably hopeless with the opposite sex. No. It's the thought of that re-heated steak and kidney pudding that's worrying me – "

"Then let's forget it and go out and get something to eat – and drink."

"Well," said Peter, "how did the great seduction scene go?"

"It never started," said Lisa.

They had arrived back at the flat almost at the same moment and instead of staying up had decided to go to bed and talk there.

"I knew from the way he managed the drinks that he wasn't out to seduce me. On previous occasions it has been the tactics of the seducer to ply me with drink until I became powerless to resist."

"Unsuccessfully, I imagine."

"Indeed. When I found that I had a harder head than the potential rapist I quite enjoyed it. In this case it didn't

164

arise. We had a decorous glass of sherry and shared a bottle of wine during the meal – a very good one, incidentally, at Petit Gervais – and when I said 'No' to a glass of port or brandy afterwards, I was not pressed. It was clear by that time that he had asked me out to get information."

"About what?"

"About you."

"For God's sake. Why?"

"It would seem that he has a very important job to offer and wanted to know whether you were equipped to do it. Always supposing you agreed to take it on. I gave him a glowing account of your many accomplishments."

"Such as?"

"I said you spoke excellent French. He regarded that as important. That you knew something about art, from your discussions with my uncle at Lambrécie."

"Practically nothing, in fact."

"That didn't seem to matter. It was much more your familiarity with Lambrécie and its neighbours that interested him. I mentioned the Deputy Mayor and the famous vinologist – I'd forgotten his name – "

"Philibert-Lucot."

"That's the boy. Also the policeman, Paul Meurice. That really did ring a bell. How well did you get to know him? What had he told you? I wasn't sure how much of your *tête-à-tête* was confidential, so I simply said that you liked him and seemed to have got on well with him."

"And you've no idea what this job is?"

"Since I knew you weren't looking for a change of job, I wasn't particularly interested."

"I'm not sure."

"You haven't changed your mind again, have you?"

"Actually, it was something that happened tonight. When we were having a drink at the Running Footmen, Len joined us. All the boys use that pub. He knew about his brother's new job and had rather assumed that this was the signal for Starfax to fold its tents. Personally, he wasn't unhappy about this, as he's been offered a share in a garage and repair shop. Stewart said, 'No. Not a bit of it. Starfax was certainly going on.' And then he switched the conversation to something else, but the way he did it, made me wonder."

"Wonder what?"

"Whether Starfax wasn't being kept alive simply to keep me out of the dole queue. And that's when I began to think that if a good job did turn up, I ought to take it."

"I see your point," said Lisa. "If you're interested in this job, I'll pursue the matter further."

They had both been lying on their right sides, Peter with his knees comfortably fitting into the crook of Lisa's legs. It was a position they found convenient for discussions. Now they both rolled over. New position, new topic, thought Lisa. What's the boy up to now?

"There was one other thing. You know you told me that you've got another Beatrice Oldfield to export."

"*Farmyard Friends*, yes."

"I gather it isn't a particularly valuable picture. Why do you need a licence?"

"Because the pictures are more than a hundred years old. That makes them antiques."

"I see. And how far have you got with the procedure?"

"We got the Ministry of Culture form about a fortnight ago and sent it off with a photograph to the Ministry of Economics."

"Did you keep a copy of the photograph?"

"Of course."

"Could you bring it back tomorrow evening, with the forms and any other documents?"

"I could. Am I allowed to know what you're up to?"

"I'm trying to prove a theory."

"Mystery for the sake of mystery," said Lisa crossly. "You're getting as bad as Stewart. Go to sleep."

On the following evening he studied the documents Lisa had brought back. Among them was a duplicate of the Ministry of Culture form. Some of the questions in it related to the artist, described as Beatrice Oldfield, born 1838, died 1898, specialising in domestic watercolours. Title of picture *Farmyard Friends*. (Lisa, he saw, had typed this as Farmyard

166

Fiends, but the error had been spotted and corrected in ink.) Estimated value six to eight hundred pounds. Photograph attached.

"Not a very good photo, is it? Looks like the sort of snap I used to take with a box Brownie."

"It is a bit blurred," agreed Lisa. "But you can see the animals all right."

"I suppose so." Peter wondered what possible attraction the picture could have for a sophisticated Argentinian. "The goat's the best of the three. He has a distinct resemblance to one of my uncles. You say you submitted this form about two weeks ago. How long, do you think, before you get your export licence?"

"When we sent in the first one they sat on it for months. Now it's all much quicker. I imagine they just say, 'Oh, another Oldfield' and we get the licence almost at once. In fact, I'm surprised we haven't had it already."

"And when you do get it, what then?"

"We book the first available flight. Chaytor looks after that side of it."

"Does he, though," said Peter thoughtfully. Some of the points in his theory which had been obscure before were becoming clearer. "As soon as the flight's booked, pick up the phone and let me or Stewart know. We'll arrange that one of us is always in the office."

"It's not a question of picking up the phone. My instructions from Meyer are categorical. If I telephone either of you, I do it from a call-box."

"Why on earth – ?"

"That policeman shook Meyer badly. He's now convinced that his telephone has been bugged."

"I am appalled," said Dr. Felix, the head of the Département des Trésors Nationaux, "at the disinterest of the authorities in the steady loss of our national heritage. Pictures and tapestries are being taken, almost daily, from unguarded churches and almost unguarded museums."

"Unlisted," said Superintendent O'Keefe, "unphotographed – and often uninsured."

167

"I must agree, with much regret, that what you say is, in many cases, correct."

"It's not much better here," said O'Keefe. "I've just been put in charge of the smallest and least important sub-unit in the Yard. It's got an imposing title – A25, otherwise the Arts and Antiques Squad. It used to be known as C.1.4. One useful thing we have inherited from our predecessors is their computer. What we need is more manpower. At the moment the department consists of me and two sergeants. One talks schoolboy French and the other has a smattering of Italian."

"It is, at least, a start."

"We should go up in the batting order if someone would be good enough to blow up the National Gallery."

"A drastic solution. But I must admit that our own position has gained in importance lately. Art theft has acquired two stepbrothers. Violence and politics. The unfortunate farmer in Normandy, who was bludgeoned and kicked to death, was only the first of a series of outrages. The most recent was in Dijon. One of the guards of the Musée des Beaux Arts was savagely attacked and is still in hospital. He will be a cripple for life. And now we have that bomb in the Café Continental. The worst incident of its kind since the bombing of the department store last September. Particularly unpleasant on this occasion since there were children among the victims."

"I apologise for speaking light-heartedly of bombs," said O'Keefe. "They are a vile and indiscriminate weapon. But are you sure that this incident was connected with art theft?"

"Not sure. No. But certain facts are emerging. It now appears that a woman, who was observed hurrying away from the café, may have been an English woman, a regular visitor to Paris, who left France that evening. A Mrs. Chaytor, wife of Colin Chaytor, who works for a certain art dealer, a Mr. Meyer."

"Right," said O'Keefe. "I'm sure that's right. The link is somewhere there."

"You have, perhaps, been able to question one or both of these men?"

"I spoke briefly to Mr. Chaytor on the night that your supposed bomb thrower, Mohammed Jemal, was killed. A report on that went through our Special Branch to your Bureau de Sécurité Publique. I hope it reached you."

"Such reports have an unfortunate habit of becoming lost in course of transmission. But in this case, I was able to see it. I found it extremely interesting. You have, you say, spoken to Mr. Chaytor?"

"Briefly. But I questioned his employer, Mr. Harry Meyer, at greater length."

"With success?"

"I succeeded only in convincing myself of what I already suspected. That he is in this racket up to the neck. He knows all the twists and turns, the dirty tricks and the legal loopholes."

"You did not find him agreeable?"

"I thought he was smooth, clever and totally unpleasant."

"If he is, indeed, buried up to the neck in this matter, could you not cut off his head? If you could contrive to do so, you would be doing a great service to both our countries."

"Find me an axe which is heavy enough and sharp enough and I'll swing it with the greatest of good will."

"I have a feeling," said Dr. Felix, with an emphasis which grew almost to passion as he spoke, "a feeling which is shared by many in our country, that the government is conducting itself towards the Iranians like a collection of old women. I correct myself. I know some excellent, tough-minded, old women. No. Our present masters are behaving like feeble, half-witted, old women. When the Ayatollah departed, in triumph, to Iran, he left behind him a number of men who are like the germs of a disease which, once it has gripped you, are almost impossible to eradicate. They penetrate our national life. The airports and central railway stations in particular. So infected are we that, at the demand of Iran, we banish anti-Khomeni activists. At their demand we liberate known terrorists and return them to Iran. One might suppose that we were a conquered nation, being dictated to by our conquerors." He added, with belated caution, "I must, of course, ask you not to repeat any of that, or I should certainly be in trouble."

"Don't worry," said O'Keefe. "I know things about our own top brass that I couldn't retail to anyone without getting stellenbosched."

6

On the following Tuesday Lisa telephoned the Starfax office. "We're off," she said. *"Farmyard Friends* is booked onto the evening British Airways' flight to Rio tomorrow."

"Who's got the picture now?" said Peter.

"I imagine it's down at Stanwell. Why?"

"I just wanted to be sure. Do you know exactly what time the flight is?"

"Early evening. That's all I know. Couldn't you find out by telephoning British Airways?"

"I suppose I could."

"Then do it. I'm in a call-box and I haven't got any more change, so if you want to know anything else for God's sake get a move on."

"No," said Peter. "No. I think that's all. And thanks a lot."

"Don't mention it."

Stewart, who had been listening in, said, "I take it that's the starting pistol. What next?"

"We go to Stanwell, in your car. If we kick off at seven, the worst of the out-of-London traffic will have gone."

"It's an easy run," said Stewart. "The A4 as far as Hounslow. Then the A30. It'll be getting dark by the time we arrive."

"Just what I had in mind," said Peter.

In fact they ran into the tail-end of a traffic block caused by a lorry which had jack-knifed across the road at the Brentford underpass. It took forty-five frustrating minutes to clear this and it was fully dark when they turned into Stanwell Road.

"We can park in that farm entrance," said Peter. "On foot from there."

They padded along the deserted road towards the house. There was a light in the front window.

"I only hope we haven't left it too late," said Peter. "Let's nip round to the back of the house and make sure. No. It's all right. There's still a light in the studio. Back to the front door."

When they rang the bell it was Mrs. Chaytor who let them in. She said, in reasonably welcoming tones, "Come in. Come in, both of you. What brings you out at this time of night?" Adding, with a first hint of suspicion, "I didn't hear your car drive up."

"We left it a little way away. We wanted our visit to be a surprise."

"A surprise?" said Mrs. Chaytor. She was standing in such a way that she blocked access to the studio. "Well, it's a nice one. Come and sit down." She indicated the open drawing-room door on her left. As they reached it, Peter moved her firmly aside with one hand on her shoulder, and said, "First things first." He stalked down the hall to the door at the end and opened it. Mrs. Chaytor started to protest, but made no actual effort to stop him.

Chaytor was in his shirt sleeves. There was a picture on the easel beside him and his palette was lying on the table. He stared at Peter and at Stewart who had followed him in and watched them in silence as they walked up to examine the picture. Then he said, "Well, well. You've surprised my little secret."

There was apology in his voice, but a hint of amusement too.

"So you," said Stewart, "are Beatrice Oldfield."

"Her reincarnation, you might say."

Peter said, "I see you're using acrylic paint for this particular masterpiece."

"Beatrice's fifth and, I assure you, her final production."

"Imposed, on this occasion, on top of Rembrandt's self-portrait."

"Certainly." Chaytor seemed to be curiously unperturbed. "What I am actually using is acrylic paint thinned with water and medium. It dries almost instantaneously and peels off almost as fast. I had to experiment to get the right proportion of pigment to filler. I found out that when the mixture was too thin to obscure the painting behind it properly I could increase the opacity by adding a little white."

It seemed to Peter that Chaytor was keener to deal with the technical side of his deception than with the consequences that flowed from it. He said, "Why don't we make ourselves comfortable next-door? Then you can clarify one or two points that I still find puzzling."

"If you like." Now that his secret had been surprised he seemed only too willing to be communicative. To his wife, who was hovering in the hall, he said, "Don't worry, love. All friends here. Suppose you make us a cup of coffee. That's right."

Peter said, "It was when Stewart mentioned acrylic paint that a faint bell rang. I knew that if you laid it on a hard surface it would tend to peel off eventually. But I'd no idea it would come off so quickly."

"It depends on the precise mix. It took a lot of experimenting to get it right." Chaytor giggled. "Do you know, the first time I did this the recipient at the other end telephoned Mr. Meyer *two months later* complaining that the over-painting was still there. That was one of my best efforts – *Cupboard Love* – but somehow he didn't seem to be appreciating it. He wanted the Titian portrait underneath. We told him to wait, and after another month it had all peeled away quite cleanly. Next time I went too far in the other direction and it started coming off after twenty-four hours."

"Awkward," said Peter. "I suppose that's why you had to be so near the airport."

"It wasn't only a question of being near. I had to make friends with a lot of the people who work there. The lorry drivers who use the Cargo Terminal at the back. I got to know most of the regulars by name and I used to ask them in for a drink at Christmas – that sort of thing. I've got a motor scooter that I use for local trips and they let me come into the airport through the Terminal. It was irregular, of course, but it meant that I could arrange the timing very precisely. Then I got to know the loaders as well. That was necessary, because sometimes a flight can be delayed for quite a time."

"As we all know," said Stewart, who had done his share of sitting about in air terminals.

"Yes. Well if that happened I could get the painting back,

172

you see, and touch it up. That wasn't difficult. I'd had to paint it twice already."

"Of course," said Peter. "A preliminary one for the photograph that went to the Ministry of Culture."

"Exactly. At the beginning, when they took months to give us our permit, I sometimes had to retouch the painting two or three times. Do you know, by the end of it, I was quite sad to see it go. I'd put a lot of work and a lot of feeling into it."

It was curious, thought Peter, how unashamed he seemed of what he had been doing. He had said, at one point, that there was nothing criminal about it. But was that true? He was certainly acting as an accomplice in – in what? Was smuggling a crime? That probably depended on what you were dealing with. Smuggling drugs into the country, yes. But smuggling pictures out of it? In breach of regulations laid down by the Ministry of Culture. The usual sort of penalty was a fine and confiscation of the goods being smuggled. Peter gave it up. He had no wish to cloud his own satisfaction. The whole thing had been exactly like solving Brindy's code. It was akin to the intellectual satisfaction of filling the last word into a difficult crossword puzzle.

At this point the telephone rang. They looked at each other. "It must be for you," said Stewart. "No one knows that Peter and I are here."

The telephone continued to ring. It calls for great strength of mind to resist the clamorous summons. Chaytor gave way. He listened for a moment and said to Peter, in some surprise, "It's for you."

It was Lisa. She said, "I guessed you'd be there. Meyer wants to see you, as soon as possible. He suggested ten o'clock tomorrow morning. If you can manage that, I'm to phone him back."

"Sounds as if he means business. Have you any idea what it's about?"

"I'd guess he's made up his mind to offer you that job."

"Now isn't that typical?" said Peter. "A few months ago I hadn't got a job at all. Now that I have got one which I enjoy I'm offered two more. One by your mother and one by your boss."

"That's because they both love you so much."

"Nonsense. Your mother may be getting reconciled to me. I hope she is. But she certainly doesn't love me. As for Meyer, he hardly knows me and has got no reason to want to help me."

"You underestimate yourself. You may not have realised it, but you've become a powerful influence in his life. A guiding star, you might say."

"Rubbish."

"It's not rubbish. Whenever he has to make an important decision I can see him asking himself, 'What would Starfax advise?' "

"Instead of talking nonsense, it would be more useful if you could give me some idea about the job he's going to offer me."

"I think it must be something to do with Lambrécie."

"But he's got no connection with Lambrécie."

"Then why, for the last two days, has he been speaking, almost non-stop, on the telephone to my uncle?"

"If you don't know the answer no one else is likely to."

"Are you suggesting that I listen in to my employer's telephone calls?"

"All secretaries listen to their employer's telephone calls. It's part of their job."

"Well, as a matter of fact, I did gather that the household at Lambrécie is in a fairly chaotic state. Almost, you might say, under siege."

"Who by?"

"Those two Iranian thugs have been seen in the neighbourhood. That was more than enough to upset Uncle Joseph. He's deposited all his best pictures in the bank."

"And what's all this got to do with the job he's going to offer me?"

"There's one way of finding out, isn't there?"

"All right. Ring him back and tell him I'll come along tomorrow morning."

"It'll be a great comfort to him. An assuagement of his anxieties. I don't suppose he'd get a wink of sleep tonight unless he knew that Starfax was on its way."

She rang off before Peter could think of an adequate reply.

*

174

Meyer said, "I understand, Mr. Dolamore, that you're a regular visitor to Lambrécie."

"Hardly regular," said Peter. "I've been there twice. Once three years ago. Once quite recently."

"And when you were there no doubt you had occasion to examine Mr. Wellborn's collection of pictures. One of the finest in private hands on this side of the Atlantic."

"Yes. I saw them. Actually I don't know a lot about art. But I did appreciate the *Madonna of the Swans*. I understand that it has been lodged in a Bordeaux bank for safety."

"That is the current story," agreed Meyer. "Unfortunately it is not true. The picture was stolen six days ago."

Peter stared at him. Realising that anything he said would be pointless, he remained silent.

"It was an obvious target for the Iranians," continued Meyer, in the same level tones. "The timing of the theft was brilliant. It took place on the evening of the day on which Joseph Wellborn received, through his New York agent, a confirmed offer for the picture of fifty million francs from a private trust, founded by the American plastics millionaire, Alexander Lafayette. In the place where the picture had hung a note had been pinned. It said, 'To recover your picture will cost you exactly five million francs in the form of a bank draft on the Crédit Agricole. If you accept this modest offer, which is not negotiable, you will insert a notice in *France Sud* tomorrow that, in view of reported art thefts, some of your more valuable pictures have been deposited with one of the local banks. You will then receive further instructions. If you do not accept this offer the picture will be burnt. We will return you the ashes.' "

"Five million francs," said Peter. "Roughly five hundred thousand pounds. Could he raise it?"

"Quite easily. Not only is his credit good, but to seal the bargain the Lafayette Trust had already caused ten per cent of the offer price to be deposited with his bank. He could not draw it out, of course, until the sale was completed, but the bank, knowing about it, would certainly advance a similar sum to him."

Peter had hardly been listening. He had no doubt that

Joseph Wellborn could raise half a million pounds. He was thinking of something quite different.

"How did they do it?" he said. "I thought that an infallible alarm system had been installed."

"No alarm system is more infallible than the people who operate it. The night guard – Michel-Ange on that occasion – had been entrusted with the master key of the alarm system so that he could un-set it in the morning when he came off guard. They had every confidence in him. But it was not a wise arrangement."

"You mean they bribed him to let them in? I shouldn't have thought – "

"One step at a time," said Meyer. "First they had to dispose of the dog. They did this with a cyanide dart. It was a big strong dog. It took three darts to kill him. When Michel-Ange appeared on the scene they knocked him silly, dragged him to one side of the garden sheds and, when they had revived him, persuaded him to show them where the alarm key was hidden and to hand it over."

"Persuaded him?"

"They soaked his legs in petrol and gave him a count of ten. I understand that he held out until they had actually clicked on the lighter. Then he gave way."

"Do you blame him?"

"The only person who blames him is himself. I understand that he has been suffering from a form of nervous breakdown ever since. This, as you will imagine, has not improved the general atmosphere at the château."

Whilst he was speaking Peter had noticed, as Lisa had done once before, that when dealing with a serious matter Meyer was a different man: harder, sharper and more self-possessed. He said, "Do you know the men who did this?"

"Goraji and Rasim. I know them well. I have had a number of dealings with them and have always found them reliable. In this particular negotiation I might almost be said to be representing them. What is needed is someone to represent the family. Not a policeman, of course, or anyone who might feel obliged to take official notice of the matter. There are, as you may know, professional firms who specialise in dealing

176

with the situation which follows a kidnapping. I mean the kidnapping of some person. Where it is a picture that has been taken, the matter is more specialised. Once I had considered the problem the solution seemed obvious. Nobody has better credentials for the job than you."

Peter, who had seen this coming, managed to remain silent. He wanted to hear the full plan before saying 'No'.

"Quite apart from your command of French, you know the household and they know you. But there is one even more important point. In such a transaction it is vital to be certain that you are dealing with the right parties and not with outsiders who are muscling in on the job. My secretary tells me that you actually met one of these men, face to face."

"I did," said Peter with a slight shudder, "and I've no desire to do so again."

"Allow me to continue. Mr. Wellborn has, sensibly I think, agreed to what is proposed. After all, he is being asked to put down five million francs to save fifty million, a ten per cent insurance premium you might call it. He has kept completely quiet about the theft, has put out the cover story of the picture being at the bank and has bound his household to secrecy. What remains is simply to effect the exchange. It has now been agreed that two bank drafts will be handed over by Mr. Wellborn. The first for the stipulated sum of five million francs. The second for five hundred thousand francs. That is the equivalent, in sterling, of fifty thousand pounds. It is the fee for the negotiator."

Peter's first thought, when Meyer stopped talking, was that he certainly understood the art of bargaining. The long, slow preamble. Then, suddenly and conclusively, the offer. £50,000 in his pocket. And what would follow from that? Certainly the goodwill of the Wellborn family. For he would have rescued the American sale. Opposition to his marriage by Lisa's mother would vanish. He would be a man of means, a suitable husband. He could see Lisa, radiant, in white advancing up the aisle. Stewart would be best man, of course. He had got as far as trying to select some bridesmaids when he realised that he had to say something.

Aware that he was being feeble, he said, "Of course, I shall have to discuss it with my friends."

"There is very little time for discussion. It is Wednesday today. The Iranians have stipulated that the exchange must take place before the weekend. That gives you two days at the outside."

Not 'would give you', Peter noticed, but 'gives you'. In Meyer's mind the matter was settled. In his mind, too.

"I am, of course, advancing you the necessary money to cover your expenses. I have here five hundred pounds and five thousand francs, in notes." It was in an envelope which Meyer pulled out of the drawer of his desk.

Peter thought, if I take the money, I'm committed.

"Come along," said Meyer impatiently. "Yes or no."

"Yes," said Peter.

"Then listen carefully. The two Iranians have been instructed by Zaman that as soon as the draft is in their hands they are to forward it to me. I have arranged with my own bank, the Banque de La Guyane in Paris, that they will exchange it, forthwith, for a bank draft on themselves, which I will collect from them."

"Less your commission," suggested Peter.

Meyer said, with the ghost of a smile, "Yes. That arrangement certainly has the advantage, for me, that I can be sure of my commission. But it also suits Zaman. As you know, a bank draft is not like a cheque. It cannot be stopped. But if some question did arise, the Crédit Agricole, the leading bank in France, might feel obliged to defer to the wishes of the French government and hold up encashment whilst enquiries were made. The South American owners of the Banque de La Guyane are, I can assure you, under no such constraint."

"In fact," said Peter, "you're washing the money for them."

"If you like to put it that way," said Meyer, who seemed unoffended at the suggestion. "Now for some final instructions. Mr. Wellborn has been told to prepare an Express Delivery envelope, appropriately stamped and addressed to me, care of the Banque de la Guyane. The Iranians have been instructed that as soon as they are satisfied that what they are getting is the agreed bank draft they are to post it off without any delay.

You will not, of course, part with the draft until the picture is in your possession."

"No, indeed," said Peter.

"Then that is all. I assume you will set out tonight or tomorrow morning."

"Tomorrow," said Peter firmly.

"One more word, then. I cannot, I suppose, prevent you from discussing this matter with my secretary and your friend Ives. Apart from them, in your own interest, you will observe complete silence. You understand what I am saying?"

Now who was it who had said that to him before? Commissaire Meurice. 'Amateurs play games for fun. Professionals play only to win. You understand what I am saying?' And he had said, 'I do understand.' Now, presumably, he had become a professional himself. He was certainly not playing for fun any longer. Meyer was still looking at him. A cold, remote look, such as an old-time judge might have given as he put on the black cap.

"Oh yes," said Peter, "I do understand."

7

The plane lifted off the Heathrow runway next morning at a few minutes after eight. It was only half full. As it crossed the south coast of England the seat-belt sign was switched off, but Peter had left his own belt buckled. He could feel that the plane was a little unsettled. No more unsettled than his thoughts.

The discussion on the previous evening had gone on into the early hours. Lisa and Stewart had started by condemning the plan. This was an instinctive reaction, but as they talked it over the points in favour began to outweigh the points against.

Peter had agreed that he was so scared of the two Iranians that any suggestion of double-crossing them was a non-starter. "But when you look at it," he said, "I'm not crossing them or double-crossing them. I'm simply helping them. They want this deal to go through. The picture's so well known that they can't have much hope of selling it openly. To get half a million pounds down, from Wellborn – "

"And no come-back," said Stewart. "That's the bull point. If the picture had been put on the market there'd have been an international rumpus. As it is, once the picture's back where it belongs, Wellborn won't complain. There's no reason for anyone else to know anything about it."

"There's a catch somewhere," said Lisa. "If it's as simple as you say why doesn't Meyer handle it himself?"

"That I can understand," said Stewart. "The last thing he wants to do is to be man in the middle in this transaction. If it goes wrong, he wants to be able to deny all knowledge of it."

"So Peter has to be man in the middle."

"For fifty thousand pounds."

That was the clincher, thought Peter. The consideration which outweighed all other considerations. Moreover, he would not have to trust Meyer to pay him. In the way things had been arranged the fifty thousand pounds would be in *his* hands. A bank draft, not a cheque. He would post it straight to his own bank. As he was thinking about this he was interrupted.

"This is the Captain speaking," said the metallic voice of God. "We have been informed that a storm centre of considerable violence has built up over Germany. It is moving south west, very slowly. The prediction is that it will be over the Massif Central in three or four hours' time and may marginally affect southern France by later this evening. We are making a small detour to keep well away from its influence and for this reason as you will see if you look out we shall be approaching Bordeaux from the west, not from the north. This will add fifteen minutes to our flight time."

The message was repeated in French. The tone was confident and comforting. But Peter shared the general relief when he was able to catch a glimpse of the steel grey waters of the Gironde, and the run-in to Merignac airport began.

"I am indeed glad that you were able to come," said Joseph Wellborn. A very different figure from the aloof, courteous gentleman who had greeted him on his previous visits. He looked like a man who had heard the first warnings of a mortal disease. His eyes were red-rimmed from lack of sleep and his hand trembled slightly as he lifted a cigarette to his lips – the last of many, judging by the state of the ashtray on his desk.

"Have there been any developments?"

"Yes. This was pushed through the door some time last night. It seems they were nervous of using the telephone."

"Possibly," said Peter. "Though I see no reason why they should be."

He was examining the document, which looked like a page torn from a child's exercise-book. On it was printed, in capital letters, 'This is your last chance. As soon as it is dark send your messenger to the old Campe Militaire de Laugnan. He will be allowed to examine the painting and will bring back with him instructions as to the time and place of exchange.'

Peter was thinking of what Meyer had said to him. The

need for expedition. He had repeated it twice. The Iranians were to forward the draft to the Banque de La Guyane 'as soon as it was in their hands'. They were to post it 'without delay'. Why was this so important? The matter had already dragged on for over a week. Why the desperate hurry? Was it just kidnappers' technique? Give your victim no time to think.

He said, "When does the last post leave Bordeaux? And when does it arrive in Paris?"

"I will find out for you." Mr. Wellborn seemed relieved at having something to do. After speaking on the telephone to someone who was evidently a senior official in the post office, he said, "The last post leaves Bordeaux at half past eleven, but to catch it letters have to be in town boxes by eleven and local boxes by half past ten. Such letters would be in Paris by five o'clock and would be distributed to addresses in the central arrondissements by nine."

"Then since it has been emphasised to these men that they must post off the money without delay, we may assume that the exchange will take place some time after I return from the Campe Militaire, but before ten thirty."

"No doubt," said Wellborn. "Do these details matter?"

"It is always useful to be able to forecast the moves of the opposition," said Peter. His reaction to Wellborn's nervousness was to assume a mantle of calm. He wished he felt as calm as he sounded. "You will notice, incidentally, that the time limits have been shortened. Previously, I understand, they stipulated 'before the weekend'. That would suggest Friday night. Now it has been moved back twenty-four hours. Tonight is to be your last chance. I wonder if something has happened to frighten them?"

"I have done nothing, I assure you. I have followed their instructions to the letter."

"I don't doubt it. But these people have the instincts of animals. They can detect a threat before it develops. It might account for their reluctance to use the telephone."

"Do you think so?" said Wellborn. Every new obstacle which stood between him and the most precious of his paintings, every delay in its return into his hands, deepened his nightmare of misery and helplessness.

"Of one thing I can assure you," he added bitterly, "they are in no danger from the police."

"You are certain of that? When I spoke to him I thought that Commissaire Meurice was determined to make a stand against these thugs."

"Indeed, so determined was he that his superiors must have become alarmed. He was posted to Corsica and departed last week."

This shook Peter more than he cared to admit. It had been at the back of his mind that if real trouble developed it would be possible to appeal to the police and that they would help. If they were now adopting a rigorously neutral attitude he would indeed be on his own.

A further point occurred to him. He said, "Then it wasn't the police who warned you about those two Iranians being in the neighbourhood?"

"Certainly not. Even if they had known of it, I doubt if they would have taken such helpful action. No, I learned of it through Hervé Gobard. He heard of it from his brother, Georges. He runs an unofficial ferry from Port de Goulée to Mortagne. This brings him into contact with the Brotherhood of the Gironde – so called. Salmon-poachers and smugglers. It was one of them, a neighbour of his, who happened to know Goraji and Rasim. No doubt they had had dealings with them before."

Peter had returned to a consideration of the note. "There are two difficulties here," he said. "The first is a practical one. How am I to find my way to the old Campe de Laugnan?" He was examining the huge expanse of green on the map. It started at the tip of the Médoc peninsula and ran south almost to Bayonne, the five thousand square miles of the Parc Régional des Landes; mostly uninhabited and in parts visited only by foresters. "It is an easy place to get lost in. You may remember that I did so last time I was here and on that occasion I was never more than half a mile from the main road. This camp is described as 'de Laugnan', but in fact, it seems to be totally isolated."

"As to that, you need not worry. I have a very reliable guide for you. Laure Gobard. She has agreed to accompany you."

"Young Laure. Do you really think she – ?"

"There are few people who know the Parc des Landes better." Mr. Wellborn was speaking, for the first time, with some animation. Possibly the result of ceasing to think of his own troubles. "When she was young – I mean eleven or twelve – she must, I fear, have been lonely. In those days we had two women who did all the housework. Having so much time on her hands she used to spend a lot of it in the woods. Her father didn't like it, but the foresters knew her and looked after her. And anyway, as they said, she was so quick on her feet and knew the terrain so well that someone who meant mischief would have had precious little chance of catching her. Mind you, they had to draw the line when she started staying out at night."

"At night?"

"All night, on some occasions. No one would have known about it if her Uncle Hervé hadn't caught her sneaking back in the early hours one morning. He told her father and they put a stop to that."

"She's a remarkable girl," said Peter. "And I'll be happy to have her as a guide. Now the second point and perhaps a rather more serious one. This theft was obviously well planned. What is to prevent the Iranians – who may have contacts in the Paris art world – from having prepared a duplicate? You often see students, in the Louvre, copying the pictures and really they seem to do it extremely well. I don't mean that a copy would get away with it for long. Any sort of expert could immediately tell it from the original. But suppose the only opportunity I have of inspecting it is a few minutes – by torch light perhaps – "

"There will be no necessity," said Mr. Wellborn, "for you to examine the picture at all."

"Then how – ?"

"All you need ascertain is that it is still fixed to its original stretcher. It is, in fact, most unlikely to have been taken off it. Any attempt to do so would result in seriously damaging the canvas. And you must remember that these men have only had the picture in their possession for a few days. That would give them neither the time nor the technical apparatus necessary to remove it neatly. If they made the attempt they would leave very obvious signs of their efforts."

"I've no doubt you're right. But if they'd got a substitute picture ready, why should they not have faked up a substitute stretcher?"

"They might, of course, have done so. It would not really be difficult to make a convincing stretcher out of suitable wood. Possibly removed from another old picture. But what they would not, and could not, have done is to reproduce in it certain features which I will explain to you."

He sounded much easier, thought Peter; now it was the professor instructing his students.

"When my father inherited these pictures from his father his attention was drawn to the fact that the canvas, in a number of cases, was not really taut on the stretcher. Close examination showed why. The pins which had been used originally were of soft metal and had rusted. In some cases they had broken right through. The solution was to withdraw them – a most delicate operation, as you may imagine – and refasten the canvas to the stretcher using new pins. These, as is common nowadays, were of copper. They were not, for obvious reasons, driven through the holes left by the original pins. They were inserted, in every case, one inch above or to the right of the old pins. All you will have to do, therefore, is to turn the picture over and examine the back of the stretcher. The old holes were filled in with some form of wood substitute, but they will be perfectly visible. If they are there, it is the genuine stretcher. If it is the genuine stretcher, it is the genuine picture."

"Then that seems to remove the last difficulty," said Peter. The last excuse, also, for not undertaking the enterprise.

Luncheon was served by Laure, who seemed unperturbed by the part she was going to be called on to play. It was a silent meal. When it was over Mr. Wellborn summoned Peter to his study and succeeded in surprising him. He unlocked his desk and produced a yellow-coloured slip of paper, printed in green, with the well-known logo of the Crédit Agricole at the top. It had been signed by two directors and was a draft on the bank for five hundred thousand francs. He pushed it across the desk to Peter.

"But," said Peter, "I can't accept this until I've done the job."

"You have done the greater part of it by coming here. I cannot tell you what a relief it has been to have someone to discuss this matter with. I felt so very lonely. Now your confidence has restored my own."

Peter folded the draft and slipped it into his wallet. It was difficult to say which was the heavier burden. The misplaced confidence which had been placed in him or the money which had been so trustfully paid to him.

He said, "The first thing I must do is to have a word with Laure. When I know how long it takes to reach the Campe de Laugnan I may be able to make some sort of plan."

He found her in the kitchen with her grandmother. Her father was sitting on a stool beside the range, crouched forward, with his head in his hands. When he saw Peter he straightened up and began to get to his feet.

Peter said, "Don't get up."

Gran'mère said, "It would do him good if he got up and went outside and made himself useful." And, before Laure could voice the protest she was going to make, "All right. All right. We are all sorry for him. But sympathy is a poor medicine."

By this time Michel-Ange was standing up. Ignoring Gran'mère and addressing himself to Peter, he said, "If it could be contrived, sir, that I meet these men once more – "

"If things turn out as we hope," said Peter. "The only person who will meet them will be myself."

Michel-Ange growled something under his breath and sank back onto his stool. He was a powerful man, barrel-chested and broad in the shoulders. In fair fight, Peter thought, he would be a formidable opponent.

He turned to Laure and said, "Can you show me, on this map, the way we shall be going this evening and explain how we propose to travel?"

"There are bicycles for both of us. We go through Queyrac and out onto the highroad."

"The D.1."

"Is that its name? We can continue down it towards Lesparre

186

and turn to the right before we get there. You can see there is quite a main road which goes to St. Isidore and out to the coast. About five kilometres along it we should be on the south side of the old camp. It was, you understand, a Campe Militaire, but that was many years ago, before the war. If we went that way we should only have a short distance to walk up the old track to the camp."

"But, for the most part, it would mean using main roads."

"That is so. We should certainly be seen."

"I'd like to avoid that if possible."

"In that case we will not use the main road at all. We will cross it at Queyrac and take this very small track – you see it? It is marked only with a dotted line." As she drew her finger along it Peter noticed that although it was the brown, rough hand of a boy, the fingernail had been delicately tinted in pink. "That takes us to Roquillac, which has been deserted for many years. After that we walk."

"How long if we go that way?"

"Half an hour. Perhaps a little more. We shall have to go slowly. It is much overgrown."

"If we leave here at seven it will be dark by the time we get there."

"Dark or nearly dark."

"So watch out for the wolves," said Gran'mère.

Laure ignored this. It seemed to be a family joke.

He decided to fill in some of the time which yawned between him and seven o'clock by going for a walk. He could make no detailed plans until the Iranians had declared their intentions, but it would do no harm to get some idea of the lie of the land. When he reached the gateway at the end of the drive he turned left and walked for some two kilometres until the road he was on crossed the main road. Here, as he had hoped, he found a post-box set in the wall. The evening collections were at four thirty and ten thirty. He had brought with him an envelope addressed to his own bank in London. The draft for five hundred thousand francs went into the envelope and the envelope, after a last-minute hesitation, into the box.

Now he really was committed.

He swung round and started back the way he had come,

passing the entrance to the château and heading for the river. Ahead of him the dusty poplar-lined road ran straight as an arrow for five kilometres, then swerved to the right. This was Port de Goulée. It turned out to be half a dozen cottages and a landing-stage with a hut at its inshore end. There were two boats moored there. Both had oars and a mast which was stepped and both he saw, when he looked more closely, had a stern fitting for an outboard motor, which had been removed and was, no doubt, locked in the hut.

There was no sign of life. A yellowing notice on the wall of the hut indicated that both boats were available for hire. One of them, he guessed, belonged to Georges Gobard. There was a tide table, which Peter studied. High tides that day, Thursday, were at 00.20 hours and 12.40 hours. Since it was then half past three they were approaching the mid-point when the tide would start to ebb. At that moment it was holding the current, but barely making against it. He confirmed his calculation by watching a clump of weeds which floated upstream, very slowly, past the end of the pier.

At his feet the broad silver-grey river was hardly ruffled by the wind. To his left he saw a single tramp steamer rounding the Pointe de Richard. It was making use of the last of the floodtide to reach Bordeaux. He wondered what cargo it was carrying. Perhaps it belonged to the Brotherhood of the Gironde which Wellborn had mentioned. The name suggested men, cloaked and masked, with rapiers at their hips. More probably a gang of bearded poachers with sawn-off shotguns.

He got up reluctantly and started on his return journey.

When he reached the château he went straight up to his room, kicked off his shoes, pulled the eiderdown over him and settled down to see if he could get a couple of hours' sleep. He thought it unlikely that the state of his mind, full of plans and possibilities, would allow this; but he had had very little sleep the night before, the room was warm and the bed was comfortable.

In five minutes he had slid into a state that was nearer sleep than waking. He was on the broad back of the Gironde, drifting slowly down stream and out to sea.

He was asleep.

8

Stewart had spent the morning in the office, in a bad temper, partly caused by boredom, partly, as he was honest enough to admit, by the fact that the interesting and heroic part in the affair was being played by Peter and not by himself.

He addressed himself resolutely to the letters, some from his own in-tray and a much larger number from Peter's. New clients were refused. Existing clients were turned off as tactfully as possible. His mind was now made up. Starfax had run its course. A satisfactory course, as the latest communication from his bank manager demonstrated.

He was trying to make up his mind where to go for his solitary lunch when the telephone rang.

It was Colin Chaytor and he was so disturbed that Stewart was unable to make out what he was talking about. Finally he managed to ask, "Are you phoning from the office? Or from a call-box, or what?"

Having to deal with a direct question produced a break in the flow of his words. He said, "Oh, no, I'm not at the office. I'm at home. The most terrible development – "

"Look here," said Stewart, overriding him ruthlessly, "unless you talk a bit more slowly and a lot more clearly I shan't have a chance of understanding what you're saying. To start with, why aren't you at the office?"

"I couldn't stay there. Not in the light of the developments – "

"All right. I understand that. There have been developments."

"Terrible developments."

"Then wouldn't it be more sensible if I drove over and heard about them? At this time of day I could do it in half an hour."

"Yes. Yes. Come as quickly as you can. The most alarming – "

But Stewart had rung off. He was not displeased at the idea of getting out of the office. In view of the upset which seemed to have occurred in the Chaytor household he thought it a wise precaution to bring his own lunch with him, and he stopped at the delicatessen on the corner to buy a packet of sandwiches.

When Chaytor opened the door to him he saw that something had, indeed, occurred to upset him. Never a very robust character he was now almost liquid with distress. Happily, as he saw through the open door of the sitting-room, Gertrude Chaytor was there. He would be able to get the facts from her.

As he made his way along the hall he nearly tripped over a bag which was standing there. There were other bags with it.

"Hullo," he said. "Are you both off somewhere?"

"Certainly. That's the whole thing – "

"Let's sit down before we talk. And I hope you'll excuse me if I start eating my sandwiches. Since I gathered that what you had to tell me was urgent I didn't stop off for lunch, but came straightaway."

"It was very good of you," said Mrs. Chaytor. "I told Colin he had no right to drag you down here. I'll get you a cup of coffee. In fact, I'll get coffee for all of us."

"An excellent idea. Now – "

Chaytor was clearly going to burst if he was not allowed to tell his story.

"It all started," he said, "a fortnight ago, when Mr. Meyer asked me to visit the Whitechapel Picture Gallery and make a careful note of their latest acquisitions. He gave me the afternoon off and said I wasn't to bother to come back to the office. I did what he wanted, though I couldn't see the sense of it. We'd never sold any pictures to the gallery and were most unlikely to do so. It was when I got to the office next morning that I realised that the carpets had been taken up and not put back straight."

Stewart stared at him. He said, "That seems an odd thing to get upset about."

"Let him tell it his own way," said Mrs. Chaytor from the kitchen. "It'll be quicker in the long run."

"It was only later that I found out what it meant. There was also the fact that Mr. Meyer insisted on my getting home in good time in the evenings. He said he'd had complaints from my wife about being left at home all day."

"Which wasn't true," from the kitchen.

"The next thing that happened was three days ago."

'Getting down to modern times,' thought Stewart.

"I had to go into Mr. Meyer's private office to locate a catalogue. I thought I should have to ask him for the key, but to my surprise the door was open and when I got in I saw there was hardly a paper there. I mean that, literally. On the desk or in the desk. Most of the drawers were half open as if Meyer had emptied them in a hurry and hadn't bothered to shut them. And you remember the press – "

"The one with paintings in it."

"Yes. But there weren't any."

"You mean they were all gone," said Stewart, really interested for the first time.

"Every one of them. Paintings and drawings. Then I remembered that Mr. Crankling had been to see him. You remember him?"

"The auctioneer. Yes. Go on."

"An evening or two ago I happened to run into him. He was arriving as I was leaving. He seemed a bit embarrassed, but at the time I thought no more about it. I now believe he had come to buy all those pictures and take them away with him. It was when I got to the office this morning that I realised what had been going on. You remember that there's a door at the foot of the stairs. It cuts off the rest of the house from the ground floor. For the first time since I had been there it was shut. And locked. I stood there staring at it and as I did so it came over me that I was alone in the house."

He stopped talking. He had told his story so graphically that Stewart could see him, standing alone in that splendid mansion surrounded by silence and doubt and, illogically but certainly, by fear.

He said, "Go on. What did you do?"

"I had to know the truth. I remembered Stanley Prior. He's one of the partners in Samuelsons, who deal with most of Mr.

191

Meyer's property matters. He's a friend of mine, from college days, so I was able to ring him up and talk to him.

"I said, 'I heard from someone that this house was on the market. He was very interested and wanted to know the asking price.' Prior had sounded surprised. He said, 'I imagined you'd know. Your friend's too late. The house has been sold.' I was astounded. I said, 'You mean that contracts have actually been exchanged?' 'Contracts were exchanged weeks ago. The sale has been completed and the money paid. Into the Banque de La Guyane in Paris, I understand. Do you mean to say you knew nothing about it?' I said, 'There was no reason for Mr. Meyer to take me into his confidence – ' 'But surely you'd know. The purchasers would have put a surveyor in. And there were people to show round. It was a turn-key operation. The woman who bought the house took all the furniture and fittings with it. Incidentally, that was history repeating itself. Did you know that when Clarence Hatry bought it from Sir Joseph Duveen, the art collector, he bought it lock, stock and barrel – '

"I didn't know and I didn't much care. I wasn't interested in history. It was what was happening now. I saw, of course, that I'd been kept out of the way so that the purchaser could look over it and her surveyor make a proper examination. What I couldn't understand was why. Why all the secrecy?"

"Why indeed," said Stewart thoughtfully. "After all, he'd trusted you in the past with more important secrets."

"Quite so. And it was whilst I was worrying about it that the morning post arrived. Of course, in the ordinary way I wouldn't have opened a letter marked 'personal and confidential' and addressed to Mr. Meyer – "

"Of course you wouldn't," said his wife, coming into the room with the coffee. "And of course, in the circumstances, that's exactly what you did. And quite right too."

"It was a letter from those travel agents he uses, Mauger & Finch. It was from their Paris office."

"Don't talk about it," said his wife. "Show it to him."

It was a folded flimsy, acknowledging the receipt of money and confirming a single reservation on the Chilean National

Air Service which left Charles de Gaulle Airport at 12.00 hrs. for Buenos Aires and Santiago.

Stewart looked at the date. He said, "That's for tomorrow. What on earth – ?"

He held the paper in his hand, waving it gently, as though he could shake further information out of it. As he looked at the two frightened faces some of the implications of what he had been told began to come home to him.

"It's a one-way ticket," he said thoughtfully.

Chaytor nodded. He seemed to be past speech. Mrs. Chaytor said, "It's clear enough, isn't it? He's getting out. There's some job or other he's been involved in lately. We know that. It's important. And there's a lot of money in it. It was something he was doing for Zaman. Perhaps you know about it?"

"Yes," said Stewart. "I know all about it. I was told in confidence, but this is no time for worrying about things like that. Very well then – "

When he had finished, the Chaytors looked at each other, appalled. Mr. Chaytor croaked, "Five million francs." And again, "Five million francs." He could hardly get the words out.

Mrs. Chaytor said, "It's what we expected, but much worse."

"Tell me," said Stewart. "When Meyer worked for Zaman before, I imagine that he took a commission on whatever money he realised. How much was it?"

Chaytor said, "It depended on the amount of work he had to do. Sometimes as little as fifteen per cent. Sometimes twenty or twenty-five per cent."

"And in this case," said Stewart brutally, "your idea is that his commission is going to be a hundred per cent. In other words he's going to pocket the lot. And take it off with him to South America."

It was clear that this was exactly what they did think.

In the long silence which ensued their minds moved on different tacks. Stewart was trying to remember the details of what Peter had told them last night. The Chaytors were thinking about Jemal, held upside down in the sewage until he choked to death.

Finally Stewart said, "I should think it was that session he had with the policeman that finished him. And I'll tell you something else. When Peter explained to us the arrangements Meyer had made – how the Crédit Agricole draft was to go into his account at the Banque de La Guyane and come out as a fresh draft on that bank – well it seemed plausible. But when I thought it over, I did start to wonder. The whole point about a bank draft is that it's a promise to pay, on demand, made by the bank and signed by its directors. Could any bank – however much pressed by the government – hold up payment on one of its own drafts? The more important the bank – and the Crédit Agricole is one of the largest in Europe – the less likely did this seem. And all that business about arranging it in that way to secure his own commission. Why shouldn't Meyer have asked Mr. Wellborn for two drafts? One for Zaman and one for himself. Then Zaman's draft could have been sent direct to him."

"It's absolutely obvious," said Mrs. Chaytor. "Meyer is concentrating all his money at this Paris bank – what was it?"

"The Banque de La Guyane."

"That's where the proceeds of the house sale have gone and his other money, too, probably. He has it turned into one bank draft, puts it in his pocket tomorrow morning and good-bye to him."

Chaytor moaned, "Naturally they'll think we were all in it. Five million francs slipping through their fingers. I don't like to think what they'll do."

"I suppose you could explain you knew nothing about it."

"Explain? They won't want explanations. They'll want their money."

Mrs. Chaytor said, "You see how it is, Mr. Ives. They know we've been involved with Meyer in all his other transactions. Why should they suppose we didn't know about this one?"

"But they must realise that Meyer is the one who planned it. And he's the only one who's gaining by it."

"How do they know that? We may have been well paid for our part in it."

It was at that point that the really unpleasant aspect of the

194

matter first struck Stewart. Was not Peter being very well paid for the part he was playing?

"Meyer is the only one of us who'll be safe," went on Chaytor bitterly. "Dear me, yes. He's looking after his own skin. Once he's in South America, he can buy all the protection he wants. They won't be able to touch *him*."

Stewart wasn't really listening. He was thinking about Peter.

"One thing I'm determined on," said Chaytor. "We're not spending another night in this house."

Reluctantly Stewart wrenched his mind back to their problems. "What are you going to do then?"

"My sister will put us up for a few days," said Mrs. Chaytor. Being less panic-stricken than her husband she had been able to divine what was worrying Stewart. She said, "I think Peter is in more immediate danger than any of us, don't you?"

"We'll have to warn him," said Stewart. "That's the first thing. He gave me the telephone number of the château. I'll get straight on to him."

But when he had finished dialling a recorded voice said, 'There is a delay of up to one hour on all calls to France and Germany. The number you dialled has been noted. We will contact you at the number you are speaking from as soon as your call becomes available'.

"Damn," said Stewart. There was a lot to think about. "The first thing I'd like to do is to get hold of Lisa. I assume she isn't at the office."

"Meyer gave her the week off. She said something about going up to see her mother."

Mrs. Shilling's number was located in the directory and it was Lisa who answered. Stewart said, "If you've got that little car of yours handy, could you come straight down here?"

"My car's in dock. But if it's important I could borrow mummy's car."

"It's extremely important," said Stewart and gave her directions. Then he started dialling again. He said, "I've had an idea which might work well for you. I don't suppose you really want to put up with your sister, do you? Not indefinitely, anyway."

"As short a time as possible," said Mrs. Chaytor. "We've never got on well together. It was a case of any port in a storm."

"Hullo. Yes. I wonder if you could possibly put me through to the headmaster. The name is Ives. Stewart Ives. Yes, I'll hang on." And to the Chaytors – "I happened to notice in the Chelborough magazine that the art master had died suddenly. He was a bachelor. He lived by himself in a little cottage – I imagine he rented it from the school. It must be empty now. If I could get you the loan of it – "

"That would indeed be splendid. Chelborough, you say. That's some way from London."

"About eighty miles – Oh, headmaster. I must apologise for interrupting you – "

"I've always expected that I'd hear from you again," said the headmaster drily. "What are you up to now?"

"I'm ringing on behalf of an artist friend of mine, Colin Chaytor. He's been turned out of his own house, at a moment's notice and I happened to read in the school magazine about Mr. Pleydell – "

"Yes. Totally unexpected. You were thinking of his cottage, perhaps."

"For a short time. If no one else wanted it."

"I'll have a word with the bursar. I think he might be glad to let your friend have it. I do know that he wasn't happy about leaving it empty. Give me your number and I'll ring you back as soon as I've spoken to him."

The idea, when Stewart had explained it to them, greatly attracted the Chaytors. Their priority was to get out of that lonely and dangerous corner as far as they could and as quickly as they could.

Soon after this Lisa arrived, having made good time from St. John's Wood. Mr. Chaytor seemed anxious to tell her his story all over again, but Stewart cut him short. He said, "If this idea I've had works, you realise you'll have to look after yourselves when you get there. There'll probably be kitchen equipment and things like that, but there won't be any fresh food. You'll have to take supplies with you. Better start packing something up now."

Mrs. Chaytor said, "That's right," and departed to the kitchen. Having a shrewd idea of what Stewart wanted she dragged her husband with her.

As soon as they were alone, Stewart told Lisa what he had heard. She listened in silence and without moving. At the end of it, she said, "If you do manage to get through by telephone, you can only tell him what you think. Not what you know."

"We can put him on his guard."

"And once he's on his guard, what's he going to do?"

Before Stewart could deal with this difficult question the telephone rang. He snatched it up. It was the bursar, a Major Caldecott, late of the Royal Marines. He said, "The headmaster tells me you've got a temporary occupant for Pleydell's cottage. Quite a sound idea. An artist, I gather. Is he married?"

"Yes. His wife will be coming with him."

"Good. She'll be able to do the cooking. The kitchen stuff is all there. When do we expect them?"

"They're anxious to get away today and they're all packed up. I seem to remember there's a five o'clock train from Paddington. A fast train."

"Gets in here at six-forty. I'll have it met."

Stewart thanked him warmly, rang off, said, "God bless the Marines," and went into the kitchen to hurry up the Chaytors.

"You'll have to wait by the telephone," said Lisa. "So I'll take them in my car. Thank goodness it's Paddington, not some station on the other side of London. I should be able to do it in half an hour."

Ten minutes later Stewart was alone in the house. Everything seemed to have happened with such speed and urgency that he found himself out of breath, as though he had been running. He sat back in his chair and started to relax. The noise of the jets, landing and taking off a mile to the north, seemed curiously muted. It emphasised the heavy silence inside the house. The Chaytors' resolve not to spend another night there seemed less fanciful now.

He was disturbed twice. Once a screaming and snarling turned out to come from the cats who used the gardens of the deserted cottages as a boxing ring. Then he thought he

197

heard someone walking up the front path and knocking very quietly on the door. When he opened the door there was no one there.

He turned on the wireless for the five o'clock news. He was in time to hear the newsreader say, in the tones of satisfaction which the B.B.C. reserves for natural catastrophes in other countries:

'The storm which was reported this morning over Northern Switzerland and West Germany has moved south west to France, increasing in force. At 16.00 hours it was over the Massif Central leaving a trail of disaster behind it. Continuous monsoon-type rain and winds of unprecedented force have already caused extensive flooding in the valleys of the Rhône and the Allier. As well as thousands of trees, telegraph poles and pylons have been uprooted. Communication between Paris and the South of France has been badly interrupted. It is anticipated that the storm centre will be over the mediterranean coast of France and Spain by this evening. Its peripheral effects are likely to be widely felt.'

Stewart took down a school atlas from the shelf and thought about this. It looked as though the storm would not hit Bordeaux directly, but if the lines of communication ran down the Allier valley and west of the Massif Central communications might be difficult.

Suppose they could not talk to Peter. And even if they could talk to him, how was he to answer Lisa's simple question, 'Once he is on his guard, what's he going to do?'

Whilst he thought about it, Stewart was elaborating the contingency plan which he had already formed and for which he had made some preparations. Its attraction was that it was dashing and possibly decisive. He turned to the collection of air timetables on the shelf and was studying them when Lisa reappeared.

She said, "I missed the rush-hour traffic going up, but, by God, I caught it coming back. People seem to stop work at half past four these days. Idle slobs. I thought I should never get off the M4. What are you doing with those time-tables?"

"I'm working on an idea which involves going to Paris. If

we can get through to Peter and tell him what we suspect he may be able to modify his own plans – "

"How?"

"I don't know," said Stewart crossly. "But if he hasn't got this vital piece of information he'll be working blind."

"All right. Sorry I spoke."

"If we can't get through to him, some more drastic action is called for – "

The idea seemed to please him, thought Lisa. Drastic action. Direct intervention. The master mind at work. Clear up the position here. Rehouse the Chaytors. Dash across to Paris.

"I have already made certain preparations. I got Agazadeh Zaman's new address from Mrs. Chaytor, a closely guarded secret, I imagine. Then I borrowed from her husband the letter from the travel agents which he annexed." He produced the flimsy and handed it to Lisa. "I've been studying the departure times from Heathrow and Gatwick. Although Gatwick's further from here, the new terminal seems very efficient. A shuttle to Paris every hour, on the hour, until midnight. I'm going for the eight o'clock plane. Gets to Paris at ten o'clock French time. That means I can stop here until half past six in case Peter gets through. If you can hang on for a bit after I go – until nine o'clock if you can bear the thought – "

"Not a moment later," said Lisa with a shudder. "This place gives me the creeps."

At that moment the telephone shrilled. It made them both jump. Stewart grabbed the receiver. The voice which had spoken before said, "Your Bordeaux number is now ringing. Owing to pressure on this line your call will be limited to five minutes. It is ringing for you now."

Someone at the other end – it was a girl's voice – said in French, "Who is that, if you please."

"*Je veux parler à Pierre*," said Stewart.

The voice switched immediately to English. "You wish for Peter? He is in his room. I will fetch him."

"Please be quick. We haven't much time."

There was no answer. The girl must already have scurried off. Stewart glanced anxiously at his watch. Two minutes gone. Three. There was a curious drumming noise in the

199

background, interspersed with crackling. Then Peter's voice, only just audible. He said, "Yes. Who is it?"

"Stewart here. Calls are being rationed. No time to waste. We think that Meyer is aiming to double-cross the Iranians. He's sold up his house, all the furniture and pictures and has bought a one-way ticket to Buenos Aires and Santiago, leaving Paris at noon tomorrow. Taking the loot with him, no doubt."

"I missed that last bit. Taking what with him?"

"The loot. His own money and the ransom money. It will all be in the same bank. He can pick up one draft for the lot. Did you get that?"

The crackling on the line was so bad that Stewart found himself shouting. The official voice said, "Your time is up. We will reconnect you as soon as circumstances permit."

A click and the purring of the telephone.

"Well," said Stewart. "That's that. I hope he understood. But we can't take any chances. I'm for Paris."

"What are you going to do when you get there?"

"I've got a valuable piece of information to sell. Zaman must have some method of contacting those thugs. If he will guarantee Peter's safety, he shall have the information. It's as simple as that."

It didn't seem to Lisa to be simple at all. It was wildly impracticable and unlikely to succeed, but she realised that it was useless to say so. She said, "All right I'll stop here in case they reconnect us, so that I can tell Peter what you're up to. But I'm not staying long."

When the sound of Stewart's car had died away she sat staring at the darkening window. She was uncertain whether she wanted to laugh at Stewart's heroics or cry for Peter's peril. In the end she compromised by going out into the kitchen and putting on the kettle.

9

The great forest of the Landes had come down in the world. A mixture of hornbeam, beech, oak and Scots pine, it had been cultivated for centuries with care and forethought; the trunks of the trees for the builder and the carpenter, the lops and tops to keep the home fires burning in a country which had little coal.

The development of synthetic materials and alternative forms of heating had seen the gradual abandonment of this careful husbandry. The neglected trees had crowded together, shooting ever higher in competition for the sun, whilst round their feet the invaders had crept in; yew, alder and holly, brambles and bindweed, the heralds of carelessness and neglect.

It was into such a forest that Peter followed Laure as dusk deepened towards night. After crossing the main road they had left their bicycles with one of Laure's forester friends and gone forward on foot.

At first they were on something which might once have been a road and which developed, after about a mile, into a main street, with cottages on either side; but they were derelict and roofless and clearly long deserted.

"Roquillac," said Laure. "My grandmother was born here."

From this point they left the road and plunged forward among the trees. Laure, who seemed to be able to pick some sort of path through the undergrowth, hardly slackened her pace. When Peter had twice tripped over snaring roots and fallen onto his knees he uttered a protest. "I don't know how you can see where you're going. How do you avoid these bloody roots and brambles?"

"I keep my eyes open."

"Then they're a damned sight better eyes than mine. Can't we slow it down a bit?"

"I thought I was going slowly."

"Then go slower still then."

He found he was arguing with her exactly as though she had been a boy of his own age. This seemed normal at the time. It was only when he thought about it afterwards that it appeared odd.

From that point onwards, either because they did go at a more reasonable pace, or because his eyes were becoming used to the dark, he stumbled but never actually fell. After twenty minutes of cautious progress they came out of the trees into another clearing which had once contained a village. This was even more derelict than Roquillac. What had once been cottages were now lumps of brick overgrown with ivy and thorn. A single chimney-stack pointed defiantly at the sky.

"Laugnan," said Laure. "The camp is named from it. You will be able to see it in a moment."

What Peter saw next was an impenetrable screen of bushes and undergrowth woven into a rusty barbed-wire fence.

"How do we get through that?" he said.

"We don't," said Laure. "There is a gate where the road enters."

"Why on earth did they bother to put up a barricade like that if the camp is deserted?"

"When the military left – it was just after the war, a time of great shortages, you understand – the local people went in and started to pull down the huts. The wood was valuable. That had to be stopped."

"Best way of disposing of the camp, I'd have thought."

"They might have wanted to use it again, might they not?"

"Simple French obstructionism, if you ask me."

"I suppose the English would have said, 'Come and help yourselves'."

"Probably."

During these exchanges they were cautiously circling the camp site. On the eastern side the remains of an approach road, deeply rutted, ran up to a double gate, topped with a roll of barbed-wire. Peter, stooping to examine it, found that, although the chain which passed through the uprights of the gate was as rusty as everything else, the padlock which held the ends of the chain together was new.

He said, "What they did, no doubt, was to saw off the old padlock and put in a new one of their own."

Laure was not listening. She was some yards away, on her hands and knees.

"It's somewhere here," she said. "I found it last summer when I was exploring."

"Found what?"

"A way in, of course. Unless you would care to try climbing the gate."

Peter looked at the roll of rusty barbed-wire on top and said, "Thank you, no."

"Come along then." She had crawled along another ten yards and was now pulling out small shoots and weeds. Peter, crouching beside her, saw what looked like the entrance to a fox's earth.

"Fox or badger," said Laure, "looking for scraps, no doubt. The bottom strand of wire is loose – I propped it up with a stick. It's still there."

The next moment all he could see was her bottom as she wriggled under the wire. He followed and found progress messy, but surprisingly easy. Emerging, they pushed on, heading back towards the track which ran down the centre of the camp.

Something loomed in front of them. A Peugeot van, of the sort used by travellers for their samples, was parked among the bushes beside the track. By the light of the moon, which had now cleared the tree tops, he could see the Bordeaux number plate and could read the legend, painted on the side, 'Gentilhomme et Cie, Lesparre'.

"Garments for women," said Laure. She was whispering now. "They must have stolen it when they arrived."

Peter was trying to work out why the men should have risked stealing a van when they could easily have brought their own car, but Laure was already padding ahead down the track.

It was evident that the pillagers had, sensibly, started

dismantling the huts at the point nearest to the gate. Of the six huts fronting the central track the first two on each side had been completely demolished, the next three partly. The only complete huts left standing were the end ones in each line. They approached with care. If the two men were there, it was likely that they were housed in one or other of them.

There was no light visible in either.

"Let's try the one on the right first," whispered Peter. He noticed that Laure, who had been in the lead throughout, had now fallen back into the shadows. He tried the hut door. It was unlocked, but sagging on its hinges. When he pushed it open it screamed a protest.

He peered in. At the far end of the hut a line of light showed through the door of an inner room. As he stepped forward something whipped round his throat.

He was unable to utter a sound and could only put up a feeble resistance against the throttling arm. There was a red mist behind his eyes and a drumming of blood in his ears. As consciousness slipped away he realised that the inner door had been opened, letting in a flood of light and that a man was speaking. It was a voice he had heard before, in the church of St. Brieuc des Caves. Now it said, in tones of amusement, "Don't kill the boy, Mahmoud. Remember, he is our meal ticket."

The pressure on his throat relaxed. He drew in grateful lungfuls of air. A hand on his arm steered him forward, through the door and into the inner room. It was bare of furniture except for two rusty and decrepit iron beds which looked as though they had been left behind when the camp was abandoned. On them, sacks full of straw served as mattresses. There was a pressure lamp and some enamel plates and mugs, on a packing case which served as a table. The three outside walls had been draped with what looked like sections cut from an army tent. This was, presumably, to keep out the draughts which would otherwise have whistled through the rotten planking of the walls.

It looked primitive, but habitable.

"You are admiring our little nest," said Rasim. "As you

see, we are soldiers. We have the art of making ourselves comfortable."

"But we do not plan to stay here long," said Goraji. "No longer than we have to. And you are going to help us. Yes?"

"Yes," croaked Peter.

"The boy has a *rhume*," said Rasim. "Doubtless the night air is bad for his constitution."

"He is somewhat pale," agreed Goraji. "We must not keep him any longer than is necessary from the comforts of the château. To work, then."

He unfolded on top of the packing case a plan of the sort which was handed out to tourists by the Syndicat d'Initiative. It showed all the named vineyards of the Médoc, with the major and minor access roads boldly plotted.

"It is the road D103 to which you will pay attention. As you will see, it runs on the west side of the Lambrécie château and alongside its vineyards. It crosses the D102 at that point."

"I know it," said Peter. His voice was coming back.

"He knows it, good. As you proceed south from that point, you reach the village of Courbian and a bridge across the canal. Right? Three hundred metres further on, as you will observe, the road skirts the south-west corner of the château vineyard. That is the place appointed for our meeting. We shall be there at ten o'clock. Do I make myself clear?"

"Quite clear."

"We shall there exchange Monsieur Wellborn's beautiful picture for a banker's draft – "

"Equally beautiful," said Rasim.

" – for five million francs. And let me warn you of one thing. Should you be so stupid as to arrange for an intervention by, perhaps, the police, it would still be quite easy – " he produced a cigarette lighter from his pocket and clicked it on " – to destroy the picture before any such interruption could become effective."

"I don't think you need worry about the police," said Peter.

"The boy is a thinker," said Rasim. "He has been educated. He uses his brains."

"One thing more. In addition to the draft it has been agreed that you will hand over an envelope, addressed to the Banque

205

de La Guyane in Paris, eighty-three Rue Etienne-Marcel. The envelope will be marked for express delivery and appropriately stamped. You understand?"

"Yes."

"This is important. Because the letter must be in the post before half past ten. There must be no slip-up on that point."

"I can assure you," said Peter, "that Monsieur Wellborn will follow your instructions implicitly, as he has done throughout."

"Monsieur Wellborn is a man of sense," agreed Goraji. There was an unconcealed sneer in his voice. "I do not imagine that he would wish to be present at the exchange."

"I'm quite sure that he wouldn't."

"In that case, you will bring the *gosse* with you."

"The *gosse*?"

"The Gobard child. Her presence there will ensure that no one starts a shooting match, yes?"

"I will see if I can persuade her to come."

"You will not see *if* you can. You will ensure that she *does* come. If we do not see her beside the road when we arrive, we drive straight through and the deal is off. Understood?"

"Very well," said Peter. "There is just one thing more. I should like to examine the picture."

"You think we may have substituted a copy?"

"The boy has brains," said Rasim. "I have already commented on it. He is a pretty boy, too. No doubt a great favourite with the girls."

Goraji ignored this. He went over to the corner of the hut and drew out, from under a pile of blankets, something wrapped in brown paper. He undid the wrapping and brought across to Peter the picture which he had last seen in the uncle's drawing-room. It was no substitute. It was the Titian masterpiece, one of the greatest pictures that master had painted. The virgin mother had a look on her face in which adoration was mingled with an unmistakable touch of surprise.

Rasim said, "You would think she is displeased with us for handling her so roughly."

Peter had turned the painting over and was examining the back of the wooden stretcher. Sure enough, by each of the new

206

copper nails was the filled-in hole where the old iron nails had been driven through and removed.

"You see something there?" said Rasim.

"Only what I have been told to look for."

"What a boon is education."

"All right," said Goraji sharply, "then if you are satisfied, we will get on with it." He led the way out of the hut. The moon was playing hide-and-seek among the black clouds and there was a tingling feeling in the air.

"Rain coming," said Rasim. "A storm perhaps."

"So waste no time," said Goraji. He unlocked the padlock and forced the gate open far enough for Peter to squeeze through. Before he could do so Goraji stopped him. "I meant to enquire," he said. "How did you get in?"

Peter had seen this coming. He said, "There are plenty of places where the wire can be climbed."

"An athlete," said Rasim, "as well as a thinker." He stroked Peter's arm, as though he were feeling his biceps. Peter jerked himself free, squeezed through the gap in the gates and started to walk quickly down the path towards the main road. He was conscious that the two men were standing there watching him. He heard one of them say something. The other man laughed. As soon as he was out of sight of the camp, Laure materialised beside him. She gestured him to follow her. Abandoning the track, she made a beeline through the trees, without hesitating and without speaking, until they were back in the ghost village of Laugnan. Here she opened her mouth for the first time.

She said, "These men are savages, yes?"

"Yes," said Peter. The muscles of his throat still felt sore. "Do I understand that you were listening?"

"Of course. I was behind that piece of canvas which they have hung up."

"You mean you were actually inside the hut?"

"Certainly. There are holes in the wall a horse could get through. Some of the things which were said I did not understand. Why do they want this envelope?"

"Once they have the money -- the bank draft -- their instructions are to post it straight to a bank in Paris. It must be there by tomorrow morning."

207

"And you are worried about that. Why?"

Peter thought before speaking. Then, having come to the conclusion that his ally was both reliable and intelligent, he told her the whole story. They were through Roquillac and heading for the main road before he had finished. Laure was silent for some minutes. Then she said, "If this person Meyer goes to South America and takes all the money with him, what will these men do?"

"I don't care to think about it. You said yourself they are savages. I think they would kill everyone in Lambrécie and burn it to the ground."

"Then why do you not tell them what you have just told me? Then, if they believe you, they will not send the money to Meyer."

"*If* they believe me," said Peter. "That's the trouble. Remember, they have most definite instructions from their own boss, Agazadeh Zaman. And I judge from what Commissaire Meurice told me that he is a very formidable man. Probably the only man in France these two apes are frightened of. They will certainly *not* disobey his orders merely because I tell them some wild story."

"Could they not speak to him? Get new orders."

"How? All communications between Bordeaux and Paris are suspended. Tomorrow, they say, they will be restored. Tomorrow will be too late."

"Yes. It is difficult," said Laure. She made no further comment until they had recovered their bicycles. As they were preparing to mount she said, "Is there any reason we should not take my father and my uncle into our confidence? They are both men of courage."

"Yes. But we will not, I think, say anything to Mr. Wellborn."

For the first time that evening Laure laughed aloud. She said, "Certainly we must not tell the patron. Poor man, he is like an ostrich, looking for somewhere to hide his head."

On this more cheerful note they pedalled back to the château. They found Michel-Ange and Hervé in the kitchen. Gran'mère, who had made all ready for the service of dinner, had retired to her room. Both men were anxious for news and

208

in ten minutes Laure had not only told them what happened, but had given them a concise and accurate summary of the difficult position they were now in.

Hervé said, "The *patron* has been speaking to his friend in the Post Office. It seems there is no possibility of telephoning Paris before tomorrow morning at the earliest."

Michel-Ange said, "I see no problem. Now we know where these men are we can go straight to their hide-out and kill them."

Laure said, "The objection to that is that they are expert assassins. They would almost certainly kill you before you could kill them."

Michel-Ange growled, but offered no comment. He was confident that, in fair fight, he could deal with one or both of the Iranians. The last occasion had not been fair. The dice had been loaded against him. Next time it would be different. If his daughter, whose brain he respected, could devise a method of making fools of them, so much the better. But it was not the final response to the affront that had been put on him.

Peter said, "It seems to me that what we have to do is to buy time. If we were to tell these men what we suspect and if they could communicate with Zaman – which they can't – he would no doubt alter their instructions. But by the time he could do so the money will be out of the country."

Laure said, "Certainly it is difficult."

"It is very difficult. I can see no clear way out of it."

"Have not you yourself propounded the solution?"

The three men stared at her. Peter suspiciously, her uncle and her father hopefully.

"You said that we need to gain time. In short, that the money has to be put in safe custody where neither Meyer nor these other men can get at it. Only, perhaps, until tomorrow, by which time the situation will be clearer."

"Stating the problem does not solve it."

"Very well then. I have a plan. Your mother was, I believe, French. She is dead, but you will have relatives living. In Paris perhaps?"

"My mother's elder sister, Christine de Clissac, lives in Paris, yes. She is old and extremely obstinate."

"Tant mieux. Exactly what we require. This envelope which has been prepared for the money to be despatched to Mr. Meyer's bank – you have it with you?"

"It is in Mr. Wellborn's desk. I could get it – only – it might lead him to enquire what we were going to do. Would that be wise?"

Hervé said, "I do not know what plan you have in mind, little one. But I can assure you of this. If the *patron* thought that you were proposing in any way to cross these men he would forbid it absolutely."

"When I saw him last," growled Michel-Ange, "he was in the dining-room restoring his self-possession with the aid of a bottle of cognac."

"Then I will go myself," said Laure. "If he is in his study I can always tell him that Gran'mère wishes to speak to him."

"But surely," said Peter, "If she did, he would come to her."

Both men laughed tolerantly. They explained that people who wished to discuss matters with Gran'mère came down to the kitchen. She was, in effect, the uncrowned ruler of the château. When Laure came back she was grinning. She said, "No trouble with the *patron*. He is asleep in the dining-room. And snoring."

She laid out on the kitchen table the unsealed envelope, addressed in clear block capitals to Mr. Henri Meyer, care of the Banque de La Guyane, Rue Etienne-Marcel, Paris and adorned with an express service sticker and two ten franc postage stamps, one of them put on slightly askew. She had with her two envelopes of the same type, a number of stamps and two or three stickers.

She said, "I have also borrowed the pen from the desk which the patron always uses. It will now be possible for you – yes? – to produce an exactly similar envelope."

"As the address is in capital letters that should not be difficult," said Peter, "but I still don't see – "

"I will explain. But do it, please. We shall need also another envelope addressed to your aunt in Paris and a letter of explanation to go in it. I will tell you about that later."

Peter obediently took up the pen and produced, without

much difficulty, an exact replica of the envelope for the Banque de La Guyane. An express sticker was affixed to it; also two ten franc stamps, one of them slightly askew. Whilst he was doing this Peter was thinking, I'm back at Chelborough. Now it's Laure, not Stewart, who is involving me in some hare-brained scheme. Only this time the stakes are higher. Much higher. Very well, he was prepared to learn what was in the tortuous mind of this wild sixteen-year-old. But, he assured himself, he would reserve the full right of veto. At no point would his hand be far from the brake.

"All right," he said, as he addressed the third envelope to aunt Christine, marking it, also, for express delivery. "Perhaps you can now tell us what goes into them?"

"In the envelope addressed to your aunt the bank draft for five million francs will, ultimately, be enclosed. Also a letter to her – oh, you can make up any lies you like about it – you won the State Lottery, perhaps. All you have to tell her is that she should put the money in some place of safety and that she must not hand it over to anyone but you. That is important. To no one but yourself in person."

"Very well," said Peter patiently. "But let me first hear the rest of your plan."

"In one of the two envelopes addressed to the bank you enclose a blank piece of paper."

"Proceed."

"The second one will, eventually, contain nothing at all. Once it has served its purpose, it can be torn up."

"I see," said Peter. He was beginning to have an idea of what she was after. It was, as he had suspected, outrageous and impracticable. "You are planning a switch."

"Exactly." Laure sounded like a schoolmistress who has discovered an unexpected gleam of intelligence in a backward child. "Let me demonstrate. The meeting takes place on the road. The men will arrive by van. This peppergrinder represents the van. You will be in front of it – we place a salt-cellar for you. I shall be standing by the road, as requested."

"A mustard pot for you," said Peter indulgently.

"Thank you. The van, as you have seen, is a large one with a heavy body. When I move behind it I shall be out of sight

211

of the men – two spoons for them please. They will be in front of it, standing perhaps together, or perhaps on either side of the road. The moment of exchange arrives. They produce the picture. You take the bank draft out of the bank envelope so that they can examine it. When they are satisfied, you take it back from them, place it in the envelope and seal it up. At that moment you give the sign by saying something – let me think – what would it be natural to say?"

"I think I should say, 'O.K. That's that!' "

"Excellent. When I hear those words – I am now hidden by the van, remember – I shine my torch. My father, who is in the woods above the road, sees the torch. He has with him his old fowling piece, loaded and primed."

"Good, good," said her father. "I shoot both men."

"You most certainly will do nothing of the sort. You will have it ready cocked. Your finger will be on the trigger. Immediately you see the light from my torch you fire, aiming well above the van."

"It would be better to shoot them," said Michel-Ange. "I do not see the object of firing if not to hit them."

"I do," said Peter. "And I want, here and now, to be absolutely clear about one point. You think that if these men's attention is distracted I shall be able to pocket the letter which I have put the draft in and hand over to them the duplicate envelope which contains nothing but a blank piece of paper."

"It would be better, I think, if you managed to pass the letter with the draft in it to me. They might seek to detain you. I do not think they will trouble about a foolish girl like me. I shall no doubt still be screaming with terror at the sound of the gun. It would be natural if I threw myself into your arms."

"Don't overdo it," said Peter. "The men are not fools. And listen, please, to what I have to say. I shall be the judge, and the only judge, of whether the men's attention has been sufficiently distracted to allow this farce to be played. If I consider that it has not, I shall simply hand them the envelope with the draft in it. If Meyer is indeed planning to steal it and take it out of the country, the consequences may be unpleasant. But they will not be as unpleasant, or as immediate, as the reactions of these men if they find us trying to swindle them. I doubt if any of us would be alive at the end of the night. Do you understand?"

"I understand," said Laure sadly, "that you will try to convince yourself that their attention has *not* been sufficiently diverted."

Before Peter could deal with this all further conversation was aborted by the reappearance of Gran'mère. She bustled in saying, "A quarter past eight. Is everyone in this house mad? Why has dinner not been called for?"

"The *patron* has much on his mind," said Laure. "I will go up at once and find out."

Dinner that evening might have been a miserable function. Although the food was up to Gran'mère's usual high standard, Peter was so distracted by thoughts of the ordeal ahead that it could have been cold meat and bread for all the attention he could pay to it. The occasion was saved by the fact that his host had drunk just enough of the Lambrécie marc to restore his spirits, but not enough to make him incoherent. He was cheerful. He could see the end of his troubles. Once the picture was back in his possession he had made plans for its immediate disposal. The thought of the money he was paying did not disturb him. It was only a tenth of what he was receiving. And there was a further advantage which had occurred to him. When the truth of the whole matter came out – as no doubt it would, in due course, such things could not be kept secret for ever – people could no longer blame him for selling a painting which had caused him such trouble. It really seemed that everything was finally turning out for the best.

The only drawback was that, though the dining-room windows were wide open the atmosphere seemed somehow to be oppressive. "I have spoken again to my friend at the head office of the P.T.T.," said Mr. Wellborn. "The storm over central Europe was the most severe recorded in the last forty years. The worst damage was above Clermont-Ferrand. The Allier burst its banks and flooded the main telephone exchange for the whole of northern France."

"Terrible," said Peter, who was hardly attending to him.

213

"It is being pumped out now. Communications should be restored by tomorrow morning."

"Is the storm coming this way?"

"Apparently not. The storm centre is now between Toulouse and Montpellier. What we feel here is the side effect. One is conscious, is one not, of a certain oppression? I trust we shall avoid any really bad weather. Happily the *vendange* has been completed, but I plan to take my car into Bordeaux this evening and I dislike driving in storm conditions."

This did interest Peter. He said, "It must be a matter of great importance to take you out at night."

"It is indeed important. For some time now I have been in touch with the Musée Claude Bonnier. The director is an old friend of mine. I have offered him six of my finest pictures, including the Titian until it goes to America. They will be on permanent loan. I chose that institution because it is well protected. As soon as you have concluded your business this evening I shall drive into Bordeaux with the pictures. Whatever time I arrive, the director will certainly wait up for me. He does not often get such an offer. When the pictures are gone I shall sleep soundly for the first time for many days."

"I hope we shall all sleep soundly tonight," said Peter.

By a quarter to ten they were in position. Michel-Ange had taken station in the woods which overhung the far side of the road and Laure had made sure that he could see the light from her torch when she switched it on.

She was standing beside Peter.

Had they not been totally preoccupied they might have taken some note of the behaviour of the weather. The wind, coming from the east, had drawn a curtain of low black cloud across the sky, blotting out moon and stars. Now, suddenly, it had ceased to blow steadily. It was coming in a series of strong puffs which flattened the leaves on the trees and whipped up clouds of sand from the road verge.

"What are they up to? Why are they late?" said Laure. Even her imperturbability seemed to be slipping.

Peter looked at the luminous dial of his watch. He said, "They aren't late. It's only five to ten." And after four minutes had crept by he added, "They daren't be late. They've got to get their letter into the post by half past ten."

"I wish they'd hurry."

Peter nearly said, 'And I wish we hadn't started this nonsense', but before this declaration of defeat could be spoken they saw the van. It was running very slowly, with only side lights showing. When it drew up alongside them there was a moment of complete stillness, before both doors opened and the men jumped out.

Peter could see from their movements and from the way they stationed themselves, one looking up and the other down the road, that they were expecting trouble. He had the bank draft ready in one hand and the envelope in the other. Goraji walked towards him and held out his hand.

"The picture?" said Peter.

Goraji said, "What a suspicious young man. Your picture is here." He half turned, opened the van door and brought out the brown paper parcel which Peter had seen before. He then pulled the picture clear of its wrapping and held it under the side lights. Peter moved forward to examine it. They were now standing quite close together. He took a quick look at the picture, nodded and held out the bank draft.

Goraji took it and subjected it to a surprisingly casual examination. It was the critical moment. Would he say, 'All right. Give me the envelope', or would he hand the draft back? Everything turned on that. And even if that went well, was it possible that the feeble diversion they had planned could succeed against two trained and suspicious professionals? Peter had noticed that, during all these manoeuvres, Rasim had never relaxed his attention. He was turning his head, looking first up then down the road, with one hand never far from the gun which lived in a shoulder holster inside his coat.

Peter held out his hand. Nature seemed to be holding its breath. Then Goraji handed back the draft.

He watched closely while Peter inserted it in the envelope, licked the gum and fastened it.

What happened next shook everyone.

As Peter opened his mouth to utter the agreed signal, a

jagged streak of blue lightning split the cloud almost immediately overhead. Laure dropped her torch. Michel-Ange, whose finger was on the trigger, pulled it without waiting for any signal. The blast of his gun was swallowed up by the drum roll of thunder which followed.

Both the men, blinded and deafened, dived for the further ditch, going for their guns as they dropped. By the time they had climbed back onto the road there had been ample time to switch the envelopes and Laure was back behind the van scrabbling for her torch.

Peter alone seemed not to have moved. He was standing, rock-like, in the same position holding out an envelope.

Goraji said, in a voice in which fury was mixed with suspicion, "That wasn't just thunder. Someone was shooting at us. Yes?"

Another flash of lightning and a thunder clap, but further off and more muted. As it rumbled away among the trees Peter said, quite coolly, "No one was shooting at you. It was probably old Gobard. He goes after rabbits in that bit of wood."

Goraji was clearly in two minds. He had a feeling that something was going on that he didn't understand. Peter decided that the time had come to break up the scene. He said, "We'd better get the picture under cover, hadn't we, before it's damaged?"

Single, heavy thunder drops of rain were now battering the top of the van and throwing up little spurts of dust from the road.

Goraji said, "The *gosse* can take it. You're coming with us."

That was the point when Peter's moment of triumph started to crumble.

Rasim handed the parcel to Laure. The brown paper was already getting soaked. She took it without a word, crossed into the vineyard and was lost to sight.

Goraji said, "Get in." Peter started to protest, but there was no arguing with the guns.

As they drove north along the road he thought perhaps they only wanted to keep an eye on him until the letter was posted. On the other hand, were they now so suspicious that they would reopen the letter to check its contents before dispatching it? When they reached the box – the same one in which Peter had posted his own letter some hours before – this fear, at least, was dispelled. Rasim jumped out with the letter, paused only to examine the legend in front of the box to make sure that the 10.30 collection had not yet taken place and pushed the letter through the slot.

"Can I go home now?" said Peter meekly.

Goraji said, "No." Rasim jumped in beside Peter and the van bumped off down the road.

Goraji, who seemed to be in a slightly better humour now that the business of the evening had been concluded, said, "You feel that an explanation is due for our detaining you. Yes?"

"I didn't see that I could be much more use to you."

"On the contrary. You may still have an important part to play." He glanced at Rasim who was smiling. They both seemed relaxed and happy. Much too happy for Peter's peace of mind.

"We observed," said Goraji, "the care with which you examined the painting."

"Care and skill," said Rasim.

"Clearly you had been instructed what to look for. Yes? We, on the other hand, do not possess the necessary knowledge to examine the bank draft with equal care and pronounce on its authenticity. We observed that the name of Crédit Agricole was at the head of it and that the sum mentioned appeared to be five million francs. But the signatures at the foot and the names and descriptions of the signers – what did we know about them? Nothing. The whole document could have been fictitious. A scrap of paper. Worthless. You appreciate now why we have to keep our hands on you. When this draft arrives in Paris tomorrow morning it will be examined by people who understand these things. As soon as they can communicate, they will be able to assure us that the draft is in order.

"After which," he added, "you will be of no further use to us."

Rasim said, "I also remembered something when I saw you

earlier this evening. Yours is a face one does not easily forget. Outside that church in Normandy – you recall the occasion – ?"

"Yes," said Peter. He said it reluctantly. He was hoping that Rasim would not have remembered him.

"It makes you very precious to us," said Rasim, sliding an arm round his shoulder. "Doubly precious."

10

It was ten past ten when Stewart stepped from the plane at de Gaulle airport.

The storm which had ravaged central Europe had passed too far to the east to affect Paris. It was a fine autumn evening. The moon, nearly full, was dimming the streetlights and the black sky overhead was full of stars.

Stewart, who knew and loved Paris, took a taxi from the airport to the east end of the Boulevard Haussmann, then transferred to the Métro for a short trip to the Gare Guy Moquet. From here to reach the end of the Rue Lamarck involved a short walk back, down the Avenue de St. Ouen. A number of the shops were still open and he found himself stopping to examine the displays in the windows. After he had pulled up two or three times it occurred to him that his slow progress was the result of apprehension about what was to come. This was an uncomfortable thought and he swung round resolutely to continue his advance. As he did so he nearly collided with a man who was coming in the opposite direction.

He said, "Mille pardons," and then, "My God, fancy bumping into you."

It was Henry Bear, but the difference that four years had made was startling. The lumpy adolescent had become a man of the world. In his expensive herring-bone tweed suit, cream shirt and suede shoes he was the epitome of the successful businessman on holiday. The only suggestion of the schoolboy that had once existed was the Old Chelburian tie.

"Stewart! Well met. Come and have a drink."

"Can't. I've got a job on."

"Then after the job is over. It can't take all night. Where are you staying?"

For the first time it occurred to Stewart that in the hurry of his departure he had forgotten to make any arrangements for sleeping. He said, "As a matter of fact I hadn't fixed anything. What about you?"

"When I'm on business I stay at the Meurice. Being on holiday I'm more modest. A bed and breakfast place called the Deux Continents. It isn't full. I could fix a room for you."

"That's very good of you."

"Not a bit of it. Did you realise that you were the founder of my fortunes? That fifty pounds you wangled for me in my last term."

"It wasn't a wargle."

"Anyway, as soon as I got home I put it on a horse."

"Silly ass."

"Hold on. It was an excellent animal. It cantered home at twenties. And that thousand smackers was the basis of my modest stake in the marketing outfit I'm with. I'll tell you all about it at breakfast tomorrow."

When Bear had left him, heading for the pleasures of Montmartre, Stewart felt surprisingly cheered. He had at least one ally at hand. And wasn't marketing something Ron had talked about? Marketing. It had a solid ring about it. And if a hearty lump like Henry could make a go of it with a mere thousand pounds as entry money, why shouldn't he, with twenty times that sum and – no point in being modest about it – with twice his brain power, soon be swimming on that warm and profitable tide?

These thoughts were in his head when he went through the door of No. 34 Rue Lamarck.

The porter was sitting on a chair beside the lift, studying the racing pages of an evening paper. He did not seem happy. Perhaps his selections had not been as successful as Henry Bear's. When Stewart asked for Monsieur Zaman he looked at him blankly.

"Cinquième étage," said Stewart. "Monsieur Agazadeh Zaman."

This time the porter seemed to understand him. He said, *"Attendez un instant s'il vous plaît,"* and disappeared into his hutch, shutting the door behind him. Stewart could hear him talking on the telephone. Then he reappeared, gestured towards the lift, sat down and resumed his reading.

When Stewart got out of the lift at the fourth floor two young men were waiting for him. The taller of them said, in passable English, "You desire to speak to Monsieur Zaman. Yes?"

"As the porter has by now no doubt informed you, that is precisely what I desire to do."

"There is a small formality first. Your hands on the wall, please. And lean forward."

Hands ran over Stewart's body. It was an expert frisking which left nothing to chance. The hands paused for a moment and pulled out the cigarette case they had detected. It was handed to the second young man who opened it, looked inside and passed it back again. The lighter in his jacket pocket was examined in the same way.

"I hope you are now convinced that I am not carrying any lethal weapons," said Stewart pleasantly.

"Only the cigarettes," said the first man. "They will kill you in due course. You may go in. The room at the end."

One of them held the door open and both of them followed him in. Zaman was sitting on the couch in front of the window reading a book. He did not get up. The two young men retired to the far corner of the room and sat down. When Stewart looked round for a chair for himself Zaman said, "I did not invite you to be seated. I did not invite you to come here. First you will explain one thing, please. How did you know where I lived?"

Stewart, who had anticipated this question and had decided that frankness would serve him best, said, "I am a friend of Mrs. Chaytor. She visited you here recently. She gave me the address."

"I see. And being in Paris you decided to pay me a friendly visit."

"That's not quite true. It was something I learnt yesterday afternoon, from Mr. and Mrs. Chaytor, that convinced me that I ought to come here."

"So – an impromptu visit, then. Did you tell the Chaytors you were coming?"

The question slid out so smoothly that Stewart had said
'no' to it before it occurred to him that it might have been
wiser to say 'yes'.

"Then no one knows that you are here?"

"That could have been the case, but in fact, quite by chance,
I ran into an old school friend on the way here."

"And you told him where you were going, perhaps."

Stewart would have liked to have said 'yes', but could think
of no plausible reason for having confided in Henry Bear. He
decided to stick to the truth. He said, "No. I hardly imagined
he would be interested."

"So if you disappeared, all that anyone would know was
that you had been in Paris."

"True," said Stewart. He added, as lightly as he could
manage for a certain dryness of his mouth, "as a matter of
fact I hadn't contemplated disappearing. What can have put
that idea into your head?"

"Oh, people do disappear in Paris. Not as often as in
Teheran or Beirut, but with some regularity. Their bodies
are placed, so I am told, in the sewers. This prevents awkward questions from arising, since the rats who swarm there
in millions can consume the soft parts of a body in three
days."

"In two days," said the taller of the young men in the
respectful voice of a student correcting a professor. "That is,
if the body, when placed in the sewer, is unclothed."

"Thank you, Yussuf. You are correct. Clothes always make
a difference, in life as in death. But we are straying from the
point, Mr. – ?"

"Ives."

"Mr. Ives. You came here on business. Then state it."

Back in England it had seemed easy. He had repeated so
often to himself the proposition that he intended to put that
the words had come pat. Now it was different. It was not
only that he was frightened. It was the realisation that he
was dealing with a formidable man; a man, moreover, who
had all the cards in his hand.

He said, coming to the point more hastily than he had
planned, "I happen to have stumbled on a piece of information

which I think might be of vital importance to you. A friend of mine – "

"Yes, yes. Mr. Meyer has told us about Peter Dolamore."

"Then you know that he has gone down to Lambrécie to transact a certain matter for you. What you do not know – and what I have just learnt – is that the affair may not now come out in the way you had anticipated."

"And this is the information you will now give us?"

"I will sell it to you."

"Oh. In return for what?"

"In return for your ensuring that no harm comes to Peter."

Of all the reactions that Stewart had expected, the last one was laughter. Zaman leaned back on the couch and shook with a spasm of apparently genuine amusement.

When he could speak he said, "Delicious. Let me be quite clear about this. You and your friend have, with unimaginable stupidity, got yourselves into positions of danger. Real danger, Mr. Ives, I can assure you of that. Now you want me to get you out of it by selling me some valuable information. Yes?"

Stewart managed to say 'yes'. He experienced some difficulty in speaking. The atmosphere in the room seemed to have become both closer and colder.

Zaman sat forward and said, with great deliberation, "You – are – a – baby. No. I am wrong. A little older than that, perhaps, but not much. Shall we say, a schoolboy. A schoolboy who tells himself stories. Stories of which he is inevitably the hero."

In a last effort to assert himself Stewart said, "If you are going to lecture me, you might at least invite me to sit down."

"You will not sit down. You will stand up straight. You will listen and you will guard your tongue. If we have any more impertinence I shall be tempted to give you a lesson which you will not easily forget."

Whilst he was speaking the two young men had got up and were now standing so close behind him that he could feel their breath, on the back of his neck.

"So. Attend to me closely. I shall not repeat myself. There are two reasons why the proposal you have made is nonsense. The first is that even if I wished to communicate with Goraji and Rasim I could not do so. When they are engaged in matters of this sort they do not live in luxury hotels with telephone numbers and receptionists to take messages."

"In any event," said Yussuf, "all communications with the South of France have been temporarily interrupted."

"Is that so? I had not heard. But my second reason is even more cogent. You propose to sell me some information. But why should I buy it? I have at my disposal cheaper and quicker ways of obtaining it. Not many weeks ago an Iranian came here. He, also, was proposing to sell me information. I entrusted him to Yussuf here and his brother Ali. How long did it take to open his mouth?"

"He was not very brave. In five minutes he was screaming and we were forced to gag him. Three minutes later, when the gag was removed he was most anxious to speak."

"But," said Ali, "he was sobbing so bitterly that we had some difficulty, at first, in making out what he was saying."

"I am sure, now that you understand the position Mr. Ives, that you will not provoke us to such extremes. Quickly, if you please. We should all like to get some sleep tonight."

Stewart had no thought of refusing. He put a hand into his breast pocket – conscious that Yussuf's hand was within inches of his as he did so – and drew out the flimsy from Mauger & Finch. Yussuf took it from him and passed it to Zaman, who read it carefully. He said, "Then it is tomorrow morning – or rather, since it is past midnight, I should say, this Friday morning – that Mr. Meyer leaves at noon for Buenos Aires. A single ticket. Are you suggesting that he means to stay there? This is not evidence of such intention. He has business contacts in South America. He may be coming back by some other route."

"Then why has he sold his house in London, with all its furniture, and lodged the money in the Banque de La Guyane here in Paris?"

"You are certain? The Banque de La Guyane. That does suggest a number of interesting possibilities."

"And it was into that bank that Mr. Wellborn's money was, in the first instance, to be paid."

"As I said, it is interesting. Fortunately – it was at my

insistence – certain rigid time limits were incorporated into our arrangements. So if Mr. Wellborn's draft, changed to a draft on the Banque de La Guyane, is not in my possession by eleven o'clock at the very latest, I shall have cause to believe that your suspicions of Mr. Meyer are well founded. In which case, I shall feel sufficiently grateful to allow you to depart. If not, I shall be forced to assume that you have intervened in my affairs for some ulterior motive. Or that you have been mischievously wasting my time. In which case you will, I assure you, regret your stupidity. But why should we anticipate unpleasant consequences which may not arise? Yussuf and Ali will show you your quarters. I cannot promise that they are comfortably furnished, but fortunately there is not much of the night left." He gestured to the two young men and returned to the book he had been reading.

The small room at the end of the hallway into which Stewart was led was neither comfortably nor uncomfortably furnished. There was nothing in it at all. The single window was shuttered and the shutters had been bolted into place.

Yussuf said, "If you make any attempt to call attention to yourself, or to escape, you will be badly hurt, possibly crippled."

Both then left and Stewart heard two bolts on the outside of the door being shot home.

Since there was nothing else to do he sat down, with his back against the wall and his legs stretched out in front of him. He hoped that he would be able to get some sleep because only if he slept would he be able to stop thinking.

His thoughts were bitter.

He had ridden out like a knight errant to rescue Peter and he was crawling home on his hands and knees. He had done nothing to improve Peter's position and had rendered his own infinitely worse. He was a failure. He was a poseur. What was it Zaman had said? A schoolboy who told himself stories.

In the depths of his self-abasement he was overdramatising the position. Nevertheless it is arguable that it was then and there, with his legs stretched out on the boards and his back against the wall, that Stewart finally came of age.

11

As the van sped along the road and bumped down the track to the Camp, Peter was examining, with no pleasure at all, the ruin of their careful planning.

It had never crossed his mind that the men would keep him with them. What was going to happen to him when the envelope was opened at the bank and was found to contain nothing but a blank sheet of paper? How long would it take the news to reach his captors? Even if telephone communications had not been reopened a fast car, using the *autoroute*, could reach Bordeaux in three hours. A succession of possibilities occurred to him, all of them unpleasant.

"Here we are, then," said Rasim cheerfully. "Safely back in our little nest." He led the way in and lit the pressure lamp. "I think we all deserve a drink, yes?"

Goraji grunted agreement. He was less relaxed than Rasim. Somewhere a seed of suspicion had been planted in his mind and was germinating. As Peter had realised, at their first encounter in the church, he was the leader. He made the hard decisions.

From a battered suitcase on the floor Rasim extracted a bottle of calvados and poured out three generous tumblerfuls. Rasim smacked his lips as he swallowed the raw apple brandy. Goraji drank more sedately. Peter took one sip and felt the bile rising in his throat. He said, "I am going to be sick."

"Outside," said Goraji.

The two men went with him and watched as he deposited his supper on the path, after which, sweating and shivering, he crawled back into the hut and sat down on one of the beds.

"It is a grave crime to waste honest drink," observed Rasim sententiously. He divided the contents of Peter's glass between himself and Goraji.

When they had finished drinking Goraji looked at his watch. "Past eleven already," he said. "But I think I will make one more attempt to telephone."

"Is that wise?" said Rasim. "Now that he has his precious picture back Mr. Wellborn may have circulated a warning."

"It is a chance we must take. I will have a word with Bernard. He is discreet. And being of the Brotherhood he is likely to have contacts in the Post Office. I may be able to find out what I want to know without even using his telephone."

Peter, who was recovering slowly, listened to this scrap of conversation with interest. Some things were becoming clearer. Mr. Wellborn had mentioned Georges, the brother of Hervé and Michel-Ange, who ran a ferry across the Gironde from Port de Goulée. It was Georges, it seemed, who had learned of the arrival of the two Iranians from one of his neighbours in Port de Goulée. It was logical to suppose that this neighbour might be the Bernard they were talking about. When he had been at Port de Goulée that afternoon he had seen two boats, both with fittings for outboard engines and both, no doubt, capable of crossing the mouth of the Gironde, particularly if the right concurrence of tide and current were observed. It was a reasonable supposition that one of the boats belonged to this man Bernard and the other to Georges Gobard. His mind was starting to work more clearly. If this was right, it explained a point which had puzzled him.

The men had left their own car on the north bank of the Gironde. They had arranged with Bernard to ferry them across. Once over, they had stolen the first vehicle they could lay their hands on. It had been kept hidden in the forest and only used, discreetly, after dark. Then, when the time came to leave, all they would have to do was to abandon it near Port de Goulée, be ferried back by Bernard, pick up their own car and head for Paris. He was convinced that he had read the situation correctly. It fitted in with the men's professionalism. They had realised that, if a hue and cry had been raised, it would be only too easy for the police to post guards at the regular crossing places of the river. By adopting this method they kept themselves clear of trouble.

By the time he had reached this conclusion Goraji had

finished his drink. He said, "I have no doubt that you can keep this boy safe in my absence. But I think we should take some precautions in case he should slip away when your back is turned." He extracted a length of cord from one of the two big rucksacks that were hanging on the inner wall. "We will remove his shoes – so. And we will attach his ankles to the end of the bed – so." He knotted the cords expertly. "Now I do not think our little bird will fly away."

He went out and Peter heard the van start up and the sound diminishing as it cleared the Camp and headed for the Lesparre road.

Rasim had followed him out, but had not gone far. Peter could hear his footsteps crunching up and down on the stones. He realised that Rasim, on his own, was more nervous than when he was backed by Goraji. He was keeping his eyes and ears open for intruders. Might this be the moment when he could slip away?

A superficial examination of the cords round his ankles convinced him of the impossibility of this. They had been tightly knotted and the final knots were below the level of the iron bar at the end of the bed.

Such chance as there might have been vanished when Rasim reappeared. He poured himself a second drink and offered one to Peter, who shook his head. His stomach had recovered some stability, but he was not taking any chances.

"You must keep up your spirits," said Rasim. "As you will be aware, our religion discourages the use of alcohol. When I am in Iran, I observe the prohibition. When I am abroad, I follow the customs of the country I am in."

"When in Rome," said Peter, "do as the Romans do."

"Rome is a fine city," said Rasim.

He came across, swallowed half the contents of his glass, put it down on the corner of the packing case and perched himself on the bed. He was close enough for Peter to see that he was sweating. The point of a pink tongue came out from between his lips.

Peter said, "I suppose it's some time since you were last in Iran."

"Alas, yes. Our work has kept us in France for a number of years."

"I guessed as much. You speak French very fluently."

Rasim smirked. "Not too badly for an ignorant man. You also speak it well."

"No credit to me. My mother's family were French. She is dead, but many of my relations still live in Paris."

"And you? You are still very young. Not long out of school I would guess. You live in England?"

"For the last ten years, yes."

"And how do you pass the time? Chasing girls? They would find you attractive, no doubt." A hand strayed onto Peter's leg.

"I'm afraid I have to spend most of my time earning my living."

"And how do you do that?"

(Keep him talking, for God's sake.)

Peter started to explain the practice of Starfax. He dragged it out as long as he could and was relieved to note that Rasim seemed genuinely interested.

He said, "So you tell fortunes. Is that it?"

"More or less. We judge what may be in store for a man, or a woman, by considering the exact position of the planets and the stars at the moment of their birth. If you can read the signs accurately you will know what course their life will take."

"Could you, for instance, do that for me?"

"I could try."

"Very well." Rasim sat back to think about it. "I was born, very close to midnight, so I am told, on the eighteenth day of February – that is by your calendar, you understand."

"A very significant date indeed. It lies almost exactly between the houses of Aquarius and Pisces."

"What does that mean for me?"

(Peter had managed to look at his watch. Goraji had left at around a quarter past eleven. He had perhaps twenty-five kilometres to cover, all on good roads. He would meet little or no traffic at that time of night. On the other hand, he would not want to call attention to himself by speeding. Say, twenty minutes to Port de Goulée. Five or ten minutes to pursue his enquiries with Bernard. Twenty minutes back. A minimum of three-quarters of an hour. It was now a few minutes short of midnight.)

Whilst Peter was thinking about this, Rasim had been watching him anxiously. He said, "I see you can read something. Is it good or bad?"

"It is equally divided. It seems you will be safe from any death by violence involving knives or guns. At the same time you will have to be very careful when crossing water – this is the significance of the fact that at the moment of your birth, you were leaving the house of the Water-carrier and entering the house of the Fishes."

Rasim chewed over this information for some seconds. It seemed both to reassure and to disturb him. Finally he said, "So be it. I must, as you say, be careful. You say that you earned your living by this skill that you possess. Was it you alone, or were there others who helped you?"

"One other in particular. An old schoolfriend of mine."

As soon as he had said this Peter realised that he had made a mistake. Rasim was smiling. "A schoolboy friendship," he said. "One has heard of such things. In our country it is very common. Before a young man discovers the attraction of the other sex he will take his pleasure with one of his own sex. Great pleasure. sometimes."

He was now lying half beside and half over Peter, who was held fast by his feet. One of his hands went down and unbuckled Peter's belt.

"Please," said Peter. "Don't do that."

"A beautiful boy like you. It will not be the first time, I am sure."

(Only once before, when two older boys had trapped him in a railway carriage. They had been much less brutal than Rasim was planning to be and had left him alone when he had started crying.)

Rasim was now trying to pull down his trousers. The cord round his ankles helped Peter to prevent him. Rasim's face, glistening with excitement, was a few inches from his own. He said, "If you resist, I may be forced to hurt you."

Then he stopped. He had heard, before Peter did, the sound

of the truck returning. He climbed back off the bed and stood up. "No matter," he said, "we have all night for our games."

Peter watched him go out, through the inner door. He heard him cross the outer room and step outside onto the path. Then he saw the knife. The point, glittering like a star in the light of the lamp, had pierced the wall-covering near the top and now came slowly down through the tough canvas, with a slurring noise.

Then Laure was in the room. Her face was white and working, but her hand was steady. She sliced the cord which held Peter's feet. He rolled off the bed, refastened his belt and looked round wildly for his shoes. They might have been put in the suitcase, or hidden away somewhere. No time to waste. Laure had already gone. He followed her, squeezing through the slit in the canvas. He heard Rasim say something which made Goraji laugh. Then he was through the gap in the planking and in the open air.

He saw Laure beckon and stumbled after her. It was not too bad whilst they were inside the compound. He followed his guide who led the way to a place where the bottom strand of the wire was loose and wriggled under it at the cost of a tear in his windcheater. The moon was hidden by clouds and he could see very little. Some yards on he fell forward, on hands and knees, into a hole which seemed, from the dampness of the earth, to have been freshly dug. It was no more than three foot deep and easy enough to climb out of. From this point the going became very difficult.

Not only did he trip over roots, but he trod on stones, some of them flints half buried in the earth with their sharp edges uppermost. First he tried putting his feet down gently to feel for a clear patch. This helped, but not much. The soles of his feet were cut and bruised. He could feel the blood soaking through his socks. Finally he sat down. He said, "I'm sorry, Laure. It's no good. My feet won't take me much further. I could hobble along for a bit and maybe crawl. But that's not going to get us to Roquillac, or even to Laugnan, if that was your plan."

"We are not far from the Lesparre road. If we can reach it, walking on a smooth surface would be easier for you."

"Much better."

"And we might stop a car and get a lift. Not that it is very likely at this hour of the night."

"Lead on," said Peter. "If you go slowly I can manage."

It took them half an hour, an agonising thirty minutes, to reach the Lesparre road. After that it was certainly a lot more comfortable walking on the smooth asphalt. And when they had been going for a few minutes they heard a car coming, from the direction of Hourtin. Peter stumbled out into the middle of the road, waving his arms. Blinded by the headlights he saw, too late, what Laure's sharper eyes had noticed as she dived back into the ditch.

It was Rasim who jumped out of the van and threw an arm round Peter's shoulders. Goraji, who had been driving, dismounted more slowly. Rasim said, "How could you bring yourself to leave us after all the care we had taken of you?"

Peter said nothing. He was too shocked at his own stupidity to utter a word.

Goraji was also silent. He seemed to have something on his mind. When they were back in the hut he said, suddenly, "Where did you hide the knife?"

"I didn't hide it," said Peter. "It was in my pocket. If you'd looked you'd have found it."

"Where is it now?"

"Somewhere in the forest. I must have dropped it."

Goraji chewed on this. Then he said to Rasim, "When I went away you came out with me, yes?"

"That's right. I did so."

"How long were you outside?"

"Perhaps five minutes. Maybe ten."

"Then he had five or ten minutes to cut himself free and escape. And at that time only you were there. So why did he wait until I was back? That was stupid, wasn't it? And he is not stupid, this boy. I think someone helped him. Someone who came from outside. Someone I fancy I saw slipping off as we drove up. I think perhaps he will tell us the truth if we ask him."

"Yes," said Rasim. He was smiling with pleasure at the thought of what was to come.

Goraji said, "Go out and cut me two or three sticks. Supple ones, about a metre long." And to Peter, "Lie on the bed."

Since resistance was useless, Peter lay down. Goraji removed his socks. They were matted with blood and had stuck to the soles of his feet. When Goraji jerked them off the wounds began to bleed again. He fastened Peter's ankles to the bar at the foot of the bed and pulled the bed away from the wall.

By the time he had done this Rasim was back, carrying two whippy branches which he had cut from an alder. He sat himself down on the other bed and started to trim them, doing the work carefully, humming to himself as he did so. When he had finished, he got up and examined the state of Peter's feet. "A touch of the bastinado," he said. "That should produce the most interesting results."

Peter was now quite clear what was going to happen. They were like two boys who had caught a rat alive in a trap and were thinking out interesting ways of killing it. They would torture him, for their pleasure, and when he was a screaming, blubbering wreck they would finish him off and bury him in the grave they had prepared. Since they must have dug it before they came to the meeting place, it was clear that they had never had any intention that he should survive the night.

Rasim came across, took careful aim and brought the stick down. The pain was horrible.

Surprised at the steadiness of his own voice Peter said, in an offhand way, almost as though he were a spectator and not a principal in what was taking place, "Before you go on, you ought, perhaps, to consider one point."

"Yes?" said Rasim.

"Had you, perhaps, overlooked the fact that my mother's sister, the Countess Christine de Clissac, lives in a second storey flat in the Avenue de Neuilly? And – " he paused artistically " – that she has no lift."

It was the tone of voice as much as the words that checked Rasim. Their earlier conversation had left him with the idea that Peter was possessed of hidden powers. Like all ignorant people, he distrusted anything he could not immediately understand. Goraji was less impressed. He said, "If you are propounding riddles in order to save yourself from punishment, do not bother. We have the night ahead of us."

"Very well," said Peter. "A further point, then, before we return to my aunt and her flat. Are you both such townsmen that you did not know that no rabbit would leave its hole in a night of storm? Because if you had realised this elementary fact you would have known that Michel-Ange Gobard would hardly have been out rabbit shooting."

"So?"

"What happened was intended, of course, as a diversion. We could hardly have known that nature would oblige us with a much more powerful diversion of its own."

"Speak plainly," said Goraji impatiently. "A diversion for what?"

"Well, I should have thought an intelligent man like you would have guessed by now. To enable us to switch envelopes, of course."

This produced a very brittle silence. It was broken by Goraji who said, in a voice compounded of distrust and dislike, "Explain that. You say you switched envelopes. I do not think you can have done any such thing. But if you did, what was in the one you handed to me?"

"Nothing. A plain sheet of paper."

"And the other? The one with the money in it."

"That is where we return to the point at which we started. The draft went, in a different envelope, which we also had prepared, to my aunt who lives in the Avenue de Neuilly; with a letter asking her to keep it safe and hand it to no one but me. She is a very obstinate old lady and will obey these instructions to the letter. If anyone else tries to get it, you may be sure that it will go straight into the strongroom at her bank."

The two men looked at each other.

It was clear to Peter that Rasim was already beginning to believe him. Goraji was balanced between belief and disbelief. He said, "Why did you do this? It was stupid and it was dangerous."

"Agreed. But it was necessary. I happened to learn, at the very last moment, that the man Meyer was almost certainly planning to play Agazadeh Zaman false."

234

Peter saw that this statement had somehow raised the temperature of the discussion. His wits were now working well and the solution occurred to him. They had not realised, until this moment, that he knew anything about Zaman. Now, for the first time, the involvement of that formidable man had made itself felt. For, suppose what he was saying was true. Suppose they had been fooled and had allowed five million francs to slip through their fingers.

Peter, reading their silence, continued with increased confidence.

"I will tell you what we had learned," he said, "and you shall judge for yourselves. Only yesterday we found out that Meyer had sold his house in London, his furniture and his pictures – including, no doubt, the ones that you had obtained for him from the church at Sassencourt. This money, together, we believe, with his private fortune, has been concentrated in the Banque de La Guyane in Paris. Hardly a coincidence, would you say, that he has now so arranged matters that Mr. Wellborn's draft also is to be added to his personal account at that same bank? You perceive the result? Immediately the bank opens for business this morning he can walk in and draw the whole amount, in the form of a single bank draft."

"And what then?" growled Goraji.

"When I tell you that he has in his pocket a one way ticket to Buenos Aires and Santiago, on a flight leaving Paris at midday, well – I expect you can guess the answer."

He had convinced Rasim. He was sure of that. Goraji, not yet. His mind was more powerful than Rasim's, but it moved more slowly. What was helping to convince him was that he had nursed a suspicion all along that something was wrong, that some of the facts did not add up. Was he now possibly being told the truth? He said, "If this is so, why did you not tell us before?"

"Why should I? It was my intention to be back in Paris by this morning to pick up the draft and keep it safe until the situation had become clearer." He added thoughtfully, "I could still do that, you know. It would offer you your only chance – by no means a certainty, but a very good chance –

to rectify the mistake you have made. A mistake which will not please Zaman, I am sure."

(Press that button as often as you can.)

"I say, your only chance, because if it occurred to you that you might revisit the château tonight and recover the picture I should tell you that it, with all other valuable pictures, is already in the Musée Claude Bonnier, which is much better guarded than some you have attended to in the past."

"Explain, then, how you think we could recover this draft."

"I should have thought it would be obvious. All you would have to do is to drive me to Paris – you have, I am sure, your own car somewhere handy on the north bank of the river – we could be outside my aunt's door soon after the post arrives. No doubt you would have a knife in my back to ensure that I played my part. But that is where we return, once more, to my first point. I must be able to walk up two flights of stairs to her door. If you are carrying me on a stretcher, she is hardly likely to oblige you – at least without asking some very awkward questions. You follow me?"

Goraji said nothing, but the frown on his face had deepened.

"Then let me add one further point. If you do decide to adopt this course – which I am sure is the sensible one – it may have occurred to you that as soon as you are across the river and have reached, say, Rochefort or La Rochelle, you will be able to telephone Zaman and receive instructions. The western lines from Paris would not have been affected by the storm, only the southern ones."

When Peter stopped, there was a long silence. Then Goraji jerked his head at Rasim and they went into the next room. He could hear the rumble of voices, but could only make out the word 'telephone'. Evidently his last point had impressed them.

By now, Peter had been talking for ten minutes. He had been talking for his life. The reaction left him feeling sick and dizzy.

It was not only having to think of the words he was using, gauging precisely what impression he was making. More important and more difficult had been keeping his voice at the right level, a level not of pleading or even of argument, but of simple exposition. The least slip, the slightest faulty intonation would have destroyed the illusion he was building. He was still uncertain whether he had succeeded.

He lay back as comfortably as his feet allowed and took a succession of deep breaths. The room which had been circling around him slowed down as his heartbeat steadied.

He was already beginning to think ahead. Even if his plan was adopted he was far from safe. When they had recovered the draft the men would certainly consider it expedient to shut his mouth permanently. Particularly now they knew that he could identify them in connection with the killing at Sassencourt. But he would, at least, be back in the public eye and out of that foul den. This must be a step forward.

He had no idea how long the discussion went on next door. Towards the end it seemed to him that Rasim was trying to convince Goraji and that Goraji was reluctantly coming round to his point of view. Then the talking stopped, the door swung open and they marched in with the air of men who had made their minds up.

They started packing, putting all their personal belongings into the suitcase and the two rucksacks. They were concerned, he guessed, only to take things which might be traced back to them. Neither of them spoke a word. When they had finished, Goraji came across with a knife. He cut the cord round Peter's feet. Then, without replacing his socks, he forced Peter's bare feet into his shoes. He said, "Stand up."

Peter found that he could stand and could even walk after a fashion. By the time the three of them and the luggage were on the van it was past four o'clock and there was a feeling of morning in the air.

If Laure had gone to the police and if she had persuaded them to move, this was where they were going to run into trouble he thought. But the van cleared Lesparre, turned right into the side road and reached Port de Goulée without any sign of opposition. Evidently the police had either disbelieved Laure, or had been disinclined to act.

The little hamlet was asleep. When the van came to a halt and Goraji touched the horn the door of the only cottage that was showing a light opened and a man came out. Bernard, Peter guessed. He was a short thickset man, almost a dwarf. He waddled to the end of the landing-stage, where only his own boat now swung at anchor and spat into the river.

He said, "The tide has turned and that storm is sending much water down on us."

"I'm sorry," said Goraji pacifically. "We might have been here sooner, but we had things to attend to. I am sure you will be able to take us across."

"As long as this pig behaves itself." He jerked on the starter. At his third attempt the engine spluttered into life. "Hurry, now. No time to waste."

Peter was pushed on board first and crouched in the bows. Goraji and Rasim each took one of the seats. "If this cow lets us down," Bernard warned them, "you may have to help with the oars and sail."

He slipped the mooring-rope and stepped into the stern to direct their course and to keep an eye on the engine, which seemed to be running steadily enough.

He was manoeuvring cleverly, Peter saw, keeping the head of the boat pointing half into the stream, which was now running strongly, smacking the side of the boat and sending an occasional burst of spray over them.

Out of the darkness, from up stream, came a boat, larger and heavier than theirs. It hit them, not squarely, but at an angle. The force of the current swung it round and held the two boats together.

Laure had not gone to the police. She had called out her own family.

Georges was crouched in the stern, Michel-Ange and Hervé were both standing, locked firmly into position, with their legs spread and their feet wedged against the bottom and sides of the boat. Both were armed with steel bars. As Goraji half rose in his seat, Michel-Ange hit him. All of his fury and all his frustration were behind the blow. Peter heard the crunch as it split Goraji's skull.

Rasim managed to draw his gun, but before he could fire it a sideways sweep by Hervé had smashed his spine and tumbled him over the side into the water. Bernard was screaming. Peter had his eyes shut. When the screams stopped, he opened them. Michel-Ange's great hands came down, grabbed him and hauled him into the other boat.

All three of the Gobards were now at work. Sitting in their own boat they were rocking the other boat, lowering one side and raising the other until the water started coming over the freeboard. Then, with a final concerted effort, they turned the boat right over.

It floated away, bottom up, towards the open sea.

12

Meyer spent that Thursday night in his apartment in the Rue Oberkampf. He was out of bed by eight o'clock.

After washing and shaving in the tiny bathroom annexe he completed his preparations for departure, which were simple. He had already booked his heavy luggage through to Buenos Aires, where he proposed to break his journey. All he had to do now was to pack his pyjamas, washing things and slippers into a handgrip which contained some important papers, a clean shirt, some handkerchiefs and a pair of socks. He made a final and unnecessary check of the contents of his wallet, which held his air ticket and a modest supply of French and Argentinian currency, slipped his passport into the slit at the back of his handgrip and was ready to set out. A quick glance around assured him that he had left nothing behind by which he could be identified. He had taken the room on a short tenancy in a name that was not his own. The rent was paid to the end of the month, after which, no doubt, it would be re-let.

One of the attractions of the block had been that there was no concierge to spy on the tenants, who seemed to be, like him, people who valued their privacy. He encountered no one as he made his way downstairs and stepped out into the street. Although it was the third week in October the weather was so unseasonably warm that he abandoned any idea of wearing his light topcoat and carried it over one arm as he set out in search of breakfast.

Over his coffee and croissants he made a few last-minute calculations. His London house, with its contents, had been sold for eight hundred thousand pounds. This was well below the market price, but he had accepted it in the interest of quick completion. In the same way, he had accepted twenty-five thousand from Crankling for all the remaining

240

pictures in his press, aware that the auctioneer would make a handsome profit out of them. Adding the money transferred from Belgium would bring up the total to just over a million and a half sterling.

And that was not all. If everything had gone as expected in Bordeaux the equivalent in francs of a further half million would now be on its way. There was much comfort in these calculations.

He paid his bill and strolled out into the street, arriving outside the Banque de La Guyane as the clocks in the Rue Etienne-Marcel were striking ten. The uniformed commissionaire was swinging open the embossed bronze doors of the bank. He recognised Meyer and saluted. A messenger took him straight up to the manager.

Monsieur Agostino was clearly expecting him. He had a number of papers on his desk and was checking some calculations as Meyer came in. He shook hands, waved Meyer to a chair and said, with a faint note of apology in his voice, "You will realise, monsieur, that in making out the final bank draft in your favour – which I have here, ready for you, as requested – I have made certain deductions."

"Yes?" said Meyer.

"The Banque Liégeoise retained a nominal balance of five thousand francs in order, as they said, to keep the account open."

"That seems not unreasonable. And then?"

"Then there was the question of our own commission. Normally when effecting transfers of large sums of money we charge a half per cent on the total involved. In this case, it seemed to me – " the manager paused delicately " – that there were certain rather unusual aspects of the matter. Added to which, the sums involved were very large indeed."

Meyer said, coldly, "So you saw a chance to increase your commission rate. To what figure, might one enquire?"

"We thought that, in the circumstances, two per cent would not be excessive."

Meyer made a rapid calculation. He said, without any particular emphasis, "Then I am paying you the equivalent of thirty thousand pounds for a few days' work."

"Thirty-two thousand in fact. The total at your disposal was, in round figures, sixteen million francs. The draft I have prepared for you is for 15,680,000 francs. If you feel that the commission I have charged is excessive, you could always appeal to our Board, who have a final decision in such matters. It would only take a few days – "

Meyer took the proffered draft, examined it, folded it and placed it in his wallet. He said, with a slight smile, "I can see why you are such a success in your profession, Mr. Agostino." Rising to his feet he added, "By the way, I was expecting a letter. I wonder if it has arrived?"

"My apologies. I have not yet had time to attend to my own post. I will ascertain."

He pressed a bell and to the secretary, who appeared from his ante-room with a speed which suggested that she must have been stationed close to the door, he said, "Please enquire of our postal department whether they have a letter for Monsieur Meyer."

Whilst she was away the manager observed, "I trust that the letter has not been held up. There is no real reason why it should have been, but you may have heard of the disruption caused by yesterday's storm – "

"I heard about it on the wireless. However, letters travel by rail, not by wire."

"True. Yes, here it is." He took the envelope from his secretary and handed it to Meyer, who slipped it into his pocket unopened, got up and said without any suggestion of warmth, "I will wish you goodbye."

The manager nipped out from behind his desk and held the door open for him. Meyer ignored a half extended hand and walked out.

When he was back at the café at which he had breakfasted he ordered a cup of chocolate and only when it was on the table did he bring out the envelope and slit it open.

Had a spectator been watching him at that moment he would have read little from the expression on Meyer's face. A slight bunching of the jaw muscles, the smallest narrowing of his eyes. He was a man who prided himself on total self-control. But the shock had been severe.

He re-examined the contents of the envelope. A single sheet of headed notepaper from Lambrécie, which had been cut in half and folded, reducing it to roughly the size of a Crédit Agricole bank draft. He held it up and examined it against the light. There was nothing written on it. He replaced it in the envelope and started to think.

The envelope had been carefully prepared, in accordance with the arrangement he had made with Zaman. The bank draft should have been enclosed in it. In place of it was this half sheet of notepaper. The fact that it was Lambrécie notepaper suggested that the substitution had occurred at the château. Who, then, could have been responsible?

He considered the possible candidates coldly.

Joseph Wellborn? Most unlikely. He had been scrupulous in following out the instructions of the Iranians. Peter Dolamore? But why should he? His job had been to put through the exchange, not to interfere with it. That left only one uncomfortable possibility. And the more he thought about it, the more did he become convinced that it was the truth. The Iranians had themselves discovered in some unaccountable way that he proposed to walk out on them.

He considered the courses of action that were open to him.

He could wait for further news from Lambrécie. Or even go down there personally and try to ascertain what had gone wrong and to recover the draft. Or he could forgo the five million francs and catch his plane that morning for Buenos Aires. He thought about this for some time, whilst the chocolate in his cup formed a thick skin as it grew cold.

He had no intention of staying long in the Argentine or Brazil, where prices were high and inflation was rampant. As soon as certain preparations had been completed he planned to cross the continent to Santiago, where he had many contacts and where prices were reasonable. Part of the money he already had would serve to purchase a modest *estancia* and the interest on the balance would be more than ample for his needs.

Within twenty minutes of opening the envelope his mind was made up. He signalled for his bill.

As well as its main entrance, the restaurant had a second

one which opened into a side street. At the moment when he stepped out this was deserted. He walked away from the main entrance, turned two corners and was lucky enough to find a taxi discharging its passengers. He said, "De Gaulle Airport, if you please." The driver thought about it and then nodded. If it had been the rush hour he would probably have refused the fare.

The airport, at Roissy-en-France, was a full fifteen miles outside Paris, on an indifferent road. Most people who had business there preferred to take one of the frequent trains from the Gare du Nord. Meyer, however, was strongly of the opinion that the less he hung around in the centre of the town the better. His arrangement with Zaman had been that he would get the draft from the bank as soon as it opened. There might, he had explained, be some delay in making it out. But he would be with Zaman by eleven o'clock at the latest. He did not underrate the Iranian's organising powers. After eleven o'clock Paris was no place for him.

He reached the airport at a quarter past eleven. He saw that Flight number 8684 for Buenos Aires and Santiago was signalled on the Information Board, but the passengers were not yet warned for boarding.

He went through the passport and customs checks and settled down in the departure lounge to read his morning paper and wait with what patience he could for the boarding signal to come up on the screen.

The two flights ahead of his, to Geneva and Rome, were already boarding. Evidently neither of them was heavily subscribed and when their complement of passengers had drifted off, the lounge was only half full.

Meyer became aware that someone was addressing him. He swung round in his seat. It was a man in the grey-green airport uniform with Air France flashes on his arms. He was carrying a briefcase and seemed to be some sort of official. He said, in fair if laboured English, "You are Monsieur Meyer, a passenger on Flight 8684, yes?"

"Correct," said Meyer.

"The man who checked your passport did not, most unfortunately, take note that you intended to break your journey at Buenos Aires. It had been assumed from your ticket that you were going straight through to Santiago."

"I'm spending a few days at Buenos Aires, yes. Is that against the law?"

The man said, with a slight smile, "It is not against the law, no. But were you not aware that, since the recent troubles, all foreigners intending to enter the Argentine, even for a few days, must have their passports endorsed? It is simply a matter, I understand, of checking them against a list of undesirable entrants."

Meyer said, the alarm evident in his voice, "I knew nothing about this. Are you telling me that I shall have to miss this flight? Because if you are – "

The man smiled again. He said, "It is not as serious as that. The Argentine government has no desire to inconvenience travellers. They have arranged that we can ourselves check the records and endorse your passport. If you will come with me, please."

Leaving his coat on the seat, but carrying his handgrip, Meyer followed the man across the lounge and through a door marked 'Administration'. It led into a short passage, with doors on either side of it. At the end there was a right-hand turn. As they went round it the man stopped, so suddenly that Meyer almost collided with him.

He saw that the man had drawn out of his briefcase a curious weapon. It was a knife, about eight inches long, with a triangular blade, each side being concave and each edge razor sharp. Using a left-handed underarm swing he drove it upwards. It slid in smoothly under Meyer's ribs and into his heart. The operation was performed without fuss or emotion.

As Meyer went onto his knees the man followed him down, keeping the knife pressed home to prevent unnecessary bleeding. It took him no more than a few seconds to search Meyer's pockets and remove his wallet. Then he exchanged his own briefcase for Meyer's handgrip and walked sedately back the way he had come.

13

"So what are we going to do about the money?" said Stewart.

In the back room of number four Bolingbroke Mews a committee of three was in session. Lisa and Stewart had the two chairs. Peter was perched on a stool. The first item on their agenda, a bank draft for five million francs, lay on the table in front of them.

With an interest which was gently malicious Lisa had taken note of the difference between the two boys.

Peter had given them a confident, minute-by-minute, account of his experiences down to the climactic moment when he had hobbled up two flights of stairs to recover the bank draft from his aunt – ('What have you been up to, Peter? And what's wrong with your feet? Gout? You wouldn't have gout at your age if you took more healthy exercise.')

Stewart, on the other hand, had been oddly reticent about his experiences Zaman, he said, had been unco-operative. He had been held prisoner until after midday on the Friday when Zaman had appeared and told him he might go. What he had not reported, among many other things, was Zaman's cold dismissal. "We have recovered the money due to us. Some credit goes to you for the successful outcome of this matter, but do not trade on it. You will, of course, say nothing to anybody about your experiences. If you open your mouth, this immunity will not continue."

"Well," said Peter, "I think he might have shown a bit of gratitude. You saw the reports in the papers. They attributed the attack on Meyer at the airport to robbery, on the grounds that when they found him he had no money on him."

"And when you think," said Lisa, "that the sale proceeds of that lovely house and whatever he had by way of private fortune must have meant that he was carrying a draft for at least ten million francs. Probably twice as much."

"No doubt," said Stewart. "But it doesn't answer my question. What are we going to do about *this* money?" He was staring, fascinated, at the bank draft. "After all, when you think about it, there aren't a lot of claimants left, are there? Zaman thinks he's got it. Far be it from us to disillusion him. Your uncle's got his picture back, so he's got what he paid for and he's happy. And as for those two Iranian thugs – "

Peter said, "I had a word with Lisa's uncle on the telephone yesterday. Naturally, the Gobards haven't said anything, but Bernard's boat was found, when the tide brought it back still bottom-up. The local theory is that the current – it really was exceptionally strong on account of the storm inland – had taken it out to sea where it capsized. Bernard and anyone who might have been with him, is assumed to be under the rocks at the Pointe des Oiseaux. No one seems keen to go down and look."

"Then I think we can regard the account as closed," said Stewart. The words rang a distant bell. Had he said it, or had someone said it to him?

Lisa said, "So what's your idea about it?"

"Well," said Stewart, "since the money doesn't seem to belong to anyone and possession being, as they say, nine points of the law, I wondered whether we – "

"Certainly not," said Lisa. "It belongs to my uncle."

"We can't keep it," said Peter. "It's a pity, but really we can't. As I told you, he trusted me enough to pay me before I'd got his picture back for him."

"That makes it two to one," said Stewart sadly. "I suppose it'll have to go back."

Lisa said, "I've had an idea about that. Mummy says that once I'm gone she doesn't fancy the idea of living alone in that St. John's Wood barracks and she's seriously thinking of moving to France. As a first step, she's planning to pay a rather longer visit to Lambrécie. Why don't we get her to take the draft back? She can simply tell my uncle that Peter succeeded, somehow, in recovering it. And she can suggest that, in the circumstances, a handsome wedding present wouldn't be out of place. She knows how to handle Uncle Joseph."

"An excellent idea," said Peter. "So that disposes of that. What's next on the agenda?"

Lisa, who seemed to be acting as secretary, said, "Marketing."

"I've been in touch with Henry Bear," said Stewart. "I had to write and apologise for not turning up at his hotel. His firm definitely wants us. There's another old Chelburian on the board already. Chap with big ears called Taylor-Walker. Do you remember him? No. Well, our money's one of the main attractions. Henry got in, on the ground floor, for a mere £1,000. Since they trebled their profits last year, it'll certainly cost us a lot more in our case."

"Have you seen any actual figures?"

"He's sent me copies of their accounts for the last three years. I sent them on to our own accountants. What do you think?"

This deference to Peter's views was something new. Lisa wondered more and more what had happened to Stewart in Paris. Whatever it was, she approved of the change.

"If your accountant O.K.'s it," said Peter, "I'm all for it. Our experience in astrology should take us right to the top in marketing." He paused, "Wasn't there something else on the agenda?"

"There was," said Lisa coldly.

"Of course. Wedding arrangements."

"Not as important, I realise, as money."

"Much more important. How are the arrangements going?"

"Well, we're a bit short of bridesmaids. I've got Peggy Ashford, one of my friends at Chelborough. Very nice girl. She was sacked soon after I got there."

"Sounds most suitable," said Peter. "And if we're looking back to our Chelborough days, what about Miss Troop as a matron of honour?"

"Don't joke about sacred subjects. Mummy and I have put together a reasonable guest list, mostly her rich friends who can be counted on for a decent present. We didn't get much help from you two there."

"Alas, no," said Stewart. "Most of my friends are impoverished bachelors."

"I've asked the Chaytors, but I doubt if they'll come. They seem to be scared stiff at the thought of coming to London. But the real snag is that mummy doesn't get on with the local vicar. He's a terrible little man with a beard and Marxist leanings. But we can hardly use his church and not him."

Peter said, "Isn't it possible, sometimes, to superimpose a really senior clergyman – an old friend – something like that?"

"Of course," said Stewart. "Let's ask Brindy to officiate."

The others considered this, but once more the vote went against Stewart.

"It's a lovely idea," said Peter. "But I think not."

"Certainly not," said Lisa. "The sight of that unctuous old humbug would wreck the ceremony. All the same, I think that we might, for old times' sake, send him a piece of the wedding cake. A small piece."